REVIEWS FOR

HARARE VOICES AND BEYOND

Daring. **Harare Voices and Beyond** is full of intrigue and brutality. An unflinching portrait of broken families and a broken society.

—Paida Chiwara

***

In this his third novel, fire brand Zimbabwean novelist, Andrew Chatora, demonstrates that every man understands the complexity of his crime and the subsequently unsuitable punishment. This is a rare story about loss and strife in post independent Zimbabwe.

This is a detective story with no detectives. It is more like Doris Lessing's *The Grass is Singing* and Ngugi wa Thiongo's *A Grain of Wheat* in that the guilty is always in your midst, helping you solve the crime but making sure the criminal is not easily found. In the end you appreciate both the crime and the cause of the crime. You see that the criminal is an ordinary man who is driven over the precipice by irreparable generational loss. This is a deft work of art.

—Memory Chirere, University of Zimbabwe

***

Chatora expertly deals with unresolved trauma, psychosis, identity politics, citizenship, and nationhood issues through the portrait of both white and black Zimbabweans' lived culture.

—Malvern Mukudu, Writer & Journalist, Rhodes University, South Africa

The land question continues to hog many African countries, South Africa being the latest to join the fray and for a black author to tackle such an issue and bring it under the literary gaze is nigh remarkable.

This could be the first book of its kind by a black Zimbabwean author to deal with this contested terrain. Equally pertinent sub strands come to the fore in the narrative like Harare's burgeoning crystal meth rampage and its devastating impact on Zimbabwean youth and adults. These are important questions the author feels deeply about as a schoolteacher that they ought to be rightly critiqued and interrogated for the greater good of posterity. Through this book, Chatora brokers uncharted territory in post-colonial literature and it stands to make a worthwhile contribution to this great tradition.

—**Gift Mheta**, Writer, Durban University of Technology, South Africa

Harare Voices and Beyond

by

Andrew Chatora

Published by KHARIS PUBLISHING, imprint of KHARIS MEDIA LLC.

Copyright © 2023 Andrew Chatora

ISBN-13: 978-1-63746-196-9

ISBN-10: 1-63746-196-8

Library of Congress Control Number: 2022948805

All KHARIS PUBLISHING products are available at special quantity discounts for bulk purchase for sales promotions, premiums, fund-raising, and educational needs. For details, contact:

Kharis Media LLC
Tel: 1-479-599-8657
support@kharispublishing.com
www.kharispublishing.com

To my father: John Chatora

A great man, a fierce ally, and most constant friend.

Rest in perpetual peace.

Table of Contents

Chapter 1

This is it for me and Mother. Are we going to die? Could there be any other way? There is the murder case of my brother Julian, who is Mother's youngest son gone rogue. Whatever happens, our defense lawyer Jonathan has done a brilliant job, eloquently pleading our case before High Court judge, Justice Chatikobo.

"Your honour, this was an act of self-defense gone wrong on the part of my clients Doris and Rhys. Both plead culpable homicide in the face of extreme provocation. They have both shown exceeding remorse for this mishap which will haunt and traumatize them all their lives.

"As we speak, my clients have experienced delirium and hallucinations, an upshot of this excruciating ordeal for them. Doris now has longstanding insomnia, as her medical records submitted to court confirm; she is now on chronic restorative medication. It is my submission to this court that it considers all the extenuating circumstances facing my clients and pardons them, for they are not murderers but are law-abiding citizens goaded into a tricky scenario, through no fault of their own.

"Prior to this, they do not have criminal records, not one, not two, none on their records. Blameless stain! No blemish! So, they deserve a second chance; we all deserve a second chance in life."

Jonathan had persuasively argued and took a respectful bow as he resumed his seat in the packed courtroom and both Mum and I gave him a thumbs up with our eyes.

"Excellent delivery Jonathan," I mumbled under my breath, as if afraid the judge would hear me.

"May the court rise as the judge leaves to prepare his determination," boomed the usher's sonorous voice as we all complied with his instruction.

That had been a few days ago, last Friday to be precise. I looked at Mother's haggard, emaciated, expressionless face and felt for her. She had gone downhill within the last eight months and had shrivelled into a wilted leaf, reduced to a pitiful shadow of her former self. Her face was now etched with perpetual pain; deep furrowed lines of misery, worry and unhappiness now creased her brow. My mind flickered to the ebullient, effervescent Doris of yester-year that I had been used to. *Where had she gone, that vivacious, upbeat woman who had a ready smile for everyone, a big heart and larger than life personality?* I have the cheek to ask, as if I don't know the genesis of her ordeal. Blame it on Julian. But he is no longer here to state his case, is he? Perhaps, I should give him the benefit of the doubt to state his side of the story, but just. Perhaps, that is for another day.

"Time to go back to court Rhys," the prison officer's gruff voice jolted me out of my reverie. I scrambled to put on my creased khaki prison garb, grabbed water from an old scrappy metal mug on my cell window and shuffled out as Warren the prison officer unlocked my clanging metal cell doors and leg irons. The noise grated on me each time the heavy steel doors were opened with that hollow annoying noise which went on and on as if to remind me of my captivity status. I felt it; I was a caged animal and it hurt my self-esteem, yet this my newfound status.

"Your mother is already in the prison van waiting for you," Warren said. "Better hurry up." I shuffled awkwardly along the dreary, dingy, urine-stenched D section corridor of Chikurubhi Maximum Prison, slowly navigating my way towards the exit under the hawkish eyes of the other four burly prison officers who had joined us to first escort other prisoners to Harare Magistrates Court. Then high-profile cases like mine and Mother's would be dealt with at the corner Samora Machel/Second street ensconced colonial-looking high court building. I must admit it still looked regal in the decrepit disintegrating Harare infrastructure.

The Harare jacaranda trees were a vivid show of purple adding to the aesthetic ambience of the streets. Although decrepit Harare buildings made a mockery of its former epithet status as "Sunshine City," the blooming jacarandas still gave the city some much needed color.

"Morning Mum," I exchanged greetings with Doris as I sat opposite her in the green prison van. She could only grunt and give me a curt nod for an acknowledgment greeting. I wasn't surprised by this new change on Mum. Somehow the past eight months' trial and incarceration, first at Harare Remand prison and later at Chikurubhi, had sapped her energy. The once voluble woman cut a sorry figure as she increasingly became morose, reticent and laconic.

"Cheer up Mum, I know it's difficult; whatever happens today, we will get some closure on this case which has dragged on for so long," I remarked as I flashed her a radiant smile trying to be upbeat. Inwardly my stomach was churning and constricting at the uncertainty of what lay ahead. Today was judgement day from Justice Chatikobo, following several gruelling weeks of intense sparring between our defense lawyers and the prosecution, with the tetchy exchanges that had, at times, became ugly and heated. Moreso our cross-examinations had been brutal and adversarial, but we had emerged unscathed, at least those were Jonathan's reassuring words to us, "Both you and Doris have done very well throughout court proceedings, believe me." Jonathan had consistently allayed our misgivings in his periodic debriefs to us.

That morning, as if to exacerbate our jarred, frayed nerves, the prison van took exceedingly long to navigate the traffic on the treacherous pothole plagued roads of Harare. Because the van itself was like our jail, we couldn't hardly see what happened outside, as it's boarded up by tiny, barbed windows at each top end. All we occupants could feel was the constant discomfort and being jolted off our seats each time the vehicle hit a pothole or crater, with the attendant pain traveling up the bum. Being handcuffed when this happened didn't make things any easier. I caution you, don't ever be in my position.

Once at the Harare high court, we had a moment to consult with Jonathan just before the expected 11:00am verdict delivery time.

"Now here are the likely scenarios which are bound to happen today," Jonathan said quietly in the private courtroom legal chambers where lawyers would confer with their clients.

"In the event of a guilty verdict, my learned colleagues and I will have recourse to studying the judgement so we can expeditiously lodge an appeal to the Supreme Court.

"Should you both be acquitted, which I am hoping will be the case, then I will quickly proceed to Chikurubhi to collect you both. Are we clear?" His eyes bored into both of us as he spoke.

"Crystal clear, Jonathan, and what does the time frame for an appeal look like, between a guilty verdict and you putting this in?" I asked, the despondency in my voice perhaps a tad too obvious. This was a far cry from my trying earlier to be upbeat with Doris in the prison van.

"We should get our papers lodged and filed within a two-week period at the latest, though I am still holding out hope for a propitious outcome," Jonathan said.

"We do as well Jonathan, and in case things go the other way, please accept our utmost gratitude from the profoundest depths of our hearts, for what you've done for my son Rhys and I," Doris butted in. She appeared to have found her voice in the end, much to my surprise.

"No worries, Doris, you don't need to even say it," remarked Jonathan with a modest peremptory wave of the hand. "Rhys and you have been through a lot these past eight months; you deserve a respite in the form of a favourable outcome. There's the court usher beckoning to us. It may well be the die is cast. Let me hear whether judgement delivery is ready."

"Judgement has been moved forward to 2:30pm this afternoon," remarked the court usher, peering at us over his horn-rimmed glasses that he adjusted each time he spoke, much to my annoyance.

"How's that?" asked Jonathan, palpably annoyed at this unforeseen delay.

"No reasons have been offered, but this is Zimbabwe you know, where the wheels of justice turn excruciatingly slow," the usher said in low tones. The last statement came in a conspiratorial way to us, as if he was on our side and afraid to be overheard.

"For crying out loud, my clients have suffered long enough for all these months to have their day of reckoning just pushed from pillar to post, just like that," remarked a visibly dejected and vexed Jonathan.

"Well, we just have to wait, don't we?" said Doris. So we did wait with bated breath, for our judgement hour, which was more long drawn out than first stated. It was not until 3:45pm in the afternoon, a further delay of an hour and a quarter, when Justice Chatikobo took his seat, with us standing to acknowledge him.

Then he commenced speaking, as the court room descended into ominous silence. Our trial had received national and global headlines, some I can clearly recall, as they are permanently seared in my psyche: *"Murder most foul committed in posh Harare's Borrowdale Suburbs. A white Zimbabwean family, Rhys and his mother Doris, bludgeoned their sibling Julian Williams, Rhys's brother, after which they buried his body in their garden, in a grisly murder which has shook the opulent, leafy, affluent community..."* jumped to my memory. There were other snippets of some of these newspaper headlines and the furore surrounding our highly publicized trial in this southern African nation, where we the white community were a reclusive minority who tended to stay in the background.

"And so, judgement will be reserved indefinitely, as I need more time to study the prosecution and defense's closing arguments..." Justice Chatikobo's droning voice roused me from my late afternoon reverie.

"Judgement reserved indefinitely?" I was confused by these events unfolding before me. I glanced at Jonathan, who looked pissed off by Justice Chatikobo's terse address made just before he brusquely left the bench and the courtroom.

That had been it, a dramatic end to a long-drawn-out day in which Doris and I had woken up looking forward, however difficult, to a day we hoped would have given us the much-needed closure to a gruelling several months which had sapped our energies and resilience to live. But Justice Chatikobo had other ideas, a judgement reserved verdict. Even Jonathan, the best legal brains in Zimbabwe, had not seen this coming. He commiserated with us thereafter. Trying to reassure us, he said, "Well, I am extremely annoyed at this whole judgement reserved thing, Rhys. I am absolutely fuming on your behalf. I am sorry and feel for both of you."

"So, what does this mean to Doris and me? So many questions," I quibbled sarcastically. "Excuse me Jonathan, but where do we go from here? How indefinite is indefinite a non-judgement?" I threw back the questions at Jonathan as if it had been his fault.

"Well, I wish I knew," he said. "I can only say, and here, I hate to say it, but can only repeat the usher's words, 'this is Zimbabwe' where the rule of the jungle prevails, *donga watonga;* rule as you please, anarchy reigning supreme. Justice is up for sale to the highest bidder. You know what, forgive my rambling. Reserved judgement is bullshit stuff! We are at the mercy of this kakistocracy system now, and just have to wait until Chatikobo is ready with a judgement. Goodness knows whenever that will be."

"What about bail? Is there any chance all this circus can rumble on while we're out on bail?"

Jonathan replied, "Not a chance, I'm afraid, especially as it's a murder case. Besides, the high media interest in your case does you a disservice. So, as much as it pains me to utter these words, you are likely to stay in Chikurubhi prison, in limbo, without having a definitive end in sight. It could be weeks; it could be months we are talking of here, but hopefully not. Look, I'm fed up with all these antics. What this country needs are judicial grit, rigour and independence.

"Reserved judgements have become the recent "in" thing, an abuse of power instrument at the disposal of this banana republic judiciary. I don't like them; no one likes them who's been on their receiving end. But that's the way it is, I'm afraid. I'm sorry to you both once again. Will keep you in the loop on how things progress. This is Zimbabwe." Jonathan was clearly deflated, and I felt for him as he left with a dejected air, his creased, scruffy tweed suit underscoring a defeated man. Even his limp became more pronounced as he hobbled off.

We trudged out of the high court buildings and made that short walk back into the prison van belly, our leg irons clanging against the high court's pavement. I felt a dark, thick cloud of despondency descend on me, amid the teeming journalists and clicks of their cameras taking shots of both Doris and me and under the barrage of their ceaseless interview requests, "Mr. Williams, I'm from *The Zimbabwe Times.* Would you like to say a few words to this adjournment of your verdict today?"

"Do you think there is rule of law in Zimbabwe given your nearly nine months ordeal in Chikurubhi prison, and now this?"

"Would you say you are being persecuted because you are white?" rang another question amongst a litany of ceaseless questions thrown at us by these vultures.

"No comment," I quietly mumbled to them, my head lowered as I shuffled toward the prison van. *Golly, these fuckers, why can't they leave me alone?* I reflected as I negotiated the dodgy steps into the prison van. I missed a step and was roughly propped up by the butt of an AK 47 and the rough grimy hands of one of the prison wardens.

Chapter 2

*H*ow *time drags on in Chikurubhi*, I reflected within myself one morning as I sat in the prison canteen for my measly breakfast. It had been close to two months since Justice Chatikobo had delivered what I called his "no-show" judgement to us. No show, because nothing happened to us, either by way of giving us back our freedom had we been acquitted or availing us some certainty in the case of a conviction. In effect, nothing of the sort had happened. Here I was, still wallowing in Chikurubhi prison, with ceaseless anxiety daily gnawing on me, not knowing how my future would pan out with Mother. Good old Doris, she wasn't taking this incarceration well; she'd been perennially in and out of the prison infirmary.

"My heart is failing Rhys; I can feel it in my bones. My blood pressure has shot through the roof, the prison doctor says. I'm not the same person anymore," she would often remonstrate with me. I did my utmost to allay her fears and anxieties, though inwardly I believed something was not quite right with Doris anymore. Her cheeks had become sunken and sallow. Looking at her now somehow reminded me of a hideous scarecrow. It was a pitiful and harrowing sight to me witnessing the woman I loved dearly as my mother in a gradual descent and wilting, withering away like a deprived flower in a desert. Within those months in Chikurubhi, she had lost considerable weight. Frailty, thy name is an austere maximum prison.

"I'm sure you'll be fine Mum. Granted, a prison is not exactly an ideal dwelling place for anyone, let alone the aged and infirm as in your case, but we can only hope this is a temporary setback, our being here." She didn't sound convinced or placated. I saw the haunting fear of prison life, cold, palpable fear of an uncertain future staring back at me with those dilated, wizened eyes. As I often did when conversation became awkward like this, I tactfully changed the subject. Inwardly, I did feel for my mother and the physical downward spiral for a woman who had given in so much, given

19

her all to her country and family, yet had been so disproportionately rewarded.

Doris's life had been a lifetime of service, from way back in Mazowe, with her brainchild Mazowe Poly Clinic, which served the rural community of Mazowe and Christonbank well. But had she been rewarded, let alone acknowledged for her disinterested, selfless service? I am not sure of this. A lifetime of service, if there was an apt accolade, then this pretty much typified my mother's life during those years.

Every now and then my mind kept flickering to Julian, my kid brother Julian. What had made him snap and set Doris's bed on fire? Why had it come to this? What had become of our close-knit family of yesteryear? These and a host of other questions constantly flooded my psyche most evenings when I laid on my narrow Chikurubhi bunk bed and stared at the grimy ceiling, where reams of rainwater scars had built up on the decrepit surface. Perhaps, what made it more jarring, and unsettling was that it hadn't been Julian's first attempt at arson.

Something weird had come upon Julian in recent years, yet equally, Julian's descent into hell hadn't been unseen either. The signs had been too palpable to miss.

"Your brother is up to no good. He won't talk to me. Have a quiet word," mother constantly admonished me. "It's a silent cry for help. He will be our bane if we don't reach out," Doris would bang on, referring to Julian's increasingly erratic, eccentric behaviour.

As I kept jabbing my fork into my hardboiled egg, I felt it; someone was staring at me within the prison canteen. Then I saw her staring at me, just as I had felt it. That feeling had lingered, even though I'd been wrapped up in my innermost trance and it was overpowering. Someone was ogling me big time over the prison cafeteria table, across the wide sitting area on the other extreme end.

So much for Governor Warren and his much-touted prison reforms. An expatriate white American brought in to sort out the mess at Chikurubhi and other correctional prisons within the country, Governor Warren certainly had a chip on his shoulder as he stood at the cusp of change with his rallying call being, *"Prison reforms, put the prisoner at the heart of rehabilitation not punishment. We aim to reform the individual when they eventually leave prison walls."* That was it, things had changed rapidly in some respects at Chikurubhi with Warden Warren's prison reforms in which he advocated for men and women inmates to intermingle. That was how it came to be; we now mingled with female inmates as on this fateful morning.

"They are doing it in America, why can't we do it also here?" Governor Warren would often advance this as his raison d'etre, as if America were the moral standard bearer for things in life.

"Pleased to meet you." I remarked as I ambled toward her and stretched out my hand to her. "I'm Rhys Williams, I'm in for murder," I said, deliberately dropping in the last bit if only so I could gauge her reaction.

"In for murder as well, Marina Thompson," she remarked, flashing me a ravishingly dazzling smile which rather disarmed me. I had been expecting instant rejection, given the nature of my crime.

"You're also in for murder Marina? Is this some flip-it-back-at-him joke?" I asked her incredulously as I sat across the table staring at her full length.

"Far from it. You heard me correctly, Rhys. Interested in my story? Be my guest then. I have nothing to hide anymore do I, given my committal here. Besides, what else can we do here in these granite walls of Chikurubhi?"

"Go on then sunshine," I playfully teased her back, taken in by her outright candour and charm. I mean, it's not every day that you come across a fellow inmate so blasé about their past misdeeds. Not only that, but one willing to share them with you. I must admit, I found that bit of Marina immersive and certainly magnetic.

"Well, here's the deal, Rhys," she resumed speaking, a naughty smile curling her luscious olive lips.

"What deal again? You change so fast. Isn't it you who just said a minute ago, you're an attention-seeker willing to share your story?" I politely retorted. She gave back my playful banter in equal measure. *She must be enjoying this*, I thought to myself.

"Well, Rhys, there must be a trade-off of some sort. I am not just going to tell you every tiny-winy bit of my life without you sharing yours in reciprocation. It's only fair we get to know each other in these four walls of mighty Chikurubhi. Besides, it would be boring to hear just my side of mishaps I've been through. So I say, you put your cards on the table, I do likewise. Do we have a deal, Mister Prim and Proper?" she remarked, a wicked glint in her almond blue eyes.

"Yes, we do have a deal, Marina," I shot back gleefully, now very much up for taking on her challenge which I found strangely, sexually alluring. *For fuck's sake, I've stayed far too long in the belly of these walls, my sexual guns are misfiring*, I mused to myself, feeling the stirrings of my manhood in my loins signalling an erection. *Behave yourself, will you?* Another counter voice politely whispered in my ear.

"Bravo!" she almost shouted, drawing glances from other inmates in the prison cafeteria. And that was how it started between us, the enigmatic Marina and me. That ravishing mixed-race girl who stood out from all within Chikurubhi prison, if not because of her exquisite looks, then for her super-posh twang British accent, certainly made you look at her each time she opened her mouth to speak. I can't say I wasn't elated to be in such exclusive company. I certainly felt chuffed, and judging by their lecherous, covetous glances at us, I know I detected envy from the other male prisoners each time they saw us together within the prison compound. Why wouldn't they be, given Marina's captivating physical beauty, radiance, and presence? Marina would light any environ she happened to grace. Tall, voluptuous with pointed nipples, these physical attributes were further accentuated by a ravishing smile and intelligent conversation which were certainly the hallmarks of this mixed-race British lassie. Many atimes, Marina carried herself with a seductive, hip swinging strut across the prison compound, much to the delight of the lascivious male eyes drooling on her frame. There was little doubt I found Marina's sexual allure and captivation magnetic and irresistible, thus I started looking forward to our usual dalliances, if not within the prison compound, then the communal library.

Chapter 3

Meeting Rhys

I warmed up to Rhys early on during my settling down days at Chikurubhi prison. It would not be an exaggeration to say I liked Rhys instantly upon setting my eyes on him. In fact, I had been staking him out for a couple of weeks, especially at mealtimes, when I would gaze at him relentlessly across the wide dining room. Much to my dejection, all the while he would not even bother looking toward my way. As weeks went by with no breakthrough, the frustration to my perving him with no tangible rewards was beginning to grate on me. *Gosh, it's like I don't even exist,* I would often remark to myself as I pleasured myself in the serene darkness of my prison bunk bed most evenings. My long fingers stroking the inner crevices between my supple thighs, this was a treat I had taken to as a coping mechanism in the dull, Chikurubhi fortress. In a weird way, part of me regarded his standoffish behavior as a welcome challenge which I found sexually alluring, especially in the throes of the evenings when I took the fantasy trip of his cock slipping in and out of me, and let my fingers finish the job as I squirted my juices on the prison bed. And then it happened, just like that, boom!

One morning, the legend that was Rhys confidently sauntered to my table, and I playfully feigned nonchalance at seeing him; I wanted to play it coy with him even though I was inwardly elated at seeing him.

There was something about Rhys which reminded me of someone back home in England, perhaps a familiar face at Blanchett's Goodhope? Rhys was an interesting man who exuded a smooth, magnetic charm. He had that uncanny aloofness which set him apart from the other prisoners and I found this magnetic. *What goes on behind those dark glasses? Who is this seeming loner of a man who hardly mingles with the others? This is a prison for heaven's sake. Do you have to be that stuck up?* All these were key questions coursing through my mind each time I glanced at Rhys within the prison compound. Above all, he exuded a certain aura of unmitigated confidence and invincibility, attributes very much at variance with our mice-like captivity status in Chikurubhi. Whatever it was that made him tick, I was determined to get to know this fella at close quarters and unravel his mystery and enigmatic facade.

For the uninitiated, there is something unique about me. I've always been one for wanting a bit of a challenge. And I found Rhys' distant persona alluring. I found talking to him immersive and enthralling, like I had known him for ages. We felt so much at ease as we chatted nonchalantly within the prison grounds. I was enchanted with this white Zimbabwean fella who never seemed to run out of amusing stories and anecdotes. I found myself hanging on to his every word. We could go on talking non-stop, regaling in unmitigated laughter and gaiety at Rhys' anecdotes, stories, and mirth. At times the prison guards would interrupt. "You two behave yourself, don't forget you're in a gaol for heaven's sake," they would remonstrate with us, wringing their hands.

That was how I bonded with Rhys. Why couldn't we, given the numerous ways our lives were intertwined? We were more like twins in many respects, as Rhys's own intimate life shone a light on mine, and we bounced light off each other like that. Each morning in the prison yard at Chikurubhi we could mingle and exchange notes on the roads we have trod, Rhys on his travails in Zimbabwe, I on my England misadventures, and how they inadvertently jettisoned me into beautiful Zimbabwe, now my adopted home for the past few years.

Initially the prison guards had made a deafening huha and brouhaha about us interacting, but they eventually relented and left us be, though with some grudging recriminations.

"Whatever you two get up to, no handholding and touching. You're not at a dating center. This is Chikurubhi for Pete's sake," barked Steve, one of the guards well known for his excessive sadism and meanness. One of the legendary stories which ran throughout the prison compound was how, at one point, Steve had to be restrained by fellow prison officers; in fact, the story goes that it took four of them to contain him after he got involved in a nasty brawl with one of the notorious D section prisoners, which earned him a broken nose and a crooked Y shaped scar on his face. For that misdemeanour, Steve had escaped with a warning from the prison board authorities, but if anything, that did not seem to have deterred and detracted him from his brutal callousness, crass character and interactions with prisoners.

"We hear you loud and clear, Steve, and we assure you nothing of the sort will happen," Rhys would remark nonchalantly. I think with the passing of time the prison establishment came to accept we were two good friends who meant no harm, so they grudgingly acquiesced and left us to our own devices. The prison library was another safe haven for us, for Rhys and I shared a deep affinity for everything literature. During our usual pass time, we would be lost, engrossed in the voluminous Penguin classics of literary luminaries of yesteryear, such as Dickens, Daniel Defoe, and George Eliot, among others.

"I come from a strong literary background," Rhys would proudly gush at me. "My dad Jim was way, way ahead of his times than most of his mates in terms of literary appreciation, and it is on me that he bequeathed his love for reading. Do you know he was churning out poetry pieces back in the days at our Mazowe farm? Unbelievable stuff in that Pops was such an unassuming intellectual. A man of mixed talents, bookish and yet a farmer of note, all in one.

"Reading though was never my kid brother Julian's forte and he made no attempt to hide his disdain for this, 'Not for me Rhys. Besides reading is boring, that's for you dull boffins!'

"Dull boffins, ever heard of such a thing? Talk of an oxymoron coming from someone professing to loathe reading." Such was the strength and testament of the camaraderie between Rhys and me as we shared up-close moments of intimacy and interaction during our sojourn at the country's leading infamous gaol, Chikurubhi, both awaiting the inevitable hangman's noose.

Chapter 4

Harare Airport

Being the nephew of Harare Airport's General Manager Aviation Department, one Jairosi Bhamu, meant I had it easy for the years I worked at this dinosaur airport in an age where other countries had upgraded their air terminals to world class standards. Harare Airport still lagged behind with its antiquated air traffic control systems. "One of these days, these ancient systems will cause an accident of untold proportions," people used to cheekily remark at this decrepit infrastructure at the airport, amid our staff meals in the airport canteen. Uncle Jairosi, my mother's brother, saw to it that a job was created for me at Harare Airport after I spectacularly flunked my A Levels, much to Mother's chagrin; she didn't hide her displeasure with me. My mother Renika would bang on relentlessly about this with her incessant tongue lashing of me. This she did on this lazy Saturday morning when I had chosen to slouch on the settee, nursing a hangover and a splitting headache, following the previous night's bender.

"I'm afraid we took it a notch further with the lads last night Mum," I remarked to her, expecting some sympathy, but this appeared to rile her further. She must have been on steroids or some noxious substance that particular morning, judging by her unprecedented vitriol.

Aaah, now you think it's a badge of honor continuously smoking weed and drinking your *mutoriro* and *brocho* nonstop?

"Seeing you decided to flunk your exams, you may as well make plans to look out after yourself, Munyaradzi. Your father is hardly here, as he now literally lives at that woman's place. I don't see how it's my place and duty to look out after a grown man like you. God knows how many times I entreated you to studiously study, but did you listen with that band of forsaken lads you hang around with. Lousy Fantan and all them lot…"

"But Mamma…"

"Don't 'Mamma' me boy, and for once listen and do as you're told, not this one-man misplaced bravado. Yet you can't provide for yourself, let alone afford your undergarments, those boxers. Beats me how you manage to fund your booze and *mbanje*. It's an expensive habit you know. Drinking like a fish the way you do and snorting that meth powder.

"Besides, you're slowly killing yourself anyway, the amount of nicotine those lungs of yours have taken in. Surely, they will be knackered by the time you turn thirty, if you get there, that is."

Mamma must have woken up on the wrong side of the bed. She was unrelenting in her vituperative attacks on me, branding me *a waste of space layabout and good for nothing sod*. In the end, Sekuru Jairosi, mother's flamboyant brother from Glen Lorne, saved the day for me.

Relentlessly tired of Mamma's incessant whining and whinging over my no job status, I turned to Sekuru Jairosi.

"But Khule, it's not like I haven't tried job hunting," I remonstrated with him when Mamma started on her auto playlist diatribe one evening Sekuru visited us in our cramped Tafara lodgings.

But as usual, Renika was gung-ho in her put downs of me and was having none of it. It was now bordering on obsession this job-hunting thing, this: *"Get a job or you are out of here,* mantra."

"The problem with your nephew Jairosi is, taking everything as a sick joke. To him life is all a laugh; that's why he doesn't see the importance of sourcing out a job to help out with household expenditure here."

"Things are tough Khule, as everyone else well knows in Zimbabwe. I've lost count of the numerous job applications I've made to no avail. Mamma would prefer I blow my trumpet on my job-hunting escapades, but really that's not my style Khule."

"That's not me. I prefer to report back when there are tangible results. See! I'm a man of results. Progress, not cheap talk, that's me," I had remarked with an exaggerated flourish of the hand and deferential bow, against a hideous scowl and evils from mamma.

With as beaming a smile as ever, Uncle Jairosi reached out and back slapped me for encouragement. He said, "Report to my office first thing Monday morning, then I can see what can be done for you, Muzaya. *Tisu tinotonga paAir Zimbabwe, tiri vene veushe,* and so people can be hired and fired at my calling." Sekuru spoke with a smug smile firmly ensconced on his puffy lips which were now maroon, courtesy of many years of excessive drinking of illegal *kachasu* brews in the township shebeens.

That was how I landed the job.

True to Sekuru's word I turned up at Harare Airport first thing that Monday morning and was ushered into an opulently furnished office by his pretty looking personal assistant, Tarisai. She must have been in her mid-thirties, based on her trim figure, which had me mesmerised as I silently undressed her in my mind and thought of all the wonderful things my hands would do on that curvaceous booty, if given the time. In no time, I felt a stirring in my loins, and I could feel a hard on building, much to my embarrassment. She must have sussed my discomfort, for she flashed me a rather disarming smile, which I took as a potential invitation for future things to come.

"Call me Tarisai. Mr. Bhamu will see you once he's done with the client he's talking to over the phone," Tarisai remarked to me. And boom! Just like that, I landed the Harare Airport job as a check-in assistant for commercial airlines passenger flights. Among other duties, my job entailed cargo handling for passengers or also doubling as a customer service representative. In no time, I acclimatized and settled down well in my new job at the airport.

A typical day in my 2-9pm shift would entail a range of beehive activities, not least of but including checking in passengers, and handling their luggage, which is how my path crossed with the gregarious Mark Instone. But each time, I kept my eyes and ears craned, harbouring hopes for a possible fling with Tarisai, that voluptuous beauty who'd made a lasting impression on me on interview day.

***

I would say it was by a stroke of coincidence that I crossed paths with Mark Instone eight months into my stint at Harare Airport as a flight check in attendant-cum customer service rep. I had pretty much settled down and established myself by then. I remember we had lots of banter with the girls and the lads in the airport canteen which underscored how everyone got along well with each other. How can I forget that poignant Saturday evening when Mark strode in frantically at the last minute as his Emirates Dubai flight was already boarding, and he was visibly flustered at the prospect of missing his flight.

"Please sir, do anything you can within your powers to ensure I board that plane. *Bloody hell!* There's no way I can miss tomorrow's boardroom meeting in London!" He appeared distressed, and I quickly jumped into action stamping his passport and briskly intervened as I expedited his check-in and luggage retrieval. I also took it upon myself to personally chaperone him to the front of the boarding que in departure lounge terminal 6, which was at the ground floor of the airport.

I could see he was beside himself, overwhelmed with gratitude that I had facilitated a flight which he had nearly missed. For a big man of such stature, he was beside himself.

"Here, let me take your number," he remarked as he fished out an imposing looking silver iPhone 14 pro and he appeared to type in my digits and name as I recited them to him.

"Here, take my business card Munyaradzi, did you say your name was Munyaradzi?"

"Munyaradzi, it is sir, and enjoy your flight with Emirates." And that was it. We shook hands as he got his carry-on luggage and started moving towards boarding gate 27. I thought nothing of him then, just another important bigwig passenger. Goodness knows, we came across them daily in our lives at the airport. I was by then losing my enamour with celebrities, still I couldn't take it away from him as I later found out, Mark Instone was a big shot, a well-known telecommunications mogul who had spearheaded mobile network infrastructure in Zimbabwe, Southern Africa and beyond. *Didn't they say he also had a thriving property portfolio in London?* I later remarked to myself as I googled his name, only to be overwhelmed by how herculean a stature Mark enjoyed online for his business prowess and philanthropy work championing the cause of underprivileged beings. At the time of our initial interaction, though, I had been unaware of the man's herculean stature.

"Gosh, this man is like Mother Theresa," Tarisai remarked to me when I broached the Mark subject.

"Really?"

"What do you mean 'really?' As if you haven't heard of his various charities and widespread tentacles spread throughout the country, community development projects, scholarship awards, you name it!" She added, "Mark Instone is the real deal in town, count yourself lucky to have served royalty."

"Aha," I remarked nodding my head as the penny dropped and I reflected at the 100-dollar tip, he'd surprised me with at our parting.

Several weeks following the Mark incident at the airport, I got what I thought at the time was a complimentary thank you email; towards the end of the email, in fact in the last paragraph, were buried the words, *"Wanna be rich, then he who dares wins, have big, massive, huge plans for you Munyaradzi. Email back to confirm interest and will furnish you the details."*

A few weeks following his cryptic email, Mark flew into Harare for our in-person meeting in which he kept saying he had life changing proposals for me. He arranged our meeting at the elegant Meikles hotel in Harare. I was visibly over-awed and enamoured by the splendour, grandeur, and gaiety of the hotel. Its imposing well-lit chandeliers brought a sophisticated glow and ambience to my discreet meeting with Mark.

A whole host of questions flooded my mind upon reading this message from Mark, a man I had, in his words, helped catch his last-minute flight by my kind intervention to the flight captain to please hold on for a special passenger.

Mark Instone began, "Let's put it this way, every now and then we will have shipments which need a safe passage at Harare Airport headed for Dubai en route to England. Let us have this hypothetical discussion, Munyaradzi; remember it's all hypothetical so that we avoid getting ahead of ourselves."

Continuing his opening pitch, Mark threw at me, "Let's just say in this proposed venture, you become my Harare local business associate.

"We always need an inside man in each county we operate. And may I start by congratulating you Munyaradzi, you are most likely to be our next Zim contact, but you need balls of steel for this demanding job. We are a big international company, GTN. I'm sure you've heard of us, a huge telecommunications company, and I am its regional co-ordinator in London."

Almost barking at me, he demanded, "Do you have balls?" His eyes bored into mine in an intimidating fashion.

"Of course, I have big balls, try me!" I goaded him defiantly, as I sought to win his confidence.

That had been over twelve months ago. How time flies. Now I had become deeply embedded in Mark's well-orchestrated criminal underworld of various activities: vice, sleaze, and substances. Yet nothing pricked my conscience at this metamorphosis I'd gone through, from a wet-behind-the-ears twenty-year-old to a career criminal, wide-eyed owl in the making. A lot had happened in those twelve months which had contributed to bending my moral arc. Somehow, I revelled in seeing myself in the mould of a fellow child prodigy criminal, Jessie Pinkman, in the famed *Breaking Bad* TV show.

Chapter 5

Smugglers Haven

Onai

As pushers, we had a free pass in Zimbabwe, moreso at Harare Airport because we were runners of top elites at the highest levels of the government. Government ministers, judges, high ranking officials within the party, and private sector big wigs were among the litany of some of our clients. Add to that spiralling web of deceit and corruption endemic within the country, my immediate boss Mark Instone, who was a highly connected man with the top echelons of power in Zimbabwe. Being a telecoms media mogul provided him the much-needed cloak and veil of darkness, secrecy, and cover, as he was a highly regarded figure within and beyond Zimbabwe's borders. Mark pretty much supped with Harare's elites with wild abandon, and for someone supping with the devil, his spoon was certainly long. Many times, among his underlings like me, he could be heard revelling and bragging, "We're connected to the heartbeat of Harare and Harare is mine. In London, they know me big time."

He relentlessly boasted with a bottle of pilsner lager in one arm, a slur in his speech, and dilated eyes to show the alcohol was now firmly in charge and doing the talking.

Interestingly, these elites like Mark's party friends were bleeding the country dry, and yet they had a knack for blaming everyone else for the country's ills or sanctions; that was their scapegoat song to explain away their political ineptitude and kleptocracy.

"It's the sanctions on us. No wonder we're being dragged down, and the economy is at a standstill," they often unashamedly opined in the face of galloping inflation and endemic hardships in the country.

Ironically, much as they pontificated on the rhetoric of sanctions, the looting of state resources continued in full swing, ad infinitum. Meanwhile, the party faithful supporters wallowed in abject poverty and penury, while the establishment carried on with their looting and scorched earth policy of national resources and asset stripping. They had perfected the art of enlisting fraudulent men of the cloth to sanitize and window dress their misrule chicanery in the grand deception of the populace.

Occasionally, a drug smuggler would be caught at Harare Airport, as was the case with our novice mule Amanda Poulter, who was caught attempting to smuggle 6kg of drugs to Dubai. And once our novice mule got busted at Harare International Airport, that was it for us. We were done, fucked, back-to-back!

Striding from desk to window and back again as he relentlessly dragged his cigarette, Mark remarked; "We have to lie low."

"Let's see how this case plays out in the courts first, before we resume business.

"Better to err on the side of caution, methinks."

A few seconds later, he gulped his pilsner and added; "I'm a businessman, I don't take unnecessary risks. If anything, I take calculated risks." We nodded, knowing he was just warming up, as he carried on, a sly-eyed grin spreading across his wolfish face.

"Right now, it would be too risky to carry on business-as-usual style; all eyes will be on Harare Airport, and we don't want to play right into the authorities' hands. Even though we do have inside backing, still we shouldn't openly flaunt it, should we?"

That had sounded a sensible approach, coming from our boss. We'd all gone underground to escape the authorities' radar.

Chapter 6

Chamu

Introspection

My problems pretty much commenced when Mother lost her seven-year battle with cervical cancer and Papa remarried in no time, as if the woman had been waiting in the wings for this to happen all along. That was how I started living with Mainini Julia, the woman father married, the mean, cruel stepmother from hell, if ever there was one. We resided in Unit K Seke Township, one of the southern suburbs in the satellite town of Chitungwiza.

Julia didn't take long to assert herself and her influence over the household. Neither did she hide it that I was her least favorite person.

"Now, listen and listen good Chamu, this here is my domain, I don't give a damn that you're Brian's son, in here, you pretty much do as you're told. You will listen and adhere to my dos and don'ts in this house. Are we clear?" There was a mocking leer in her voice as she spoke to me, with an unmistakable loathing registered in those dark harsh eyes. And she had this annoying, condescending habit of waggling her index fingers at me each time she spoke, as if to demean me further.

"Whatever, Julia, be my guest," I derisively replied. That had been several months down the line, and true to her words, Julia had been running the household with a heavy hand. She certainly brooked no nonsense, and since she took over my mum's position in the house, Dad seemed to have been emasculated and somehow lost his voice. The man hardly spoke. He'd wilted from his former ebullient, abrasive self, and I felt for him as he increasingly withdrew into his inner shell and took to alcohol as a coping mechanism. Part of me reflected philosophically, *what is it with mature men when they marry these young, nubile women that they end up losing their senses and voice?* I mean, the man obtaining before me now was different from the dad who used to throw his weight around, bossing Mummy and at times brutalizing her. This was not my dad but a far cry from good old Brian, the so-called township maverick, well known in Chitungwiza for his hard man stance and style which made him the stuff of legends across the length and breadth of Chi-town.

"Phew," I couldn't help sighing in exasperation. I often tried engaging him in conversation, but it was like he'd lost his tongue. If anything, I noticed his drinking had gone a notch up; mostly, he would reek of the acrid, rancid smell of the illegally brewed shebeen and township high alcohol content brews commonly known as *kachasu*. It now appeared, where he demurred in talking, he made up by incessantly drinking like a fish. *"Mudhara akasotwa uyu*, your old man has been well fixed by Julia's juju." I would often overhear the mocking snide remarks from some of our women neigbours, in apparent reference to dad's sudden change in demeanour.

In tandem, in my other life with the lads, outside of this domestic raucousness, my litany of problems quickly came to a head. This was exacerbated that fateful Saturday evening when police swooped down on us and busted our well-oiled, choreographed push syndicate which had been flourishing for well over three years since I had come under Mark Instone's wing and octopus-like grip. Even now, I can't understand how things went spectacularly wrong that Saturday night.

What could have caused this?

How did the police know about our drugs syndicate, considering some of them, particularly the top cops Harare bosses, were on our payroll to look the other way round each time we used Harare air terminal as a safe passage to transport drugs to the four corners of the world?

Hadn't our contacts at the airport always managed to switch off the closed-circuit television cameras each time we wanted to smuggle our loot out?

So many questions in my mind, so few answers, I silently sighed to myself, *perhaps this, in itself, underscores my perplexity and despondency at losing both my day job and lucrative side job that had elevated me to a new celebrity-like lifestyle status among the down and outs of Harare.*

My mind revels in the adulation and accolades I had gained from my notoriety in Harare: *"Aaah vakuru ndeipi? Dzauya dzega huruyadzo mbinga paTaundi,"* they were wont to address me in the Harare socialite circles, popular drinking holes, and night clubs on account of my infamy as Mark Instone's lap dog.

True to form, I was a fox bull terrier as we connived and conspired, plotting, traversing the length and breadth of Harare. And Munyaradzi, our insider, our airport link man, was always the reliable work horse. Onai was our lackey, and of course the man himself, Brian Wharton, was our linchpin fixer. We were a formidable drug running and brothels team, or so we liked to revel and perceive ourselves as such. Then Onai's cataclysmic phone call that evening pretty much upset our hitherto serene calmness, and the carefully stacked house of cards spectacularly tumbled down.

"It's done, boss!" he'd cryptically remarked over the phone line, not shedding much light.

"What do you mean it's done? I am not in the mind reading business as you well know Onai. A little bit of clarity is needed here," Mark had sarcastically replied.

And then, just like that, without warning, he uttered those words: *"numero uno."* Just like that, I knew the die was cast. He need not say any more. *Numero uno* had long been our tried and tested, drilled code phrase in case of our drug empire being busted.

"Should that ever happen, you all lie low and go underground as you await further instructions," Brian and Mark had inculcated in us. And here I was. Onai had just uttered the magic phrase, *numero uno*, which loosely translated in our parlance meant: Look out for yourself first. Things are about to get really bad, as the old Bailey are after our asses.

Perhaps all these developments contributed to hastening my personal downward spiralling descent to hell. To what else can I ascribe my fall from grace?

It's a free world. People choose what they want to do with their lives. I did not choose drugs; they chose me instead. If drugs didn't want me, then they should have not made Mama lose her fight against cervical cancer. Nor should they have implicated me in our Harare airport drug bust.

But why pick on me, a mere cog in the wheel? People who are selling drugs in Mbare, Mufakose, Fio, Dangamvura, Magwegwe, Lobengula Warren Park D are well known. They are connected to the party's district members, and they fund the party. It's a common secret. So, why come after me, a mere small underling?

These people are known by the police. They buy police lunch and airtime. People bringing cocaine? So, why should I be the fall guy? We have been no exception in our collusion with the police.

I have heard so many myths and untruths about drug misuse or substance abuse from various so-called opinion leaders. Doing drugs is an individual choice. I have seen people with good jobs doing drugs and eventually losing their jobs. Drugs have nothing to do with social or economic situations.

It's a choice and I consciously made that choice to enter this murky world as some of you call it. But you know what? I'm okay with it.

So, take your sanctimonious faces elsewhere. I don't need them or your haughty stares.

What these pontificators and mountebanks forget is, people like me and my gang once had hopes before. *Hear me, listen to me. Chamu also had nursed hopes that one day, in a free Zimbabwe I, like any other youths, would get a decent job, marry, and have children in the full cycle of life. Is that not how life goes on in its mundane trajectory?*

These people, some of my fellow druggies, also had hopes and aspirations just like you and me, but with over 90% unemployment our government has failed us.

But tell you what, despite all the deafening virtue signalling from roof tops, people may as well carry on till their voices go hoarse. Participating in the supply chain of drugs is a major contribution in destroying our future! So, I hear all the time!

This might be crystal meth *(Mutoriro/Guka)* a very dangerous drug being abused by our youths these days. I am one of those youths, taking it by choice. No need to rub it in. How many times do I have to assert my agency, freedom of choice, so to speak?

But we are not dumb; ask my mates in downtown Harare and we'll all tell you what's going on here behind all this drug facade. Truly speaking, we don't have a government. Let's be honest. Zim is a mess! Only those in the government are benefiting from the system. The rest we are suffering.

Some of these youths I snort cocaine with have degrees, diplomas, or certificates but they are jobless; they have no capital, and they end up doing this to ease stress. And why should I feel guilty at facilitating this drug cycle? Let alone partaking in it? My rationale is simple: if I don't get involved in drugs, they'll still get them from somewhere, so who am I to break the chain? One way or the other, someone's gotta do it.

"Most certainly elder, this is a disease on its own," said Kudzai, one of the lads who would often spar with me in our rare moments of clarity, like now.

"Corruption at its worst, Sir, the most notorious drug peddlers are well known.

"The system wants to keep the youths ignorant so they can manipulate the system without accountability.

"Chemical warfare this is blud. Enough respect!"

"The youth are despondent There's nothing for them to look forward to; no jobs, no food, no dreams *zvisekuru zveZANU/zvemusangano* have destroyed and broken the country. Our generation knew if I finish school, will get a good job ava, unlike now *kuno vakapedza vanoita mevendor nemahwindi* so drugs are a way to escape the harsh reality. Who can blame us?"

"There is always a root cause before the drugs gets into the hands of the user; there are always people behind that. It is said if you want to destroy a tree completely make sure you target its roots. So, until, they target the roots, we're just dilly-dallying in silly children's games here. Drugs are here to stay in our communities."

"In our country, many police officers know where to find these dealers, but instead of arresting them they get bribed. Why? Because they want to feed their families, or maybe confiscate the push only to put them on sale too. Those push dealers are now known, but they are protected because they pay bribes. So, if you want to tackle this, spare me the bullshit, and start at the top!

"Cut the supply chain completely, because as we speak, some drugs are in transit. Cut the supply first. If they are people who manufacture these drugs, that's where it should start. But how will we get our cut if you do that? People like me will fight to preserve our sustenance.

"Look, Kudzi, these people make me sick with their revolting hypocrisy and double standards. You know they've recently launched the aptly misnamed, *Zimbabwe Drug Masterplan* by the Ministry of Health. It is one step, but it's all paper if there is no capacitation financially and human resources to implement it. How many times have we been here before? Walked this road?" I sniggered with derision as I laughed this off as another government publicity stunt to hoodwink the public into thinking we're doing something to stem drug trafficking.

"Well, there's nothing you can do really, as long as the system stays broken. Corruption at the top trickles down to create these horrors when a system does not function the way it should," he replied.

"Where are the jobs to keep the youth off the streets? They're educated, but there are no jobs, so how do you heal that? Do you see now why I would rather be on the streets? At least I do make something being Brian's underling slave than seeking and waiting for a job which never materialises."

"Whichever way you look at it. People are finding comfort in either fake prophets or drugs...it's a sad scenario. We all need our fix, whether it's spiritual or a physical craving. So why is it a big deal we chose drugs? No one is yet to give me a clear-cut answer to this one Kudzi, I shrug my shoulders in bewilderment."

Chapter 7

Seedy Harare

This is what life in seedy Harare has become for me and my mates. Older men preying on us, getting hooked into substance abuse. At least, that's how I remember it. That's how it started for me.

So many things happened to me during my teen years that it meant I'd spend less time having to resist the influence of the older men in my life, many of whom turned out to be addicts, domestic abusers, murderers, and child molesters.

That laced blunt at Graniteside industrial garage where I was a general hand was my first direct exposure to any recreational drugs.

I shudder to think about what kind of direction my life would have headed if I'd listened to my elder male cousins from my mother's side *wana Sekuru* - even once. Their now clearly well-intentioned entreaties were often said: "You've joined the wrong crowd Archie, it will all end in tears, trust me." They reprimanded me each time I flaunted my newfound fame and proximity to none other than the only game in town, Mark Instone. For it was through Mark that I met his alter ego, side kick, lanky Brian Wharton, the man who was to have such a reverberating influence on my own life.

World-renowned media mogul Mark Instone's friend Brian Wharton could well fuck very hard as an initiation rite of passage to Harare's Crystal meth criminal underworld and underage sex trafficking ring around the Avenues area. At least that's how it was with me when he found me on the dingy Harare streets.

"I have to fuck you first, back-to-back, so I seal your loyalty. Is that clear?" Brian said.

I could only nod my head in submissive acquiescence as he went rambling on. Meanwhile, his crotch was getting visibly excited, as I licked the ketchup from the fries he'd given me. I hadn't had a proper meal in ages and was only too glad to have a hot meal for once.

"You see, loyalty is everything to me in this game, Matt," Brian said. "I will just call you Matt, forget about your real name. You're not really a person to me. You're just some other dumb ass Harare piece of ass, and once I'm done with you, I own you. Henceforth, you would have passed your rite of passage and it will now be your currency and duty to prowl the streets of Harare and get more black asses for me, for my Borrowdale Brooke clientele.

"Just so we're clear, I'm doing you up the arse, no two ways about it.

"My punters are rich, very rich and powerful men, I will require utmost discretion from you Matt," and even as he spoke, he advanced toward me. That the sexual frenzy had got the better of him was nigh evident in his maniacal, blazing red eyes. He was still babbling away, even as he gleefully took my virginity that evening at his Avondale bachelor flat pad.

I never saw the "father your sons" brigade talk about the fathers who abandoned their children like my own father did to me, or the male mentors who fucked their mentees up as some kind of rite of passage, like Brian did to me.

What did "father your sons" really mean to these people?

And that pioneer sordid violent sexual encounter with Brian was how I got sucked up into Mark's duplicitous world of sexual shenanigans with the high and mighty of Harare, the big wigs of mostly the northern affluent Harare suburbs. There were big names involved in this underworld lucrative sex-cum drugs ring.

I'm talking of big people within the higher echelons of Harare, both in business and politics. The stakes couldn't have been higher and were nigh risky, had I broken Brian's confidentiality clause; he followed that up with a written agreement he forcibly made me sign under threats of: "You are working for me, so may as well make it legit, Matt. We need this well-choreographed facade for obvious reasons. During the day you continue prowling the streets under your assumed identity as a street kid, but in reality, you'll be prowling around for more street urchins for my clients."

And as business expanded, we decided to dabble in recreational drugs. This was where it got interesting, as members of the ruling party and law enforcement were also intricately involved in this illicit web of well-organized crime and drug trafficking from the deprived streets of Mbare, Chidzere, Mabvuku, Fio, Tafara and many other southern suburbs of Harare.

I am one who speaks now with the benefit of hindsight, as cliched as the saying goes, *hindsight is a wonderful thing, isn't it?* In retrospect, my story with my peers' stories strengthens my resolve to be as present and positive as possible to my children, so that they won't be as likely to follow the Mark Instones and Brian Whartons of this world.

If my sons really need to know how to be "a man," I'm right here to show them. Looking back, I can clearly see I learned the hard way. There are two specific points that I need to explain from my experience with these vile men.

The first is that there is a link between toxic, violent masculinity, the homophobia that goes along with it, and direct child abuse. I can only say there is a special place in hell for grown-ass men like Brian and Mark who groom children into sexual candy for their selfish perverted desires. It is more like those widespread sects which use the façade of religion to prey on under-age girls, knowing full well their perverted debauchery is protected by the crooked state in exchange for political votes, come election time. Aaah Zimbabwe, my heart breaks for you, my homeland. How have we allowed ourselves to sink to this level as a nation where we turn the other way in the face of sexual predators to posterity?

There's a big overlap between the grown-ass men who spend so much time policing people's sexuality, gender, et cetera, and the grown-ass men who do shit like groom children, trick them with laced blunts like they used to do to lots of boys at the Avenues safe house.

And so, I will remain Matt, *the best piece of ass in downtown Harare,* for isn't that is how the mighty Mark, the man whose face appears on all major newspapers and news channels, characterised me? The man whom society looks up to. Why wouldn't they, given he's a well-known benefactor up and down the length of the country? I doubt they know his seedy side and the underground, underworld cartel he runs. But then, this is Harare, isn't it, where anything goes and is up for grabs to the highest bidder.

In many instances, myself and my mates met these men through our fixer, Brian Wharton, a lanky white man from Borrowdale Brooke. A taciturn man, we all knew he was the fixer for our predators. No one dared cross his path for, *"he's nigh powerful and connected to mighty Mark Instone,"* was the often-whispered words among my harem of other down and out youngsters trying to eke out a living from the austere streets of Harare.

Most of my ilk in our downtown Harare gang had lives similar to mine stemming from a broken home devoid of a father figure. Those who ran away from home were living on the streets. Ben was one such fellow; he was brought up without a father, his mother struggled to make ends meet, so he used to do anything for a living. He used to guard a prominent Zanu bigwig's house in Chisipite.

Perpetually used and discarded like a condom by the party or whoever was the highest bidder, that pretty much typified our Harare existence. We could guard their houses for the measly crumbs they scathingly threw at us. At times we would attend the party rallies, pissed to high heavens, having imbibed the most toxic of brews by the party's commissariat and propaganda unit, in between taking spliffs of weed, known in local parlance as *mbanje.* Then we could engage in an orgy of glaring violence against perceived enemies of the party, ordinary people, citizens going about their mundane lives in central Harare and surrounding areas. As sadistic hoodlums, we took comfort in knowing all our horrific acts of thuggery and violence would be blamed on the other side, opposition party activists. At times we would plant incriminating evidence at opposition premises just to let them get harassed by the state. Talk of gas lighting the opposition, we were masters at this chicanery and subterfuge.

Our detractors would lampoon us as "nodding dogs" appendages of the party. Just barking, though empty bellied, protecting the big fish as they enjoy. *Apo kana future hapana."*

Chapter 8

Blanchet Years

I have vague memories of my mother, Sophia, a wild, hedonistic, eccentric party-loving Bohemian was Sophie's modus operandi. I recall, though fleetingly, the drinking sprees, interspersed with drug-fuelled orgies and a string of partners one after the other, like she was a revolving door, churning and spitting out boyfriends ad infinitum!

There's no one like Sister Tendai, my mother. Isn't that what every child says about their own mother? But you see, Sister Tendai wasn't my biological mother, which makes her extra special for sticking by me when my very own mother saw fit to throw me to the wolves, into social care at the tender age of eight.

The sanctimonious English social services deemed a designated children's care home-cum orphanage was the next best thing for me, as opposed to Sophie's hedonistic lifestyle. "She's not a fit mother," the family judge decreed through the state appointed family liaison officer, Gill. That landmark ruling catapulted me into a new habitat. That was how my fleeting love affair with Goodhope institution commenced one wintry morning, when social services dumped me at the stifling prison that was Goodhope.

My memories at Goodhope Convent are quite bright for an eight-year-old mixed-race girl who experienced different reactions to my ethnicity. Not that I was conscious of my race at the time. *How can race, skin color, mean anything to an eight-year-old?*

Goodhope Girls Convent was a Catholic Church run orphanage for unfortunate little devils like myself who had no abode of their own to call home. Ensconced in the English West Midlands on Solihull hilly terrain, Goodhope Convent was quite imposing with its regal, majestic looking, sprawling, three-acre white buildings, which made us nickname it: The White House.

Altogether Goodhope convent housed 45 girls of different ages ranging between eight and eighteen. We had school onsite, and the place was run by the strict disciplinarian Madame Blanchet, an old school goose, a tall imposing French geezer with aristocratic blood in her veins as she so wanted to constantly remind us. "Now listen and listen very hard girls. Goodhope is my dominion, let's get this straight first! Everything else is secondary. Your souls are my prerogative, in addition to your intellectual fulfilment. You're damned, and I am here to save you," she would rumble on non-stop in one of her recurring assembly addresses to us.

"At Goodhope convent, you will do as you are told like a proper Catholic girl. Are we clear on this?" She posed the question as she surveyed the college's vast great hall like a bull terrier scanning her dominion for any undue opposition upon which she was ready to pounce.

Sister Tendai came into my life a few years into my early years of settling at Goodhope. I must have been eleven or twelve when she and her zany husband, Walter, adopted me.

"We'd been trying for a baby over a decade and are now resigned to the futility of this ever becoming a reality, so Marina will just do fine by us," remarked the woman I later knew was Sister Tendai to Madame Blanchet the day she came to sign the adoption paperwork. This signalled my imminent departure from Goodhope, a place which had been home to me for over many years.

Strangely enough, Sister Tendai's husband, zany Walter, had remained aloof and detached from the proceedings. I could say I detected an air of boredom and resignation in his body language. *Perhaps I'm reading too much into nothing here*, I inwardly remarked to myself. So, after the completion of the paperwork, I soon moved into Sister Tendai's Brade Drive residence in Coventry in the West Midlands. I remember being elated at leaving Goodhope then; it felt like a crowning moment as the others crowded around me in the reception foyer with their warm wishes in my soon-to-be new life outside Blanchet's gaol.

"Good luck, I am so, so envious of you Marina," remarked Gill, one of my roommates in the dormitory we shared.

"Please don't forget us," shouted Jenny across the dormitory, another girl, I got along with.

But my newfound freedom was a pyric victory. In no time, I was catapulted back to Blanchett "concentration camp" in spectacular fashion on account of an unsavoury bathroom encounter I had with Sister Tendai's husband Walter the weirdo. For the first few weeks following my moving in with them, Walter ogled me in an uncomfortable way. I always felt uneasiness, as though I'd been violated each time he was within the vicinity of the house, all the more when Sister Tendai happened to be away. So, on this evening, the bastard crept up on me in the toilet, exposed himself in a grotesque way, and as he started rubbing himself, told me to put his manhood in my mouth, calling it, "Daddy wants a massage, Marina. Now be a good girl will you and give Daddy a blow job."

For a moment, I stood absolutely transfixed, my powers of speech and sobriety having spectacularly abandoned me. My eyes were quickly darting sideways looking at possible escape routes from that monster, his lecherous, covetous eyes ogling me. "Come on Marina, you know you want to give Daddy a massage, a warm tender kiss," he repeated as I could see him becoming increasingly hard and excitable. At that very moment, something came on me quick and fast, and I summoned the inner courage to bellow at the top of my voice like my whole life depended on it.

"Help! Quick! Bathroom!" I repeatedly and frantically shouted, all the while my eyes transfixed on the monster. And within a split-second, Sister Tendai dashed into the bathroom at breakneck speed. Quite a hideous spectacle assailed her, and she couldn't get beyond the overbearing shock of witnessing her husband in the nude with a teenage girl toward whom he was supposed to be providing the duty of care.

That spectacle was enough to tip Sister Tendai over the edge, and in no time, I found myself back at Goodhope. Ms Blanchett, however, would not ever have me talk about this incident. She'd insisted in her office on my return, "Under no circumstances whatsoever, Marina, will you ever repeat what happened at your foster mother's place. Do you get me?" She'd bored her eyes right into me in an intimidating fashion as she spoke to me, her body language too palpable; she meant business.

"Yes ma'am, I get you," I acquiesced. And to drive home her points, I was made to sign what she termed non-disclosure forms.

"Just so you know, Marina, these are legal documents which seal your mouth on whatever transpired during you short sojourn out of here. I have a convent to run, and I will not brook any undue adverse publicity. We don't need it! I don't need it! I can only speak on your behalf that you've heard me as you said earlier on, and indeed we're singing from the same hymn sheet." And with that and a peremptory wave of her hand, she dismissed me from her office.

"So, you mean in all these years you haven't said a word?" remarked Rhys as he leaned forward to pour himself a glass of water.

"Oh yes, I respected Blanchett's words after that mishap. I didn't want to upset her I guess, and it is only now that I'm opening up about it. But what does it matter? In a few weeks' time I am likely to lose my life as well, so no more secrets I would say. What good is it if I don't share some of my experiences? Take them to the grave with me? What for? Happy I have someone to talk to in these grim walls of Chikurubhi."

"One other hazy bit for me Marina. Sister Tendai, right? What kind of a person calls their mother 'Sister'? I get that she wasn't your real mother, as in biological mother, but why the moniker 'sister Tendai'? Please enlighten me."

"Aah, good old Rhys," I remarked, chuckling at his inquisitive streak. "Well, at least, it shows me you're concentrating and listening to me then. The 'sister Tendai' moniker is a bit of an oddball one. It is rumoured my transient surrogate mum, foster mum, whatever you want to call her, used to be a Catholic nun, known by that name Sister Tendai, until one day, she ran into wily Walter, who corrupted her. And boom! The good sister fell short of her vows. The rest is history, as they say."

"Holy shit!" ejaculated Rhys amid a whistle. "And here I am, used to thinking those nuns were proper chaste. Frailty, thy name is pussy!"

"Thy name is dick, you mean," I cheekily retorted, as we regaled in raucous laughter.

"Well, takes two to tango, I would say."

"Funny you say this Rhys, but here is the thing. The story goes, randy Walter was one of the usual handy men lift engineers at the convent where Sister Tendai plied her trade. On many occasions, the duo would have their quickie, frisky romps within the sacred, convent building, but things apparently came to a head when the insatiable sister act was caught right in the thick of it, in a compromising nooky in the elevator by visitors who had come to the home."

"Oh, my word, Marina! You're joking, right?"

"Far from it. That's why she ended up quitting the convent and, in that action, called time on her vows."

"What an ignominious end! And I died," Rhys remarked, becoming tangled in derisive laughter.

Chapter 9

Goodhope

The Early Years

Being a blooming teenager who hadn't known any other home life than mother's chaotic life, I guess it wasn't difficult for me to resettle at Goodhope Catholic convent for girls following the weird Sister Tendai-Walter mishap. Goodhope pretty much became my new life, being an abode which promised stability, as the powers that be constantly rammed down our throats. Besides, the shenanigans by Sister Tendai's weirdo husband made me have a grudging acceptance of Goodhope as my home, not that I could be choosy on what I could term my rightful habitat. Perhaps my experience with Sister Tendai's randy husband taught me I should be grateful for the scraps thrown my way.

A typical school day at Goodhope started with breakfast in the large dining room, morning prayers, and assembly, with Blanchett pontificating to us on the rigours of bringing up a proper Catholic girl who would serve society well. We would accomplish this, "by being morally upright as is befitting of Goodhope's ethos and values." She would intone, "I will not have you bringing a stain and ruining the sacrosanct name of this institution. Do you hear me girls?"

"Yes, ma'am," we would all bellow in a thunderous affirmative in the school's great hall as we were expected to, lest we were prepared to face dire consequences like being deprived of our breakfast. Amongst all the other girls, we reckoned demurring wasn't worth losing our breakfast by trying to be a smarty pants goody two shoes to Madame Blanchett. She was too fastidious and keen to immediately lay down boundaries.

I knew from interactions with other girls that they were not happy; there was often talk of wanting to escape from this hellhole. This tended to be the case with June, a buxom, pretty black girl I gravitated toward. She put me under her wing and we became close buddies over the years we sojourned at Goodhope.

"I can't wait to turn 18, so I rid myself of this shithole," June said, as she pulled on her cigarette, then exhaled smoke from her nostrils.

"Go on, pass me the fag; don't you finish it all, psycho," I chided, stretching my arm to get my fair share of a few drags on the cigarette.

We had devised our own sneaky ways of buying cigarettes from Goodhope kitchen staff, who were only too happy to oblige on account of their meagre salaries. This meant their morality bar was very low and needed no further lowering of its rungs. Each time we wanted to have a quick ciggie, like now, we could either hide or do it in the shrubbery and bushes behind the school toilets. Once we got busted by Mademoiselle Dupont, we tended to use parts of the disused school dungeons, as in today's case, the music classrooms in an isolated building.

"I say, did you hear me, dummy?" June said, as she prodded me in my rib cage.

"Aw stop it! I heard yaa! You don't like it here. Fancy, me having such a choice would be an unheard-of luxury and certainly out of the question. Where else would I go, Sophie? My mum has now been officially committed, sectioned to a loony's place because of her drug binge gone awry. No hope for me in high heavens there. Looks like I'm here to stay for good, mate."

"We just have to wait until we both turn 18, then we're considered adults and our voice matters."

"Possibly, or university entry will certainly mark our freedom. It's not long to go now, is it? Another two years, boom! And it will happen!"

"Golly! Two years already?" My mind flickered to the past six years, particularly my first two to three years of settling down at Goodhope whilst I tried to establish myself amongst the brood of girls, trying to fit in. It had not been without hurdles though. The road had been nigh tough getting accepted into the fold by the girls. Goodhope was more like Alcatraz, where one had to prove oneself first before she was accepted into the fold.

There was that initial suspicion and scepticism surrounding my reception by the other girls. On one too many occasions, I stumbled upon them gossiping about me. That was how things panned out that Friday evening in our television common room where we all congregated after dinner, to unwind and see out the evening in between taking sneaks outside to smoke. Smoking, yes, I was already smoking by nine; there's no need to be judgemental over choices I willingly made, even though some of you may try to play the minor card at me. I'm afraid it won't wash.

But I digress. Where was I? Aaah, the common room incident, when I caught June bitching about me with the other girls.

"She's a stuck-up bitch! That's why she keeps to herself. She doesn't talk or mingle with us, for we are far too inferior and beneath her ain't we?" That was unmistakably June's gruff, booming masculine voice. No wonder the others called her "Jim" behind her back.

"I can't stand her, she's too skinny for my liking! Must be anorexic," Paula remarked aggressively. Paula was always spoiling for a fight with all and sundry. She reminded me of a bulldog, given the constant snarl etched on her face. Paula the bulldog, the epithet fit her very well.

I politely coughed to announce my presence as I confidently sauntered into the common room and boldly declared, "It can only be spineless cowards who don't have the mettle to confront a person they despise, like you two idiots, Paula and June." I spoke wringing my hands in a deprecating derisive way to both.

The entire common room went dead quiet, save for the intermittent sound of the telly, which I proceeded to switch off nonchalantly, amid wild gasps and howls from the other girls. I could tell some of the gasps and expressions of surprise were at how confounded the girls were by my brazen bravado at openly challenging and disparaging two revered big guns of Goodhope, the mighty Paula and June-Jim! All eyes were now on the duo and how they would take my humiliating public dressing down, which had shattered their hitherto flawless stock of invincibility.

53

Even as I stood defiantly, squaring up to the much-feared bullies amid bated breath from the common room crowd, I saw Paula lunging at me with clenched fists. I had well anticipated this. I skilfully ducked and instead floored her with a scissors kick on her groin, which elicited a loud yelp from her, much to wild applause and adulation from my newfound common room mates who were now excitedly chanting, "Get her! Give it to her! Stick it into the bitch, Marina!" This fired me up. For once in my life, I was in charge of a situation. I was the center of attention. I was the story. There was something searingly beautiful about this and I loved it. I revelled in my newfound glory. Their wild cries and deafening screams of adulation and cheerleading were the aphrodisiac I needed; they energized me further as I pummelled strong jabs at both Paula and June to the raucous shouts, "Get them! Get them!"

I was certainly transposed into another world that evening as I relentlessly fought off two feared bullies at Goodhope. It took the might of two burly security staff and Mister Powell, who doubled as groundsman, to restrain me into a pin hold. All the while, the common room crowd cheered me on. And boy, did I not revel in my newfound notoriety and celebrity status. I sure did savor every moment of it. Never mind the next morning I found myself sitting across the desk from a stentorian Ms. Blanchett, who did not appear at all amused by my wild shenanigans of the previous night. She took it upon herself to school me once more in the ethos of Goodhope Convent.

"Now listen and listen hard, Marina! I am thoroughly disappointed with you. In fact, what makes it worse is I'm not angry with you, but there is huge disappointment written all over my face! Can you not see it?" She spoke peering into my eyes, as if I were a lost soul who needed salvation.

I didn't know whether to respond to her question or whether it was a rhetorical question, so I just stared back at her, but there was no mistaking the sense of triumph in me. I was the new Goodhope kid on the block! The hero of the moment! I had arrived! Following the common room fight, all the girls were now gravitating toward me, even my two nemeses, Paula and June, who'd been reduced to shadows of their former selves, courtesy the kick-boxing prowess of my common room thumping of them.

"Are you even listening to me, young lady?" Blanchet's face roused me out of my momentary reverie and contented glow of self-adulation.

"Yes ma'am. I'm sorry. I've let myself down, I've let Goodhope ethos and sacrosanct ideals down, and for this I am thoroughly ashamed of myself."

"Very well, Marina. I'm glad you see the error of your ways, which will certainly receive a stiff sanction. I will not have you soil Goodhope's name and brand I've worked tirelessly to build and sustain over the years. So, for your misdemeanour you will be banned from the TV common room for a week. In addition, you will assist Mr Powell in tending the flowerbeds by the grand entrance to the convent. Is that clear, young lady?"

"Yes, ma'am," I said, nodding demurely to Ms. Blanchet. This appeared to rile her further, as she let rip into me, guns blazing. "Don't get sassy with me young lady," she bayed, menacingly baring her fangs and claws. Still boring into me with blazing eyes, she said, "You have a bee in your bonnet like the other trouble causers here. Moving forward, show me you're truly repentant of the error of your ways!"

Though outwardly cowering in her presence, I inwardly remained defiant and celebratory of my newfound status. Henceforth, I was the new center of power at Goodhope. Even former bullies Paula and June kowtowed to me, and that was how my friendship with June was sealed, in those strange moments of acrimony and infamy. Talk of interesting paradoxes, a friendship was forged in violent aggression. As June, Paula, and I gradually became close buddies, it became increasingly clear we didn't really fit in at Blanchett's Goodhope. We were considered clearly too cool by the other girls, a far cry from the book freaks they were. We hated it when Madame Blanchett sermonized everything like we were Sunday school kids. It made things sound so formal and dull. Perhaps that explains why our rebellious streak was always kicking in. "Bloody bitch!" I scowled after her as I exited her office. "She's so entirely negative. What a sad cow. All she does is nothing but criticize, criticize ad infinitum. Can't stand her," I hissed under my breath.

Unbeknown to Madame Blanchett, for all she lauded him and apart from the kitchen staff, Mr. Powell also provided an additional conduit for cigarettes and weed to the girls at Goodhope. I was all too eager to go out and assist with the flower bed chores with alacrity. Regardless, I could never reconcile his dodgy dealings with us with his counter point of constant encouragements to do well in our studies. These contradictions inherent in the man always left me agape with surprise and wonder. Mr. Powell was gifted with sheer brilliance in mathematics, which rubbed off on me and other girls during our usual interactions. Each time I was put in detention, Mr, Powell would offer to help me with any math and science homework I had. I must admit, from him I learned a lot about problem solving skills in math, particularly those agonising quadratic equations.

Though my scepticism at his Dr. Jekyll and Mr. Hyde duality in character kept coming back haunting me, I found myself pondering like the other girls, "Is the man for real? On one hand, he feeds our smoking vice, yet he goes on pontificating how we ought to do well in our studies. Who is he kidding, with this brazen hypocrisy?"

Ever so daring, once I took and won a dare with the other girls and summoned some inner guts and bravado at asking Mr. Powell pointedly about his blowing hot and cold character. I opined, "I don't know. You're a huge contradiction, Mr. Powell, but the girls and I were wondering whether you could shed some light on the mysterious contradictory vibes you give out with your character." Somewhat taken aback by my brazenness and candor, Mr. Powell quickly regained his composure and went on to offer a rambling explanation about his conflicting persona.

"Aha, I see, you're brave Marina; the other girls sent you to bell the cat," he remarked in raucous laughter at his joke, exposing the natural gap between his teeth. He resumed speaking, "So yes, my life is a contradiction. You see, I never had the chance like you girls do. I lost my daughter early on, and this can be one way I atone for Elli's memory, by ensuring you girls do brilliantly at school." Mr Powell would often opine, "So, here we go again Marina, quadratic equations are easy peasy if you do it this way, not the long circuitous way you go about it." He would chuckle at me, meanwhile making a seemingly gargantuan mathematical problem fizzle into nothing, much to my bemusement.

So, in the end, as the years flew by, my mind was set on going into Durham university, I knew early on it would have to be a math degree or something to do with electronics or chemical engineering, but the stakes couldn't be higher. Durham was a top-notch competitive uni, with well-nigh high entry requirements. And I was determined to land a place there.

"Do you think, we can make it into Durham, June?" Many atimes we would both share our disquietude and Mr. Powell was always at hand to shore up our fledgling confidence. Once I remarked, "Thank you for all you do for us. Why don't you retrain and be a teacher, as your passion in helping youngsters is clearly palpable Mr. Powell?"

"Aaah, it's too late for that now. I love what I do; the flower beds need me," he would remark, the usual friendly glint in his kind eyes.

Chapter 10

In the Trenches with June

"And here we are now, looking forward to the two years' timeframe likely to give us our freedom from Goodhope. How the time flies."

"You never told me the real story behind your kick-boxing escapades," June chuckled, as she handed me a cigarette.

"Well, what is there to know, *massa*?" I replied, the malevolent glint in my eyes all too palpable. *Massa*, a corruption of the name, "master" was an annoying inside joke between the two of us. I constantly derided June, "You think you are my master on account of my mixed-race heritage? No way will you ever be my massa June! This is 21st century Britain, not the anachronistic colonial empire bullshit anymore. Get that!"

"Of course, I am not your master. Did I ever say I am? How dare you insinuate such horse poo?" June would strongly remonstrate, feigning exaggerated annoyance.

"And now, coming back to your judoka question, I never really got to open up to you, but Maurice, one of Mum's string of endless boyfriends, was a black belt judoka who taught me the fine art of judo and martial arts. He would take me with him to the Jonathan Page judo practice sessions in Aylesbury.

"Hu ha hu ha." It was all hu-ha with Maurice," I said, as I theatrically gesticulated with my hands to June's laughter.

"Well, I must say, I owe Maurice a large debt of gratitude, then," she said.

"What for?"

"For teaching you judo. How else could we have been friends, had you not floored me in the common room that eventful night?"

"Oh, there you go again, typical June hogwash," I said, as our laughter carried us away. What pleasant memories June and I had, and a strong friendship bond shared and forged through the years growing up at Goodhope Convent. Increasingly, we gravitated towards each other and became more of sisters over the years.

Chapter 11

Doris

A Mother's Ordeal

By the time I arrived at the casualty department, I was bent over in excruciating pain. I could hardly make sense to the hospital receptionists. Both receptionists could see I was not well, and they hurriedly triaged me to the front of the que.

"I feel like vomiting," I blurted to them, as I felt bile and nausea rising in me. The words had barely left my mouth when I started retching uncontrollably and vomited a copious amount of blood onto the casualty floor. The entire A and E department sprang alive.

The surgical registrar was immediately paged. As I continued to vomit blood onto the floor, I could see everyone was running around for me.

"Theater," they called. The surgical registrar was barking orders. "Theater NOW!" Drip sets were going up. An intern was running to the blood bank. My clothes were being cut off my body as everyone sprang into jaw dropping action.

Meanwhile I continued to vomit. And vomit. And vomit. And vomi ... and vom ... and vo ... and v ...

"You're gone. We couldn't save you." And then I could see Dad's face, waving at me. Good old Jim; he approaches me, his smile dwindling as he realizes I'm hanging on a precipice, one arm outstretched for him. Much as he tries stretching toward me, he can't reach me...and boom...

"Sorry son, I can't do it. I'm sorry I tried."

Meeting with the deceased's family. Surgical registrar presents your case. "I am so sorry, Mrs. Williams, Doris, Rhys…" The doctor was struggling to speak as the lump in his throat got bigger and bigger.

"It was a perforated ulcer. Caused by many years of drug taking. We tried everything. Bled out in theater."

I passed out. I was in heaven meeting my Maker.

"Now is your time to account for your transgressions, Julian." I heard a voice address me in a peremptory tone, but I was too dazed to turn around. I was struggling to regain my usual affable self.

But how is it my fault? I ended up in a situation where I was taking far too many ibuprofens and aspirin on the run up to and following a recent operation for testicular pain. Soon as I healed from that, I went back to work and, BAM! perforated ulcer. They got me in time, and I survived, just!!

But how did it come to this? There must be a genesis in every story, ain't there? Would it make sense without a background story? Bring in Munyaradzi my fixer and supplier all in one. If anyone should shoulder any blame for my demise, then this rests squarely on Munyaradzi's shoulders. I rest my case.

How else have I been able to access my supply chain?

✦✦✦

It had been crushing, witnessing this surreal spectacle of Julian crumbling right before our eyes. That had been a right proper scare for us, Rhys and me. Julian's hallucinations precipitated the breakdown, and he stayed in hospital for over a month as the nurses and psychologists tended to him round the clock. We had hoped this was a defining moment for him, the magna carta moment when he would finally have seen the light and come to his senses, something I inwardly prayed for daily as his doting mother. But Julian had other ideas, as he appeared hell-bent on his self-destruct trajectory.

Chapter 12

Mazowe Citrus Fruits Farm

As a recovering addict, I know I have made poor choices which have brought me here. But I have always tried. In fact, I did try to confront my demons after mother dragged me to see a shrink at Harare's Rock Foundation medical center in Mt. Pleasant.

"Please hear me out, Julian. Things can't carry on like this, son."

"I need help, you're going to say, Doris. Save yourself the needless effort and breath," I sarcastically retorted, but she was not daunted.

"You forget I'm your mother for heaven's sake, the woman who brought you into this world. Why don't you just humour me and agree to see Dr Hinckley?"

"Oh, so you think emotionally blackmailing me that you brought me into this world will do the trick. I don't think so, Doris. Try another tack, not this one. It won't work and it's certainly wearing thin," I said, as I retreated to the backyard garden shed where I kept my crystal meth/*guka* stash as we called it in downtown Harare Street lingo.

This constant haggling with Mum, arm twisting me to see her doctor became long and sustained with Mum ratcheting up pressure. To quieten her, I gradually acquiesced. *Just so you make her happy, good old Doris,* an inner voice whispered to me.

Interestingly, it was because of that Hinckley visit that I came face to face with my demons.

Surprisingly, I warmed up to Hinckley, a vivacious, spirited white doctor of the few remaining psychiatrists in Harare. I think I did like her from first encounter. It would be fair of me to say so. Perhaps I was enamoured by her immersive charm and wit, and that she had time for weirdos, druggies like me, the scum of Harare as my brother Rhys used to demonize me in his constant put downs.

Much to my relief, she requested Doris excuse herself, and so it was only her and me in her consulting chambers. I felt disarmed by her calm demeanor, and I found myself chatting to her quite at ease, babbling away like I had known her before.

We chatted at length about the nature of addiction and the effects of substance abuse on the mind and body; surprisingly, I found my tongue loose with her.

"So, how did you get into this, Julian if you don't mind my asking?"

And that had been it, as I poured my heart out to this stranger I had been resisting to see for months on end.

"I know I sound defensive, Doctor," I began, after clearing my throat of phlegm.

"Helen will do, just call me Helen. Pray continue," she said, motioning with her hand encouraging me to open up.

"The thing is, Helen, it's not really my fault that I abuse drugs. Look at the underlying back story you need to know, and don't you tell me you don't see it. But as a fellow white Zimbabwean, I'm sure you appreciate things have not been easy for our lot!

"And don't you dare deny it, Helen," I looked at her again, this time askance. She could only beckon, "Please carry-on, Julian, I'm listening, and just so you know, I'm not here to judge you. In fact, I have a duty of care to you as my patient."

"Thank you, Helen. So I was saying there are many variables which have brought me to this dark place, not least the broken and toxic politics in this country, as I'm sure you well know.

"Look, I'm not trying to politicize my addiction here. Far from it, but I have never felt truly Zimbabwean since the politics of exclusion, violence and vindictive reprisals started in the early 2000s. We had a viable citrus fruit farm in Mazowe. We lost that at the hands of gun-toting, machete-wielding marauding youths masquerading as this country's war veterans. And before you start, this is not me shouting and pulling out the victimhood card at all. Far from it. Hear me out first, Helen."

In fact, I vividly recall the events of that day at our Mazowe farm as if it were yesterday. We were witnessing something extraordinary, whose unfolding we dared not disturb as the "war veterans" crowded around us and some of our farm workers' milling around.

"Iwe mzungu, you white man and your children. You leave today, do you hear me?" one of the gun-toting youths spoke menacingly, prodding my dad's ribs with an AK 47 rifle. Even though Dad tried valiantly, brandishing his title deeds to these pseudo war veterans, they were not for turning.

"You have to listen to me son," ever so polite Dad -Jim- went on. "I bought this farm soon after independence in the early Eighties in the government's willing seller-willing buyer scheme. So, there's nothing like I stole your land as you're saying, and all I'm asking you to do is to take a few minutes to look at all the bond paperwork here, of the loan I borrowed from Standard Chartered Bank to fund my purchase. It's taken me twenty years, *twenty years I say,* to settle this loan." Dad pleaded as he raised his ten fingers twice, waggling them as if to emphasise his point to the restless war veterans' mini crowd, which now filled our fore courtyard, with some farm labourers savouring the unfolding melee.

"Okay, old man, *mzungu,"* remarked the bloodshot lunatic who was probably high on some substance. Funny I'm saying this, since we seem to have exchanged places with him, and as now I also dabble into substance abuse.

"Okay *mzungu,* I will hear you out as you so request. Let me have a look at your title deeds and then we should resolve this little misunderstanding in no time," barked their supposed leader, whom we later knew was Mujubheki, a local school dropout.

"Here is the paperwork," Dad politely said, thinking this would placate this marauding gang of sadistic hoodlums, and he handed Mujubheki a wad of papers tied by a now mangled blue ribbon.

Then quite bizarrely, Mujubheki asked, "Does anyone of you here smoke?" It was a somehow odd question, given the sombre nature of the occasion.

After what seemed like an eternity, Mother came out of her shell.

"I do smoke," she timidly remarked.

"Very well then," boomed Mujubheki excitedly. "Can I borrow your lighter then?"

No sooner had Doris fished her lighter from her bag than Mujubheki ignited the lighter and, right there and then in front of us, he set ablaze the entire title deeds paperwork Dad had just given him as proof of ownership of the Mazowe farm. Soft plumes of smoke wisped upward.

Just like that, Mujubheki acted without so much as flinching his eyes, and as if he was doing something mundane and part of an everyday chore; he was oblivious to the array of incredulous wild gasps, groans, mouths agape, bewilderment, horror and surprise which marked our faces as we witnessed this surreal development.

It was then, after what seemed an interminable eternity, that Dad bellowed in remonstrance, springing into action, and trying to wrest his prized legal paperwork from Mujubheki's flames. But within a split second, boom! Mujubheki's revolver fired and caught Dad right in his left chest. I cannot begin to tell you the commotion that followed this kerfuffle. People jostled and scuttled in various directions in the melee that followed, with wild screams from Doris, my brother Rhys, and the other folks - our farm workers - whom we had always regarded as family.

I rushed to Dad's defense, but even I could see there was not going to be any reprieve for that lifeless body which now lay limp, sprawled on the grass in our fore yard amid small rivulets of blood. Meanwhile, Mujubheki fired more rounds into the sky, bellowing to everyone to calm down, as if we had to, following his cold-blooded murder of my dearest father, Jim.

Up to now, it beats me how someone could have so much hate and negativity imbued within them. What kind of person would find it within themselves to want to hurt Dad, especially after all he'd done for the Mazowe community? What kind of attitude is that? Good old Jim, a man of unparalleled depth and substance. For as long as I can remember, Dad was always generous, bonkers, and kind. He was one of a kind. I say this without patronizing anyone, but I think I'm correct in my estimation of how lofty the black community in Mazowe and far afield perceived Dad and held him in high esteem. I know his lofty status among them had also been confirmed by Sisi Maria and M'koma Eddy, our farmhouse helping hands, even when I overheard their conversations, oblivious that I was listening.

"Aaah baas Jim wouldn't hurt a fly, *ndarwadziwa fani, mkoma* Eddy," Sisi Maria had remarked as she attempted to console M'koma Eddy over our family loss. "There was no need for that, such a gruesome death, to shoot a man in cold blood and then proceed to hack him, all before his family and workers! As if that's not enough to proceed to shoot his dogs also, as if to make complete the whole macabre incident. Why have we debased ourselves to these levels?" went on Sisi Maria, her grief and anguish profound on her tear-stained, grief-stricken face.

And then the gut-wrenching sobs followed, as M'koma Eddy stepped in consoling her. These were two people who had worked closely in our employ and dined and wined with us at very close quarters. They were more like family to me, to us. See, that's just a measure of how my father Jim was held in such high esteem by those who knew him and had interacted with him over the years.

I started dabbling in crystal meth about several months following the violent seizure of our Mazowe farm. Perhaps seeing my father Jim being hacked to death contributed to tipping me over the edge. I had been clean till then, but one day, I just couldn't hold it together anymore. Through Munyaradzi's downtown Harare connections, I tried it and never looked back thereafter. I have tried to stop several times, believe me, but it only lasts a few days. Then the urge for my constant fix overwhelms me. Does that make me sound pathetic? Your call!

"Do you see, where I'm coming from, Helen?"

She nodded by way of acknowledgment as I carried on, lost in my treatise and personal agony. By the time I vacated Helen's surgery, it was already dusk. The spring crickets were chirping in Harare's streets, as the stray dogs hobbled off to find another refuge for the night. I could see the litany of Harare's ubiquitous street kids huddled in corners and little groups.

"Thank you for being patient, Mum," I remarked as I got in the car beside her, flashing her my warmest smile of gratitude.

Chapter 13

Addiction Battles

My visit to Helen was certainly not to be a one off. I had warmed up to her. Much to my surprise, talking to her had done me some good, considering my earlier misgivings at visiting her. Uncharacteristically, I felt a great air of relief, like a load had been lifted off me. I kept in touch back and forth with Helen, and we kept on talking about the nature of addiction and the effects of substance abuse on the mind and body. Then I was making progress, I thought.

But one day she put me in contact with an addicts' support group, Mt. Pleasant Diamonds, more like Alcoholics Anonymous, set up where we sat in horseshoe formation during our fortnightly meetings and poured out our stories to other like-minded sods. That's how I met Jess; she warmed up to me and asked my advice on how I could help somebody who was battling with addiction in their relationship. Fancy asking me that, as if I were a trendsetter myself. That was another superpower testament of your prowess, Helen, in seeing goodness and potential in every human being. You connected those in need with those who could help.

Jess and I spoke for a long while on the phone. I shared my experiences about the effects of addiction on the addict, from the addict's point of view. We spoke about the harsh truth of interventions and how rarely they worked. I told you and her my story, so you could help others. Interacting with Sophie did help. Another fellow addict, battling her demons like me.

And in that telling of my story of addiction, you showed me another superpower: absolute compassion/zero judgement. Your only intent was to listen, learn and help. And that was you all over, Helen, you lived your life in service of others.

That was how our friendship started. After that, we'd message each other from time to time, to check in, to celebrate wins, to share stories, connect. You really made me feel seen, and loved, and worthy. But how can I tell you, it was that uncanny friendship with Jess which was my undoing? I can't face you with the honest facts, can I? For Jess and I had our relapse moments when we cavorted with the holy powders again and again.

"Oh, don't be such a wimp, Julian, this is hot off the market, the magical blue pill. Try it," Jess had egged me on, and I was only too happy to oblige her, playing to the gallery.

"Go on then, Jess, let's see who the wimp is," I said. And thus marked the commencement of my ruin and degradation as vile Rhys and my mother Doris put it.

I am sorry Helen; I was lying to you at all those subsequent follow up consultation therapy sessions we had. I am surprised, you didn't pick it up, my well-choreographed subterfuge, for you were gushing in your praise of me. But you missed it. I had relapsed into drugs again.

I've been slipping, slipping on my meds, going in a dark frame of mind.

"I cannot tolerate all this pressure on my shoulder. It's killing me, you know, it's killing me. I cannot breathe."

"Good job, Julian, you're making palpable progress," you were wont to say, without even a whiff of suspicion, I was playing you, both Jess and I were playing you, stringing you along. Meanwhile, our wild sexual orgies commenced aided by Mt. Pleasant Diamonds, which provided nocturnal cover for our sex romps as we played the field in the gym's changing rooms and bathrooms. Gosh, you should have seen us fuck! "Fuck me back-to-back," Jess would wail at me, deliriously caught in a wild sexual frenzy and vortex of unbridled ecstasy.

Chapter 14

Doris

I don't want to wallow in the sadness. That's not the Julian vibe I remember. Instead, I want to remember the powerhouse that Julian was before this fine madness set in. I want to remember all the laughs, the compassion, the love – everything that made you the adorable son you were in Mazowe all those years.

They say as long as your name is on the tongue of those whose lives you've touched, you will live on. Julian, you live on in all of us. Thank you for you. Rest in Peace, my cherub. Will you ever forgive me though? I wonder.

What an amazingly touching and beautiful human being you were, despite our eventual falling out. Still, I give you that; you were a phenomenal force who touched many people. I love that you had a beautiful and meaningful relationship with her, the love of your life, Evie.

We are hurting as a family, our pain has abased us, and we were prepared to do anything to save you, Julian, from your downward spiral. I hope, Julian, wherever you are, you see this for what it was: our genuine desire to retrieve you from the dark abyss that engulfed you.

Even now, as my end is nigh, I hope you forgive me, Son.

As a mother, sometimes I blame myself. I did not fully attune myself to all the challenges you encountered in your youth, moreso adult life, during those dark years of the farm invasions and the tumultuous aftermaths. Could that have been the trigger which set you off? Your descent into a hell hole? I am so overwhelmed with emotion; grief has wrung me out. I spent the greater part of my days in my cell in the serene confines of Chikurubhi prison, as I strive to find inner peace within myself.

I am wracked with seismic guilt. I should have done a bit more to save my son from ruin. Far too often, I've had this interior monologue that's kept looping through my head that something just wasn't right with Julian much earlier after our forcible Mazowe eviction and I should have stepped in urgently to stave off his eventual ruin.

"Why don't you come out into the sunshine and mingle with the others?" your brother, Rhys perennially asks. He doesn't get it, does he? This is out of choice; I don't want to mingle with anyone. Why should I? I have to finish this conversation with you first, so they accept me in the other world. I don't have long to go, Julian, so we better hurry up in this, our restorative daily conversation, if I am to get the much-needed closure I'm seeking.

Do you hear me, Son? Aaah, well, suit yourself by remaining mute; as long as I've said it, I'm sure you hear me loud and clear where I stand.

I want to make atonement and seek closure with you, even though you sought to end my life that fateful night. It didn't have to come to this, Son. Forgive me Julian, the stain of your blood is on my conscience for ever, and I hurt at this.

But we had a vibrant mother-son relationship back in the day, as you grew up at the farm in Mazowe, - *chubby Julian* - as Jim and I playfully teased you on account of your large build. We were all happy families then. Remember how *Sisi* Maria nursed you from boyhood till your teens at the farm? How *Sisi* Maria always defended you each time you started those boyhood fights with your brother Rhys? I also fought in your corner, remember, with Jim always reprimanding me, "You know it doesn't do the boy any good, Doris, making up excuses for his poor choices and silly behaviour?"

"He's only a kid, Jim, give it a rest, will you?"

And then the melancholia came. Julian's melancholia was nigh depressing and sucked dry the joy of others. In hindsight, perhaps I ought to have understood, empathized with you more, and sought to unravel the mysteries behind your brooding character which eventually exploded into mayhem.

Was it losing Evie which set you off?

Now I may never know; you're not here anymore.

Evie, a lovely flower, what did death gain from such cruelty, snuffing out her life prematurely like that?

All these years, Son, I have lived through unadulterated sadness and anger at how soon my husband's life was equally snuffed to an early end.

Talk of a glutton for pain and grief, that is certainly me, the story of my life in short. There is this unspoken sense of loss and sadness that engulfs us, experienced amongst our culled family. The loss of a husband, father, and daughter-in-law in one fell swoop is just about overwhelming.

Chapter 15

Julian-Helen Therapy Sessions

Men do suffer from depression, right? I resigned from my government job of twenty years' service, invested pension money in four businesses that failed, got divorced after a 20-year relationship, and that triggered my depression that was traced back to my childhood. I do relapse and still attend therapy. That's why I'm back here, Helen.

Lately, I've been suffering, slipping on my medication, mixing it with alcohol. I know I shouldn't be doing this, veering in a dark frame of mind, and you need to know this as my therapist, shrink, whatever you call yourself. There's only so much I can take. I'm sorry about the escalation in my drinking. There are things I've been hiding from you. I've been drinking daily. Unwise I know; flies in the face of your medical guidance to me.

I was sick of faking smiles in public, I was sick of letting my kids and myself down; I was sick of feeling like a failure; I was sick of crying myself to sleep every night, and I wanted the pain to go away, but it wouldn't. My mind and body were tired, and it was 3am in the wee hours of the morning. If I can't sleep naturally, insomnia. Then I have to find solace elsewhere. Can't I?

This was a man who was known to be doing well, always dressed well and looking the part in public. How can he be sick? Maybe it's just a phase; it will pass, as I was wont to convince myself. It didn't. It went on for days that turned into months.

Story of my life. Can't even talk about it, and I can't remember when it started, because every day its struggles galore, I have to contend with; being unemployed as a man can be very depressing, most especially if there is no one to turn to ...I'm just living in my own reality.

But then, Jess came into my life, sent by Evie to ensure I cope with Evie's going away, my loss as Evie keeps saying in the dreams. But that's a story for another day, Evie's constant haunting of me. Will tell you about the recurrent dreams another day. Another day, right?

"I'm really sorry for everything that you've been through. I pray God restores everything that you lost in the process. Love and light to you, Jess had said to me, lovingly patting my shoulders to show her support. I warmed up to Jess for her kindness, and that was how our relationship started, on the foundation of my downward spiral of alcohol and drug addiction affliction.

"The first step is to accept and realize that you're not tracking on a normal path, which is very difficult and needs very caring family support. I know you've said this to me before, but then I had Jess for me. Only problem, Jess was an addict like me, so we were no good for each other. How could we be?

***

"Do you hear me, Helen? Are you even listening to me?" I remarked petulantly, jabbing my index finger toward her.

"I am not making any judgments about anything that you are saying, but allow me to say this," Helen replied. "You've been through a lot, Julian, and I think you need to talk to someone who can help you through that. Is that a fair observation, do you think?"

I could only nod my head.

"I believe I am that person willing to listen to you and offer you appropriate advice and help. Your family and I go back, in fact, way back in time. I've been your family doctor from time immemorial if I may put it that way. Let your mind go back to your childhood. Were you happy, would you say?"

"Tell me, Helen, I mean Dr. Hinckley, how would you feel each time your very own family constantly dismisses you as a paranoid schizophrenic? That is the story of my life, if I may say, Dr. And you know, Jess has the nerve of accusing me of stalking her? Can you believe this?"

"So, this is your new thing now, appearing outside windows. Stalking me?"

"Kind of is."

"You might want to sit this out, Jess, because you don't know what the fuck, you're talking about," I hissed at her between my clenched teeth. I could barely suppress my seething anger at her."

"Helen, I'm sure you know this yourself. It's disheartening the way things have become for our lot, the white community in this country. Given the way we were violently ejected from our Mazowe farm, settling here in Borrowdale, I have worried every time I left home. Perhaps that's why I started teaming up with the Chipangano lads of Mbare, possibly for protection, or so I thought to begin with."

"What do you mean, 'or so I thought?'"

"Aha, I can see, you can't make the connection between my drug dalliance and Munyaradzi's infamous Chipangano lads."

"But who is Munyaradzi and what are you on about with this Chipangano talk… dare I call it mumbo jumbo bullcrap? I can't, for I am your doctor."

"Munyaradzi and Chipangano clique may well be another story for another day, Helen. Just like Evie's dream. Humor me, will you?

"It's so disheartening that these racial tensions continue festering many years on after independence. One of my friends told me she worries that someone in power will harm her white sons every single time they leave their home. "I have two white sons, and yet that has never once crossed my mind. It makes me despair for our country. I hear attacks against whites have escalated a notch further in the past few months?"

"I hear you, Julian. Things have certainly changed in this country, if not completely flipped. I'm white like you. Born in Zimbabwe, then Rhodesia in Shurugwi, near Ian Smith's farm. I grew up playing with Ian Smith's children as we lived in a neighboring farm, and my daddy used to go to Shurugwi Country Club with then Prime Minister Ian Smith and other white settlers. Look, I don't want to bore you with a history lesson, but the point is, there has been a reversal of fortunes for our lot in this country, especially under successive post-independence governments," Helen said.

"Like you," she continued, "I don't feel I belong anymore. Each time I leave my Chisipite home to go shopping at Bon Marche, I find I am constantly looking over my shoulder all the time. Now, this is not living, if you ask me.

"I feel I'm a racial target in many ways. Gone is the leeway I used to enjoy, growing up first as a white Rhodesian, and in the early years of independence, during those reconciliation phases. It is all gone!

"So, I hear you. I think I have an idea of what it means being white in this, the second republic, or however you want to call it. Yet the gross, rank injustice I see has now been flipped over. Like you, I see black on white racism, or xenophobia if I may call it that way. Sometimes it just feels like everything is too much…too much evil. There's too much hate out there in the streets of Harare. Evident even in the emaciated stray dogs of Harare. It's like they, too, are experiencing the spiritual malaise of the land that is Zimbabwe.

"So, yes, I have walked this road you've also traversed, Julian. Rest assured; I hear you. Please carry on. I just had to get this off my chest, just so you see we are in this together."

Looking at Helen now, I felt for her. There was a certain sincerity in her candor and voice inflection which made me believe her. From that moment on, I knew she would be someone I would continuously want to come back and talk to.

Raising my head and looking her straight in the eye, I said, "Thank you, Helen. Thank you for your honesty. For once I don't feel like a piece of junkie shit, the way everyone treats me. Is it okay if I can visit you periodically?"

"Of course, you can, Julian," and that had been it. Doris and I left Helen's medical chambers and I really thanked Mum as I had taken a real liking to Helen.

"So, how did it go this time?" Doris inquired peering at me intently.

"Quite all right actually. For the next visits, I would like to see Helen by myself if that's all right."

"Of course, you can, Julian. I'm only too glad it worked out well. You did take an exceedingly long time in there, but such is Helen's modus operandi. She's very thorough with her patients."

"You're telling me," I said with a broad grin creasing my face. "So, how long have you guys known Helen?"

"Oh way, back," Doris said. "We go a long way Helen and our family. In fact your dad was the first one who introduced me to Helen at the rare exclusive white functions we had in our little Borrowdale or Helensvale meetups in Harare. Gosh, how time flies. That has been ages ago. You were not even born then, as we used to stay mostly at the farm in Mazowe only coming to Harare on an ad hoc basis."

"She seems a well-to-do and connected person; she was name dropping Ian Smith and having grown up with his kids. Is she that old though? She doesn't look it."

"Oh yes, she wasn't exaggerating in any way. She did rub shoulders with the then political establishment class of Rhodesia on account of her proximity to the children. You're right though, age has been kind to Helen. For as long as I've known her, she's ever been so youthful."

That had been great, meeting Helen. We were to meet several times as she sought to help me navigate my demons and voices.

Chapter 16

Blurred Boundaries

In the quiet comfort of our Drew Road, Kambanji, Chisipite home, I reflected on the home truths I had been gleaning from my new patient, Julian. Rarely, do I ever take my work home, as in dwell on a patient after hours, but then Julian was no ordinary patient considering my connection to his family. Inwardly, I felt for him, particularly his fleeting moments of hallucinations which tended to plague him like the Jess incident in our last session, when poor Julian was convinced he was talking to Jess right before me in my surgery!

Perhaps I ought to swap his medication to an alternative psychosis drug, I ponder within myself. *An alternative drug to water down his escalating side effects, acute paranoia and the intermittent panic attacks accompanied by his incoherent ramblings.* Julian's psychosis medication causes him to hallucinate and have conversations with people who are not physically there in his space. But he is unaware of this. So as painful as it is to me, sometimes I've had to go along with these pretend conversations, too afraid to burst his bubble.

Notwithstanding Julian's difficulties, I look forward to my therapy sessions with him. A troubled soul. He is scarred and pummelled by the weight of history and the politics of our nation. I commiserate with him. I felt it was my professional duty to minister to and right this troubled soul. And so, with time, I became overfamiliar with him. I broke the doctor/patient cardinal rules by getting up close and personal and invited him to my Chisipite home, as transpired on this Saturday late afternoon, when Julian graced our presence. *There's nothing untoward with this,* I rationalized within myself. *After all, there is a personal touch. I know his family. They know me as well.*

Get a grip dear Helen. Stop this ethics silliness, I chided myself. I snapped out of my afternoon reverie. I resumed speaking with Julian.

"So, I was saying, Julian, my second husband is black. We've been married almost eight years now. I can say I had no idea how much I didn't know about black life. It hurts on a psychological level. I am still learning how to process it all.

"On the other hand, we are living our best life now, and no one can take that from us. Even though being married to a black Zimbabwean male in the current climate hasn't come without its difficulties."

"You're telling me," Julian said. "This country has gone bonkers for want of a better word. Whatever became of 'the jewel of Africa,' reconciliation la-di-da...?"

"Forget about that rhetoric, Julian, politicians are slimy foxes; they can say anything in the heat of the moment for expedient ends, as you well know from our recurrent electioneering backlash. Just like a man when he's horny, he'll say anything to get his dick into that hole," I said.

"I have lost count of the black on white prejudice I have encountered at times, thrown right into my face because of my marriage to Nhamo. He can speak for himself there. But this racial prejudice, bigotry, parochialism, whatever you want to call it, cuts both ways. My husband Nhamo has been the butt of uncouth racist jokes many atimes at social functions we've been to.

"I've stopped being appalled at the racist remarks thrown at both myself and my husband on account of his ethnicity. Here I was, thinking our interracial marriage could bridge the racial gap in our post-independence nation. But I am not sure we're there yet. Even from my side, this malaise is prevalent. Nhamo has not been well received by some of my fellow white kith and kin within and beyond Harare.

"It's all too palpable. At the country clubs we both visit and frequent are still the suspicion and distrust Nhamo is subjected to, the odd snide remark always conveniently dropped within our earshot, possibly to hurt us. 'Here comes the bitch who debased herself marrying a kaffir,' is among some of the unkind remarks. Hell! Alternatively, Nhamo is at the receiving end himself at times, being lampooned as 'the gold digger who married an old dowager, with an eye on inheriting her estate.' Really, folks, why can't we see beyond this and celebrate diversity even in relationships.

"The thing is, I love Nhamo; we're so much in love and he's the best thing that ever happened to me following the passing of my first husband, Chris. I don't get why people see ulterior motives where there are none in a relationship, and more so they are not privy to the finer details of the relationship. But perhaps such is testament to the broken nature of our nation, where either every minute, miniscule facet of life is politicized or seen in binary terms of a black and white paradigm skin colour prism.

"And how do you deal with that, in a supposedly enlightened country with one of the highest literacy rates in Africa? Don't we pride ourselves as such? I know we do. Zimbabweans we're a proud lot!"

"It's difficult terrain to navigate, but I'm not one for playing victimhood. I just get on with it," boomed Nhamo in his usual effervescent way as he joined in the fray, his face creased in a wide can't be bothered grin.

"Many atimes, I've been mistaken for Helen's chauffeur at social outings like Borrowdale Racecourse, and each time Helen has stepped in to save the day. Haven't you, darling?"

"Of course, muffin. I won't hear of it, this needless pigeonholing of people according to anachronistic stereotypes."

"You know what hurts me the most?" I asked Julian, refilling Nhamo's whiskey glass. "Sorry, Julian, you're on soft drinks. Doctor's orders," I told our guest.

"So, I was saying, this was a nation with so much potential as we flourished in the heydays of the early Eighties with the euphoria of independence. Far from it, I'm not a die-hard Rhodie as we're bound to be characterised in the daily *Pravda*. If anything, I'm a super patriot of this country."

"No one can tell how super-patriotic you are, Helen, other than myself as your other half," Nhamo said. "By Jove! You've certainly done your fair share of promoting this nation each time we used to go abroad when we could afford our annual holidays, back in the days."

Nhamo went on, "I remember well the now-defunct scholarship program you launched as you encouraged UK-Zim Africa venture links as you called them, encouraging pre-UK university students on their gap year to come visit and consider taking up their undergraduate degrees here."

"Oh, you remember all that, muffin?"

"Of course, I do, love."

"Then we were onto something as a nation in those days. Must admit this felt like a promising place for career-minded young people to study and flourish."

"Indeed, I remember Sally and Nina Morris, the two lassies from West Midlands, England, who ended up enrolling at the local UZ university and we used to host them many weekends."

"Oh, Sally and Nina, the two medical students. They absolutely loved it at UZ. They're now eminent surgeons in the United Kingdom and that tells you how lofty we were once. Our loss is other countries' gain."

"We once had greatness amongst us," remarked Julian. "There's nothing unpatriotic in calling out the shambolic fall in public service infrastructure obtaining now."

"Exactly, Julian," Helen replied. "Why can't we shy away from politicizing every facet of our lives, and just live harmoniously as fellow citizens? No one owns Zimbabwe! Zimbabwe is certainly bigger than this or any one individual's inflated ego."

"To be honest with you both, I am fed up to the eyeballs with this rampant, unwarranted racist abuse meted out to anyone who dares disagree with the current establishment, and I do not say this lightly," Nhamo said. "Drawing on my own experiences married to Helen, I have equally faced social opprobrium and censure. What for? My only crime, 'marrying an old white woman,' as they say. So, I am branded a traitor, gold-digger, nigger, all those colourful epithets, you name it. I am so done with this senseless shit!"

"Well said, Nhamo. In all this, who qualifies to be called a Zimbabwean? I've often pondered this pertinent question to myself, many atimes," Helen said. "My gripe with some of my fellow citizens was this often-peddled big lie that they were more Zimbabwean than I, or our lot, simply because of our skin pigmentation. My God! Such misplaced thinking and nothing could have been further from the truth! Talk of jingoism gone awry. This misplaced jingoism has certainly gone bonkers. Look at South Africa, Johannesburg; they elect a South African born black mayor but won't have it because of his foreign parentage. His father is said to have been Zimbabwean! When will we ever learn to shy away from this needless hair splitting of issues?

"My grandparents, the Todds, fought alongside African nationalists supporting the collective war effort. I therefore take exception to this, what I term effrontery of the highest order to insinuate all white folks were lesser Zimbabweans on account of their skin colour. No, I refuse to accept such hogwash.

"For crying out loud, I love Zimbabwe. I'm a true patriot to the core and no one could take that away from me, whatever vile propaganda or hate speech peddled against our lot. I am done with such naysayers like the government's misfiring spin doctors."

Chapter 17

Recurrent Rhodies Slur

Ghost of Integrated Zimbabwe

"It's nothing new in our fledgling democracy, this scapegoating mantra. Racist warm-ups and press-ups against us all the time, and "Rhodesian" name calling both as a slur and an insult are hurled at us," Helen said. "Of course, it's unnecessary," she continued. "Who is technically not a Rhodesian by birth, of those of us born before1980? Why can't we ever debate matters of national consciousness without bringing race into it? So much talk about politics of rationalization and national disputation!"

"Makes you wonder, doesn't it? Julian quipped in acquiescence. "Talk is cheap; all this hullabaloo about diversity and inclusion from the establishment is mere rhetoric, my foot."

"Haven't we heard it once too often bandied around in mainstream media among other fora?" Helen asked. "Nhamo here is my witness. The view propagated by some amongst us, i.e., 'The presence of white Zimbabweans in Zimbabwe is a hidden secret, only to rise in numbers when it matters to them. Diversity and inclusion are what some of us stand for, but such scenes confuse the mind in a country with a dark history due to past injustices.'"

Julian said, "There was a song about this a few years ago; Simon Chimbetu if I'm not mistaken. Words to the effect of *Kwedu kwatinoswera havauye,* i.e., they, the white community don't want to mingle with us. Have you ever seen them at Sakubva Stadium, Rufaro, Rudhaka at Independence, or

Heroes' Day celebrations? Why not? Ask yourself that question, and when you get to the bottom of the answer, then bingo, you're onto something boy!"

"Well, Julian, for starters, I'm impressed that as a white Zimbabwean you're familiar with one of our Sungura music greats, Simon "Chopper" Chimbetu. We also call him Master of Song. Really impressive stuff there," Nhamo said amiably, his trademark grin on his chubby face.

"You know what gets to me is when those mandarins in the establishment's office, like that gobby chap, the supreme leader's spokesperson, who hurls racist vitriol, stoking hate at us as Rhodies, yet Rhodie was the historical name of the country then, nothing short of acknowledging this historical fact is needed," remarked Helen.

"That one is a loose cannon, though I'm afraid, the screws are getting looser by the day. Of late, he's taken to his Twitter handle where he lampoons and vilifies with wild abandon, the leading white public figures aligned to the opposition as Rhodies. Isn't that inflammatory, I ask you?

Isn't this an assault on their person as fellow Zimbabweans? Very sad coming from the supreme leader's spokesperson," Nhamo said, his dejection all too palpable on his face.

"The police are just ineffectual; no matter how we report these hate-fuelled crimes, nothing is done to redress them. And you tell me we're moving forward as a nation with such hate mongers amidst us? But our Zimbabwe was born out of hate, wasn't it? I often wonder if black ruled Zimbabwe is not a direct product of white ruled Rhodesia!" Helen carried on, now visibly fired up.

"A guy who was born in Rhodesia and acts like the Rhodesian government official is calling new integrated Zimbabwe born patriots Rhodies. Guess who is stuck in the past 40 years later? No prizes for guessing, folks. The jury is out in full force."

"Perhaps, because he knows the toxic nature of his racist bile, that's why he uses a ghost account to escape accountability. But all is not lost. On looking back, I am emboldened with lessons drawn from the past. Once citizens were successful in lobbying Twitter to have another hate-spewing account under a false name and avatar as Matigari eviscerated. That shadowy, toxic character is no more," remarked Nhamo in unison with Helen's sentiments.

The current rabble rouser knows it's racist bile, the shit he spews. He knows all he tweets there are poison more than anyone else. That's why he uses a ghost account, because, deep down, he's more ashamed to be associated with that account than anyone else in the Twitter universe," said Julian.

Well, you say that, Julian, but some of my fellow whites, like my sister Lauren in cabinet, have decided to sup with the devil. She's not the only one. Other fellow opportunist whites have done it before, from way back during the early days of independence, collaborating with the 'enemy.' But be warned, fellow compatriots, you have to keep this maxim close to your hearts. *The devil has a long spoon to stir the gravy and there's no mercy and atonement for those who lay down with dogs when they get fleas. They have only themselves to blame. Be warned my fellow white colleagues, going to bed with these wily politicians. I rest my case.*

So, like I'm saying, my sister Lauren in cabinet is no exception in her collusion."

"Forget about Lauren, she's only a mere cog in the grand scheme of things. Lauren is just serving her self-interested parochial interests. Like all people in the supreme leader's party, she is now one of them, besmirched, contaminated. Accept that and move on," remarked Nhamo as if he sought to reassure my cynicism."

Equally animated by the upbeat way the conversation was going, Nhamo went on, "Thing is Helen, any person in the nasty party is capable of poisoning the whole country, including family so he or she can be left alone in the whole country to enjoy empty factories, supermarkets, farmland, mines etc.

"I know a few enablers to the current regime whose families are all economic refugees, but they don't give a damn!

"These party cowards will always want to utter words of hate, discrimination, and division when they are pushed against the wall. Party apparatchiks will never repent, and they are so predictable. They will never bring superior logic to the table, it's always race, tribalism and partisanship.... never a solution. No wonder their politics of hate and toxicity is informed by rabid racism and bigotry.

"These geriatrics are responsible for the mess brought onto us by their policies. If you know, you know, but he, the Twitter rabble rouser, is the one responsible for racist, false bravado politics of the party. Remove him and you'll see a better or more modern leaning party."

"Well Nhamo, your optimism is nigh staggering," remarked a bemused Julian as he sarcastically joined in the fray. "I am actually surprised you envisage this lot as being modern and forward looking as a party, with a chance to redeem themselves. Anyway, enough of politics for today, lest you're charged of spreading alarm and despondency by the powers that be. The whole charade makes my blood boil. Moving on, changing the subject quickly folks, who's up for a cricket match at Harare Sports Club? Could do with something less depressing than politics."

"Happy to join you Julian, but not until we wrap this up," Nhamo said, the trademark mischievous glint in his eye. "There is a whole administrative malaise which sees nothing wrong with the cancerous racism endemic amongst our nation. I have accepted that expecting poise and dignity from this government is as futile as expecting mercy from the devil!"

"That's Nhamo for you," Helen playfully teased. "Be careful the whisky is now not doing the talking. I know my husband once he's had one too many. The tongue loosens as he increasingly becomes philosophical like he's some sort of Confucius."

"There you go again, love," Nhamo said, pretending to ignore Helen's playful banter.

He continued, "Anyway, I fully concur with you in your noted sentiments. And like you both, notwithstanding the misdirected racist vitriol rampant in this country, my wish is for Zimbabwe to just be a decent functional country with good leaders that care enough about everyone's welfare. Leaders that are there to serve, uphold the constitution, innovate, develop and not there to get rich quick or oppress. That's all.

"There is no Rhodie-ism or race in this. These are legitimate expectations for any citizenry. After all, I am black myself, married to a white Zimbabwean, my adorable Helen, but I have also been at the receiving end of this racism mega-monster. And we're saying about time this whole thing ends."

Helen jumped in with, "And you know what gets to me most, given the prevalence of endemic political violence amidst our nation? Our lives as the white minority have been lived in fear or punctuated by fear for so long.

"How could we not, when we've borne the brunt of government threats, scapegoating for the country's ills. Have we not heard it before from the previous administration's electioneering braggadocio statements: *We have degrees in violence. Let us strike fear in the hearts of the real enemy, the white man.'* Where were the courts when this hate fuelled vitriol was being spewed against part of the citizenry?"

"For all their bluff and bluster, they, the establishment ought to know better. Life is a fragile thing. We are constantly hanging in the balance between life and death. Sadly, that seems to be the tragedy besmirching our nation, a culture of glorifying violence, God help us, as if we haven't learned anything from yesteryear's history of the unfolding mayhem and genocide in Rwanda and other troubled hotspots in Africa." On that note, you two can go to your cricket match," Helen said as she shooed us away.

But Nhamo was not yet done with this emotive subject as he resumed his treatise, whilst driving me to Harare Sports Club. He said, "Come to think of it, Julian, what surprises me with these party geriatrics is their rabid racism, whereby they deliberately act confused and conflated, calling someone born after 1980 a Rhodesian. Yet amongst their ilk they have white Zimbabweans who collaborate with them out of self-interest to guarantee immunity for their farms and assets. Makes me wonder if the Rhodie slur is only meant for whites who defeat you in an argument or holds divergent political views?

Is their co-opted cabinet minister Lauren, for instance, also a Rhodesian or that slur is only reserved for whites who do not openly support them?"

I said, "It's bonkers stuff, Nhamo, with these lot in charge. They couldn't organize a pissing contest in a brewery, and I swear they make up some of their policies on the hoof as they go along. It's always self-interest with them, nothing to benefit the general populace. More like party ahead of the national interest."

"Exactly," Nhamo replied. "People that have destroyed the economy should not come here and lecture us about race. They've done more harm in their tenure than a million whites put together."

"Each time, things are not going their way, they throw a tantrum and start talking of Rhodesia. Rest assured, if it's not Rhodesia, then they're scapegoating sanctions for their misrule. Peddling tired narratives is their forte, these old *madhalas*. And just so you appreciate their hypocrisy up close, do you know what they would call our sister Lauren if she was from the other side, serving in a predominantly white cabinet?"

"Aaah, these people never cease to amaze me anymore. I know boundless epithets ranging from *Uncle Tom, traitor, puppet* would abound; anything to belittle and delegitimise alternative voices. But tell you what, any idiot can see this country is on a one-way ticket to disaster. It's been on autopilot for far too long..."

I could hear Nhamo's voice droning on in the background as my mind veered elsewhere, and I got lost and entangled in the cacophony of my thoughts: After everything we went through in our white farming communities during those violent land seizures now this? No wonder I find solace in crystal meth. My point? Who are you to judge me? Had you gone through what I've been then? My dear friend, you wouldn't be standing in your high heels perched on that so-called moral pedestal, passing sanctimonious judgements on me.

I've been backwards and forwards to hell, I tell you. So, let me tell you this, and tell you this for good. Wipe that malevolent, conceited smirk off your face, for you surely don't know what I've been through. I wouldn't wish my experiences at the hands of those pseudo war veterans on anyone at all, let alone my sworn enemy.

Our lives had been broken irreparably by the chaos of the land reform. And before you start on me, I am not an anti-land reform Rhodie. It is complicated, so don't even say it; it won't wash. No, it won't. I am not against the land reform. I am against the chaos.

But this is home for us, just like everyone else, Dr Hinckley, the affable Nhamo. I was now equally tired and annoyed by the constant "go home" slurs bandied around by political leaders, more so at election rallies. Why can't we peacefully co-exist as fellow citizens?

Chapter 18

Distant Mirage

At the time the marauding "war veterans" invaded our Mazowe farm, my then wife, Evie, was heavily pregnant expecting twins, but sadly it was not to be. She miscarried.

"The trauma of witnessing your father-in-law Jim murdered in cold blood, right before your eyes, must have got to you, Evie. I'm sorry the twins didn't make it, despite our valiant efforts to save them," the bespectacled Dr. Jenkins said to us in his medical chambers at Belvedere Maternity hospital.

We couldn't really say anything. What else could we say in the face of such earth-shattering news? I for one was in a state of numbness and shock, for I knew what this pregnancy meant to both Evie and me. What did death have to gain from this brazen act of cruelty? Hadn't we been trying for a baby the past four years of our marriage?

And now, by a cruel twist of fate, just like that, Dr. Jenkins had thrown the guillotine at us.

"Why does it have to be like this?" asked Evie, finally finding her voice.

"I'm sorry Evie. I'm so sorry for your loss," Dr. Jenkins said.

"Well, it's all very well saying you're sorry, isn't it? Did you try hard enough to save my children? I don't think so Doctor," Evie said. "Where were you when I was screaming in agony at your staff, yelling at them I couldn't hear any baby movements at all?

"'It will be fine dear.' That's all I kept getting, and where has that brought me? Loss of my two flowers, my two diamonds, Jeff and Julian Junior."

"I really get you; I totally understand how you're feeling Evie and..."

It was at that moment that Jenkins got what was coming his way from Evie, as she launched into an unrestrained blistering verbal tirade of hurled invectives of all sorts at him.

"Don't you dare patronize me, Jenkins. You can take your stethoscope and shove it up your dark place where the sun doesn't shine. You know why I am angry with you? Your pathetic excuses to try to placate me at your hospital's failure to save the lives of my two children.

"That is a clear case of medical malpractice and negligence, and to me, that is unacceptable, Jenkins! For crying out loud, I will take you and your entire board to the cleaners if that's the only thing I can do to reclaim my sanity and paper over my grief.

"I have lost my two boys after four previous miscarriages, and now at 42 I doubt I will be able to conceive again. So, don't you dare patronize me and tell me your bullshit about knowing how I feel.

"Eeh, excuse me, no you don't! At the end of your shift, you go home to your wife and kids. I don't get all those luxuries because I don't have the children I so want."

On saying that, Evie's trembling voice broke. She began choking on her emotions and an overwhelming downpour of tears, quite a heavy torrent of them. I sprang into action, hugging and smothering my wife with kisses, to a befuddled Jenkins who hadn't fully recovered from Eve's diatribe.

"I will give you a quiet moment to yourself," he sheepishly mumbled as he retreated from the room.

That had been five years ago, but it could have been yesterday. I also bore the collective pain of losing my sons, though I had valiantly concealed my emotions. But what good did it do me? Evie ended up leaving me after this ordeal and the *"Lovers fall in love to stay and stick by each other come what may,"* mantra? Well, that didn't happen between us, and now my Evie is but a mirage in my memory. I struggle to blink away the tears moistening my eyes, as my mind flickers to the road I've travelled.

Chapter 19

Onai

I was part of the party's national service youths tasked with terrorizing perceived opposition supporters, and especially the white community whom we had to target for violence adhering to our dear leader's instructions. Hadn't our dear leader said it well to us?

"You must strike fear and terror in the hearts of our enemies the white men, so they return to their forefather's land."

That was vintage, populist Mugabe churning out his usual rabble-rousing electioneering speeches and fiery rhetoric which, I must say, at the time, as a boy of sixteen, I was awe-struck by the man's oratory. I found the speeches inspiring, stirring me into action. Thus, it wasn't difficult for me when I was approached by the local Highfields party youth chairman, DJ Fantan, to join the party's youth wing. I gladly acquiesced.

"We will be involved in the commissariat of the party, ensuring the party's support base grows in leaps and bounds," said the pot-bellied Fantan. *Fancy, having such a big belly, yet so young,* I chuckled within myself, clearly taking pot shots at that pot belly on Fantan's obese frame.

Unbeknownst to us at the time, of course Fantan's protestations had been subterfuge, as the events of several months fronting and fomenting the party's well-orchestrated election machinery proved. Fantan was no genuine party supporter! As I soon discovered, this was all a charade by Fantan and his underlings and acolytes to gain immunity from prosecution for their underhanded criminal shenanigans. We were comrades in arms in the illicit and flourishing substance abuse trade, a trade now rife in most of Harare's high-density suburbs. The calculation of Fantan and like-minded sods was, once you joined the party, the Mafioso, there unto you were granted infinite immunity; one became a law unto oneself with no fear of prosecution or accountability.

"Go ye and pillage the resources of Zimbabwe in the name of the party, and you will be protected, my sons and daughters," seemed to be a perfected axiom, we learned well. Besides, our ideological instructors at Nyamazi School of Ideology had taught us well in this respect. We pretty much stuck to the party-infused ideology they religiously inculcated in us.

It is only now, as a recovering substance abuse addict, that I fully realize the damage done on us by that gargantuan party apparatchiks machinery; I now wholly appreciate that young people don't need patronizing indoctrination hogwash as they shovelled to us during those purported nation-building classes.

Young people don't need a military style indoctrination camp. Young people need an economy that allows them to thrive, an education system that fosters creativity, tech hubs, art centers, modern sporting facilities, recreational facilities and a government that doesn't declare war on aspiration.

In truth, is that much to ask for?

We surely didn't need all this baloney. For some of us, as it became clearer what this baloney really was, is it any wonder we also fell by the wayside as we became one of Fantan's crystal meth *Mutoriro* casualties? But to prove ourselves, we were employed as errand boys for the rich and mighty bigwigs of Harare North suburbs.

I vividly recall when Fantan initiated me and Alex, another teenage dropout from school. Alex and I had teamed up in downtown Harare streets after his stepmother kicked him out for allegedly ogling his stepsister Anesu "inappropriately," as she put it.

"So, you listen and listen to me good, lads," Fantan began, clearing his throat. "I have this punter from Borrowdale Brooke; he likes them young and fresh. Do you follow?" As he spoke, he surveyed our faces to check our comprehension, and I took it upon myself to speak on behalf of my new street recruit Alex.

"Yes, yes... we follow, boss, just let us meet this white man and we will deliver, boss, I promise you."

"Very well then. Come back around 8 pm this evening and I will introduce you to him. Remember, discretion is of utmost importance from you both. If this ever comes out, both your heads and torsos will be seen floating in downtown Mukuvisi River. And you know what? Your macabre deaths will only be news for a day or two in Harare Metro, and after that Harare moves on for that matter. That's how trite your lives are. Harare moves on at breakneck speed, scurrying for the next bit of fodder news. No one cares what happens to dumbasses."

That had been an especially chilling threat, and one not to be taken lightly, given Fantan's sadistic cruelty and well-known connections with the party's violent machinery, particularly its sadistic Chipangano thugs.

So, true to our pledges by 8 pm, Alex and I met Fantan at 204 Charingira Court where he had a flat, an easy central conduit for his criminal underworld, which marked it well for that matter. That was how I first met Brian Wharton, a lanky middle-aged white fella from Borrowdale Brooke.

As long as we pleased Brian and other punters, there was more dope for us, more crystal meth *Mutoriro*. It was difficult in the early days, the sort of things Brian wanted us to do, but did we have a choice?

"Once you close your eyes it becomes easier, and let him get on with it," Alex would later remark to me as we sat zonked out with a combination of crystal meth, *Mutoriro* and *Broncho*, a cough medicine for infants we also abused. This was a potent drug combination, I tell you. "Haaa *iyi inokurova kahwani mudhara*, so potent is it that it will completely knock you out," I said to Alex.

"For me, as a coping mechanism, I shut my eyes and think of the money and the drugs thereafter, and before I know it, Brian and his lot quickly come, and I have to clean myself up. Job done! How on earth would I make that money on the streets of Harare, let alone get access to my wide array of drugs?" Alex would nonchalantly say to me as he blew smoke from his drug-infused joint.

101

"True, Alex. We have no jobs to speak of. It's not like we really have a viable option going. I would rather do Brian's white ass than starve to death."

And so we carried on, unaware how we were gradually debasing ourselves as we sank further into our physical and moral depravity on the streets of Harare and in the secret safe houses in Harare's northern suburbs. There both Alex and I lost our virginity at the hands of Brian and his allies, other well-to-do, high-ranking Harare residents, some of whom were well-known big guns connected to the ruling elite.

"Hello, Onai, can I come in?" Amanda, my caregiver, popped in her head, her lovely voice rousing me from my nostalgic reverie of yesteryear.

"Oh, certainly, yes, do come in, Amanda." I liked Amanda – Mandy - as I called her. I had a lot of time for her, and as a young carer she got my vibes of interest.

Many times, I found myself perving on her luscious, voluptuous body. Not that there was a chance in high heaven for me, a recovering junkie convalescing at White Cliff Rehabilitation Center. No way would Mandy ever look at me.

"Glad you look brighter today, Onai. The resident doctor, Dr. Peel, is pleased with your progress. Who knows? If you keep on this upward trajectory, you may even be discharged from this place."

"Really?" My eyes sparkled as I spoke.

"Of course. I don't see why not. The doctor says you're one of the rare success stories, given how far gone you were when you were admitted here. You were out of it. I'm sorry about your mate Alex. He will have to exist in that vegetative state for the rest of his life."

I shifted awkwardly in my bed, as if it was full of pins and needless, at hearing this, how crystal meth had robbed my friend of his viable future ahead. Just like that!

What good is living if you're just reduced to an immobile vegetable? I mused within my inner self.

Seeing my consternation, Mandy moved closer to me and patted my forehead. "I'm sorry again, but look at the brighter side, Onai. Touch wood, you've kicked this filthy habit and the greatest challenge for you will be to avoid a relapse. And tell you what, I don't mind constantly checking on you once you're released from here."

"I would be delighted, Mandy," I said quickly, in case she quickly changed her mind. I couldn't believe what I was hearing; that Mandy certainly harboured thoughts of wanting to see me post White Cliff Rehabilitation Center.

Sensing my euphoria and elation, she carried on speaking after glancing over her shoulder first to check no one was listening. "We're both young, Onai; we're more or less of similar ages. I don't see any harm in us meeting up, but be a good lad and keep that to yourself, will you?"

"Of course, yes, Mandy. My lips are sealed. *Silencio*," I said, with an exaggerated flourish as I made a sign of locking my mouth.

"Very well then, we have a deal, cast iron deal if I may say," Mandy said. She flashed me one of those disarming smiles of hers which had warmed into me during my stay in this place, and she exited my room, leaving me in a joyous stupor. I am ashamed to say I felt a stirring in my loins that left my undergarments wet. But that had come to typify my interactions with Mandy in this rehab clinic.

A few weeks following my rehab discharge, it wasn't difficult to get Mandy onboard; she was young like me, impressionable. With a measly carer's wage at White Cliff, it wasn't a tall order for Munyaradzi and Brian to dangle the mercenary carrot to her. Never underestimate the mighty pull of thirty pieces of silver, and boom, just like that, my Mandy was aboard the lucrative meth train. And that weekend, Munyaradzi and Brian arranged that Mandy would be our Harare Airport mule. She was tasked to carry the drug cache through Harare Airport, en-route to Dubai for sale to our purported dodgy friends in the Middle East.

Besides, how could she have said no, as we'd quickly transitioned to become an item following my discharge from rehab. In the end, I had no proper abode in Harare, and who am I to have declined the warm bosom of a young nubile woman I had been crushing on throughout my rehab stay.

The only problem was, she took long to say it. Otherwise, I was all too enamored and sold out to the idea already. I bet I can hear some of you sanctimonious lot denigrating me for living off women. Why shouldn't I if it was an open invitation she extended to me? Afterall, we both liked each other, and I reckon the attraction was purely physical and mutual. Many times, we found post coital solace in each other's arms as we lay spent after our usually fiery and rough tumble of frisky sex.

Many times, in the darkness of her Avenues flat, I strummed Mandy's voluptuous body like I was playing an acoustic guitar, thrusting in and out as she gyrated her hips in ecstatic unison, her inner warmth and juices further egging me on. Then, I would wait for her to catch her breath before we resumed another feverish marathon lovemaking session. Her hands wandered expertly on the erotic zones of my body, mostly the nether regions of my crotch, with me reciprocating, as she purred in ecstatic delight. The sheer pleasure of her hands on me made me groan with unmitigated pleasure. Our hips moved in sync, gyrating together till we climaxed. And then we started again, she softly nibbling on my nipples as my manhood became increasingly hard.

Chapter 20

Julian

For all these years she's not here, I've been shadowed by my wife's memories. Memories galore actually. Limitless memories abound. Evie plagues me relentlessly as if she's punishing me for those miscarriages. Once in a while I see her scolding me in my dreams, waggling her little fingers at me as if I'm a naughty schoolboy caught with his fingers in the cookie jar. Sometimes, I see her in my bathroom mirror in the morning as I shave, smiling, at times taunting me.

How dare she do that to me, as if it was of my own making? God knows, I also wanted to have a family, our children together. Was that not the dream we shared from our nascent courtship?

"Boo, I so want to have a big family," Evie would often remark to me, my head resting on her belly button in our post-coital glow and contentment.

"Big as in five children, then I'm done. So, if I have my way, by thirty-five I should be done with making babies."

We would regale one another with laughter over this, but deep down we agreed it was something both of us wanted. How were we to know it would never be?

I also feel the pain of what could have been. Lost opportunities, what could have been as a family, had we not lost our twins, been deprived of our family farm... the list is endless. I could go on and on. God, I miss you, Evie! The stupid jokes we had, pet names we had for each other, my "sweetie pie" among others, our laughter and gaiety at Mazowe before those brutal farm attacks. And you know what, it's been hard going!

This brutal carry-on-as-if-nothing-is-happening hard man facade just doesn't cut it for me. It's bollocks! Solid gold shit! Something's gotta give in the end. That's why I love my powder and nocturnal release with the lads in downtown Harare.

I started with cannabis and cocaine, then graduated to LSD and hallucinogens among my many stashes of drugs. But nothing does it for me better than crystal meth, *mutoriro, ndicho chirikurira pataundi,* Harare's talking point powder.

Milestones amid loss are always going to be bittersweet. All I want is for my Evie to be here to see me through this storm together, like we did before as a couple.

"Evie, I'm in love with you. You're creative, hot, in fact awesome in everything. I'm so much in love with you."

"Really?"

"Yes, Evie, believe me."

"I'm in love with you too, Julian."

"Evie, I think we're good. Are you up for this?" I playfully teased her.

The mind is a haven for memories. Those were the days, during our courtship, but all I hold onto now is a mirage, the road I could have travelled with my dearest Evie.

Reminiscing, my mind also courses down to good old Pops, Jim, growing up at the Mazowe citrus fruit farm. Dad always fought in my corner, whereas Rhys and Mum seemed to gravitate toward each other like they were siblings. Nothing seems to have changed for me, other than that I have now lost my ally Dad. Mother would constantly lose it with me, as I had this nagging habit of relentlessly thumb sucking and boy, she would bellow at me in that belligerent voice of hers, which always seemed to rattle and strike terror in me. No wonder I felt dread and unease in her presence.

"Will you desist from sucking your thumb, you lazy bones minstrel! Wastrel! Miscreant! Do you hear me, Julian?"

"Lay off the poor lad, Doris, will you? He's only young, and means no harm," Dad would assert, and for that I was eternally grateful; such occasions tended to happen once too often. Sometimes I would flash him my coy smile as a way of giving him a thumbs up for his enduring support, sticking by me like this in the face of Mother's military regiment discipline standards. "And here we are again," I could hear her voice kicking off in the adjoining room, alerting me to what lay ahead for the remainder of the evening. I can't say I hadn't seen it coming. How could I not, when I was the architect of the looming tornado in the Williams household? The black sheep of the family as I'm constantly reminded, perpetually put down.

I associate my stuttering impediment to how Mum thought the best way to talk to me was constant shouting and put downs. By Jove! She had a way to make me appear worthless. One would think I didn't come from her loins! I sighed in utter frustration, just thinking of those dark years in my formative stages growing up at the farm. Sisi Maria was always at hand in the midst of my fear, to talk to or run to for a kind word and bosom. Sisi Maria and M'koma Eddy, our long-standing domestic help, we have certainly come a long way, and they're like family to me, Rhys, and Doris as well.

On days like this, I certainly miss Dad, good old Jim, who could easily disarm you with his infectious humor. Frailty, thy name is death! If only both Dad and Evie had lived longer, I wonder if things would have turned out this way. Would my life have taken this trajectory?

Many times, I wake up during the night drenched in sweat and with palpitations, seeing those sadistic faces, hearing that cacophony of singing voices and axe wielding pseudo war veterans at the Mazowe farm the day they murdered my father in cold blood.

I doubt things will ever be the same for me. How can I talk of closure when I have these recurrent problems and flashing images? Time and again, the establishment has spurned repeated calls for a Truth and Reconciliation Commission akin to South Africa's own TRC.

How can we move on?

We need to have this conversation as a nation.

We need healing.

But I sometimes think this means that the blacks had not exactly healed after the long bush war in 1980. How could they heal? The war had not provided what they had fought for in the first place, land, fortunes, jobs, you name it. Sometimes I see it all and do not know what could have been done from the word go. You cannot say I do not see it.

It's simply devastating to think of the way Dad's life was snuffed out in such cruel, sadistic fashion; just like that, at the drop of a hat, he was no more. Yet those responsible are still roaming the streets of Harare scot-free. Tell me, what is the basis for healing? Was history repeating itself?

In the brief time of his sojourn, hanging out and interacting with Dad he was just everything you hoped a father would be - no airs or graces, generous, naughty, kind, and total class. He lit up my life with his kindness. Perhaps that's why I certainly believe something snapped inside of me with Dad's brutal killing. The screws further loosened in my psyche following Evie's death a few months later. How was I supposed to cope, were it not for Munyaradzi and the syndicate? The Chipangano lads? The crystal meth connection saw me through the dark morass of my sorrow.

I feel exhausted by the state of this country. I feel exhausted by all the lies.

I feel exhausted by all the injustice. I feel exhausted by the incompetence.

I feel exhausted by all those who cannot see the truth. By Jove, I'm suffocated!

I am not alone, some of you say. Is that reassuring? I wonder. We are enfeebled by fear and hunger in this our nation. I sometimes think that 1980 failed to bring together black and white, and what happened at the Mazowe farm was bound to happen somehow. We white people in Africa have had to repay what history had offered us. What can I say? What can I see?

I can't say I couldn't clearly see the falling out coming from miles away. Now that I couldn't afford anymore dope money, I had gradually started pilfering Mother's little valuables from our shared Borrowdale Brooke home. It could be little items like her jewellery, kitchen utensils, china she had sentimental value on, Nan Anthea's donations to Mum's wedding many years back. And today appears to be my day of reckoning with Doris, as she's ranting and raving the whole house down, huffing and blaring, shouting my name, bellowing in fact at her discovery of my pilfering habit.

"There can only be one suspect behind all this, my missing household cutlery and now jewellery, Julian. Don't you dare deny it." She approached me menacingly baring her fangs at me. But I stood my ground, giving it back in equal measure.

"Oh, I see, it's always my fault, isn't it? The black sheep of the family. It's gotta be Julian. Who else? Has it ever crossed your mind that it could be someone else other than me behind these unsavoury disappearances of your items?"

"Hear me out, Julian, who else in this household is a crack addict who needs a constant fix? Come on, man up, and admit to your foibles, son. Goodness knows how many times I've warned you to refrain from this road you're trudging, but do you ever listen? I might as well be having a monologue the way you bang on with your shit life!"

"Aaah, Mother of the Year, is that the way to talk to your son? Such colourful language, Doris; you should be thoroughly ashamed of yourself! I am ashamed of you, Mum," I sarcastically mocked her with an exaggerated accent of an irate parent.

"Look, Julian, for crying out loud, you're in a bad place. Look at yourself; you've become a relic of your former self in one fell swoop. Just like that! What for? For the love of meth, *Mutoriro,*" she said, shaking her head. I could see the pity and contempt in her demeanor, dismissively shaking her head at me as if I was a piece of horse poo and all she needed was this needless putting me down.

I exhaled deeply, my frustration with Doris palpable.

"Look, Doris, you and I are never gonna see eye to eye on this. We have to agree to differ, as cliched as it sounds. Leave me alone! I do my meth, you do your shit with your trusted, goody two shoes son, the mighty Rhys." I sarcastically threw this at a flabbergasted Doris.

"Don't be ridiculous, Julian! Both Rhys and you are my sons and I treat you equally as your doting mother."

"Oh, really, Doris? You must think I'm a mug, don't you?"

"Whatever! Time you look in the mirror and sort yourself out, son. What are you going to do with your needle ravaged arms? Soon, you won't have any more veins to inject yourself *Mutoriro*, believe you me."

"I know what I'm doing; let me be with my life, Doris," I angrily shouted at her as I'd had enough of her relentless put downs.

"So says the junkie. Is that you or the meth speaking inside you? Tell me Julian? But as you are obviously zonked out again, a lesson on your indulgences is certainly in order! It's a shame you are not clued in to the carnage your so-called powder is wreaking on the streets of Harare."

"Go on, give it to him, Doris." I turned to see the smirking face of Rhys, my annoying brother, sauntering into the living room much to my chagrin.

"Here comes Son of the Year," I sarcastically shot back at him as he grabbed a seat next to Mum who carried on with her tirade unabated.

"So, where was I? Aaah," she said, biting her lower lip as if she was looking for something to jog her memory. "Aha, it's come back! It's the statistics you need to be aware of, Julian."

"What statistics are you on about now? I didn't realise you're now a government statistician-cum spokesperson, Doris," I sniggered at her.

"I'm glad you are closely following and now onboard, son." I hated it each time she repeated the word "son" as if she had to constantly shove it down my throat to remind me of my maternal link with her.

"Can't you ever speak without having to blackmail me about being my parent?" I shot back at her, but she completely blanked me out as she resumed her moralizing sermon. She must have come in psyched up for me that evening. Part of me even wondered whether this was a deliberate stitch-up, with her beloved son Rhys to join hands in dressing me down again. Was there nothing else they liked to do better, other than this?

"If only you knew what's happening on the streets of Harare. The unfolding drug inferno, if I may put it that way. I tell you, you would quit immediately, Julian. This too is an epidemic killing Zimbabweans, left, right and center. It's fucking enough!"

"Takes one junkie to tell from another junkie," I angrily retorted.

"How do you mean?" she countered.

"Well, why don't you find out from your partner in crime, role model son, Rhys there? You think I'm daft and I don't see how you two are raging alcoholics, yet you single out my only guilty pleasure as if it's some heinous crime. Tell me, how am I hurting anyone by snorting whatever stuff I need in my nasal passages, huh? Tell me, you sanctimonious lot!"

After a beat of silence I continued, "See, you have nothing of substance to say! And so, you resort to your usual bluff and bluster!"

"Cut this crap will you, Julian?" Rhys said. "And while we are at it, I don't like the tone of your voice and the way you speak to Mum. For a junkie, you chat a lot of shit!"

"Get out of my sight, Rhys! You don't own me and get to tell me what to do. I will damn well speak to Doris the way I want, till she equally knows how to speak with me well, and not disrespect me willy nilly like she does."

I left my corner, slamming the door after me to drive home my point.

Chapter 21

Brothers in Arms

Allow me to speak my truth for a moment before you jump in and tell me how I should feel. How does one celebrate freedom when they do not feel free? How does one celebrate independence when they feel oppressed? How does a nation grow when it silences criticism?

To ask your country to live by the ideals that it has set out for itself is not a crime, neither is it being a disillusioned white Rhodie, as I have often heard my lot being demonized and vilified each time we talk politics.

What my fellow citizens seem to forget is, Zimbabwe is also my country. I was born here in Bindura by white parents. So what? Does that make me less Zimbabwean? And by whose standard? So, what does this 'Go home' mantra mean when I'm already home? Excuse me, but this is home for me, folks.

'Go home white man!' I hear that everywhere. Of course, I am white. Of course, you are black, but can't we see that we are trapped together by a sad history? Can't it be negotiated amicably, now that we agree that we fought each other for too long? Can't a dignified way be found?

I remember vividly when Rhys and I attended the opposition leader's open-air rally at Borrowdale racecourse, and Rhys donned his cap with the words inscribed: *Nelson my man*. Pictures of him wearing the cap went viral on Twitter and Facebook as my brother was catapulted into instant stardom, plucked right there from obscurity. But that daring act of brazenly exercising one's freedom of choice in matters political earned us a 3 am visit to our Borrowdale house by men in dark glasses and dark suits, who made it evident to us they wouldn't brook whites taking part in the political discourse of their country.

"Let us make it crystal clear to you lot, this is not Rhodesia anymore. And we won't brook any whites trying to reverse the gains of independence and land reform by funding the opposition, do you hear me?" they said menacingly to us, baring their ugly protruding teeth, deliberately exposing their guns to us, possibly as a subtle form of psychological coercion and intimidation.

The seeming leader of these dreaded operatives, an ugly man who spoke with a lisp, growled at us as he chatted his bullshit, but Rhys wasn't just going to roll over for them and be cowed just like that, despite the four goons' bulging AK47s protruding from their suits, a subliminal message itself to coerce us into acquiescence.

"And what exactly is our crime?" Rhys inquired. "And how do I even address you? Are you police officers? Intelligence operatives? I wonder, were you proper, legitimate police officers, would you come threatening law-abiding citizens at the dead of dawn. Would you?

"If we have committed a crime, why not follow due process and summon us to court?" Rhys gave it back, his bravado clear, a complete contrast from Mother Doris' face, which had gone white as a sheet during these protracted hostile exchanges."

For a moment our living room went quiet following Rhys' lengthy diatribe. Then the seeming leader of the goons shot back. "I commend you. You do have balls of steel *mzungu*, to say this bullshit to us, the owners of the state, *vene venyika*. But your bravado is misplaced, young man. We have guns, we have everything on our side. The system is powerful, the system is armed, even the judiciary is on our side. And what have you got to defend yourself? Your bare hands. Look at you! Look at how pathetic this is yourselves," he said, surveying the room before carrying on with such undisguised contempt.

"*Mzungu*, your time is over; this is not Rhodesia anymore and we're now running this country, so our word goes. *Ndisu tirikutonga mwachewe*. We are running the show, whether you like it or not. Better get used to this new shit!"

114

"Officer, can I call you 'Officer?'" Rhys asked.

"My name is Black Jesus. I make people disappear and I decide who lives or dies, so just call me BJ."

"Well, BJ, much as you may think you're intimidating us, I for one am not fazed by your bigotry and blatant racism, which should have no place in our contemporary world. However racist you are to me and fellow white Zimbabweans, we're all Zimbabweans at the end of the day," Rhys said.

"To demand an end to corruption and access to quality healthcare and education for all is the right of every Zimbabwean borne of the sacrifices of those who came before us.

"Many years on, you dare talk of independence. Yet you come here with your racist innuendos, calling me *mzungu*, seeking to insult me, intimidating my family. But tell me, how can you be free if those who speak out are imprisoned? There are those who will have you believe that patriotism demands your silence in the face of oppression. However, in my mind, our most patriotic act is to never allow the wealth of our nation to be squandered by a few.

"Zimbabwe belongs to all of us, and our most beautiful celebration of our independence is in our continued perseverance in the pursuit of freedom, in all its forms. That is our inalienable birth right."

BJ sneered, "Are you done with your monologue *mzungu?* Right, you keep that bullshit talk all to yourself and other white Rhodies. Just know from now on, we've got tabs on you, and if you step out of line, we won't hesitate to strike.

"Nice little speech, by the way. Did it take you long to rehearse it?" BJ sarcastically mocked Rhys as he and the other goons quietly exited into the shadows the way they'd come. For a few moments after their exit, we had to pinch ourselves to ensure that it hadn't been a dream we'd just experienced with accompanying apparitions.

Looking back at the operatives' visit and how Rhys stuck to his guns, remains permanently etched in my memory, and in a way, it also underscores those rare moments of unanimity I did enjoy with my brother before the rift finally set in. For the irony was not lost on me. It was our brazen attendance together at the opposition leader's Borrowdale racecourse rally that had brought this upon ourselves. Still, it was great to know, at one point, that Rhys and I did get along well and could pretty much do things together as brothers in arms. How we did laugh at the operative's weird name, BJ. "Like he was going to give us a blow job," Rhys would constantly remark, amid guffaws on days following this Nikodemus visit from agents of the state.

Chapter 22

Durham University Forays

Landing a place at Durham University, a majestic looking uni steeped in rich architecture, old English buildings, regal culture, wide expansive countryside, green fields, and traditional history in an exclusive English county, was a dream come true for both myself and my long-time mate, June. Elitist and considered posh by some, our ascension there was no mean achievement, an accolade we both regaled and revelled in. Durham the city was lovely, a mixture of pristine beauty and decadence.

"I can't believe we've made it into Durham, poppet," June said one afternoon as we hugged in euphoria at our newfound beckoning freedom from Blanchett's prison.

"Me too, sweetheart. Goodbye, Blanchett years, I'm sure I won't miss you with your horrid memories," I said in unison with my partner in crime, good old June.

That was a few months back when we rejoiced in our post-A Level exam results, basking in the glory of our achievements. We'd gone on a bender that weekend in central Coventry city's drinking holes, downing lagers and cocktails one after the other like there was no tomorrow.

"Let's turn Coventry pubs flowing with splosh Friday. Who cares what grumpy old git Blanchett will say," I suggested, and June concurred.

"Now that our days are numbered at this hell hole, perhaps Blanchett may well do us a favour by expediting our leaving. Possibly chucking us out would do us a favor." We'd both chuckled at this in our brazen defiance and bravado, now that we knew our Blanchett exit was imminent.

Still, inwardly, in our heart of hearts, we had to grudgingly accept that Blanchett had shaped and nurtured us over the years, whatever disdain we had for it. Looking back at my ten years' stay there, I had evolved and developed as a person. "I'm grateful at the inner tenacity the rough and tumble of Blanchett's gaol bestowed on me. Those fist fights, June!" I said with my usual cheeky grin. "Who knows where I might need this in later life? Time and again I have pondered over this."

Thus, two semesters on at Durham, both June and I had settled into our new life and habitat, a far cry from Blanchett's West Midlands "prison," given the freedoms we enjoyed as boisterous undergraduate university students, from our heady days of freshers' week to the now raging alcoholics some of us had become, even though as our students' union maxim went: "We drink daily and pass annually."

A typical day at Durham commenced with our attending lectures, interspersed with weekly tutorials in which we had to do presentations and get quizzed by fellow students, as happened this Friday morning. I ended up snapping at the relentless put downs from some of my electronics engineering classmates.

"If you're going to criticize me, just say so openly, Gill, instead of this needless tiptoeing around me, throwing your well-rehearsed politically correct soundbites," I angrily replied to Gillian's relentless onslaught of questions against me.

"Not at all, Marina, I am just probing you further to get to understand your line of argument, that's all. Nothing personal here."

"Oh bollocks, sorry. I didn't mean to swear, but I get the vibes you're biased and morbidly negative against me."

"Far from it, Marina. Nothing could be further from the truth. I'm surprised you get emotional in an academic argument."

"Oh, stop patronizing me, will you? Emotional my foot! So, I'm supposed to roll over quietly while you pillory me left, right and center at will? What kind of an unbalanced academic debate is that? You tell me, Gill, because clearly I have no idea what you are banging on about."

"Aaah, can we conduct ourselves in an appropriate, adult manner please," Dr. Chennells intervened in his usual amiable way, a flickering smile on his face, which helped cool frayed tempers and tensions that morning. Matters had proceeded somewhat amicably following this frosty start to our fortnightly tutorials. Such were the mundane occurrences in our undergraduate days at Durham University. Weekends were pretty much taken up by the drinking and partying, which I must admit had escalated a notch. Still, we immensely enjoyed our university forays at Durham. They were certainly memorable encounters we had.

Chapter 23

Piccadilly Circus

There was a bright moon that evening, its serenity intermittently interrupted by the crickets chirruping nonchalantly as we sat in the opulent Jewel Piccadilly restaurant terrace by Piccadilly Circus in the borough of Westminster in central London. Guy Fawkes celebratory firecrackers flared in the dark silhouette horizon and were constantly bursting in the night with staccato punctuation.

"You look terrific!" Mark said admiringly, eyeing me up and down as if I was some ornament at an auction.

"Are you trying to seduce me?" I blurted, looking straight into his eyes.

"Of course, why not," he threw the gauntlet back at me, a wicked twinkle in his eyes. This momentarily disconcerted me, though I did like his guts. Mark poured himself a glass of wine, took a long sip, savoring the crisp flavor as he proceeded to pour me my share.

"Thank you. How do you do, Mark?" I remarked, quickly regaining composure, and flashing him a dazzling disarming smile. As he studied the menu, I decided on the steak filet with mushrooms dipped in sweet chilli sauce.

"Couldn't be happier at seeing you. Tell me about yourself, Marina," Mark said through a mouthful of pizza from the starters.

"What do you want to know? Fire away; my life is an open book, for want of a better cliché. I have no secrets," I dared him, much to his delight. And that had been it; we'd chatted away the night like we'd known each other for ages. This man had a way with him, which made me feel self-assured and at ease with him. In no time we were cackling away, with gales of laughter at his jokes.

"I am pleased to have offered you a scholarship, Marina. In fact, you can't attribute it to me personally. Call it GTN corporate ethos facilitated by our Philharmonic Trust Department. We strive to assist disadvantaged members of our society. And I say this without the slightest hint of insult to you, believe me, Marina."

"No need to apologize, I totally get you…er…"

"Call me Mark, Mark Instone will do for me," he reiterated, his face creased with that trademark boyish, grin. "I want to offer you a job at GTN, Marina. How is that?"

"A job? But I'm still to do two more years of my undergraduate degree," I replied petulantly.

"Yes, I'm very much aware of that, but I'm thinking ahead here, Marina. I'm talking of your post-university phase in two years' time when you graduate. I don't expect an immediate response, but I want you to go and mull it over." Then he asked, "Will you do that for me please?" his piercing eyes beneath those bushy eyebrows mesmerizing me.

To me it felt more like a command, and it felt flattering, getting a job offer from GTN, a reputable telecoms company. Still I needed some quiet me time to think things through first, before committing myself. In any case, I also wanted to share this gem of brill news with my inner circle at Friday's student union pub, June, and Elise among the gang.

Clearing my throat, finally finding my voice, I looked back at Mark confidently and gave him my reply, possibly unsettling him by what he hadn't thought he would hear from an undergraduate student in a world where many would have fallen over themselves just to land a job at prestigious GTN, let alone be considered as temps.

"I must say, I'm flattered with your offer of a job at GTN Telecoms, Mark, but like you said earlier on, I need time to consider this. Post-graduation my mind had been set on an internship down under in Melbourne, Australia."

That seemed to jolt him further into unfamiliar territory.

"Melbourne, Australia? Why on earth would you want to do that to yourself?"

"Do what to myself?" The pity and condescension in his voice grated on my nerves. *Who does he think he is?* I said inwardly.

"I mean, Australia, who the hell leaves England for flipping Australia?"

"Well, what is there to live for in England, if I may throw that back at you, Mark? Ever since the Brexit shit, this country has gone to the dogs," I sniggered, not giving a monkey's at Mark's grimaces.

I'm not sure whether this was meant to be a "get to know each other" or a date night. Whatever different dimensions it was in our disparate minds, I'm sure it wasn't going well. Besides I hadn't really warmed up to this, "just go and meet Mark" talk from June, Elise, and the brood.

"Just go and meet him, Marina, you have nothing to lose but everything to gain," they had egged me on as they crowded around our shared flat.

"Just don't shag him on a first date though," June had mischievously added as an afterthought, not to be outdone.

"But I really don't know this fella. Besides the age difference is stretching it far, even by my standards," I had said as they baited me further.

"Oh, stop being a bitch, Marina! For heaven's sake, why can't you loosen up and be fun like everyone else? Besides, it's not like you've been the prim and proper sort, given your campus reputation," Elise had butted in, chiding me.

"Oi, watch it! What do you mean "given my reputation?" I gave it back to them in this increasingly one-sided verbal sparring.

In the end I had grudgingly gone along with it, against my will and better judgment, and here we were, mighty Mark Instone, telecoms mogul, sitting together with me in London's Jewel Piccadilly restaurant. I was obviously bored and doing everything to antagonize him so he could quickly call time on the date. But it appeared, try as I might, I wasn't succeeding with Mark. Perhaps he had come with a pre-set agenda, but the thing is, I wasn't remotely interested in this man who was far older than me anyway, and his ginger beard was a further turn-off.

"So, Marina, will you have another drink?" His gruff voice roused me out of my reverie, his lecherous lips all too intense.

"Okay, one more, then I should be hitting the road. Agreed?"

"Agreed," he acquiesced, a naughty conspiratorial smile curling his lips as if he had some secret hold on me. Like a predator, Mark held my gaze as if daring me to make the first move. I could swear I saw him salivating and drooling over me. Throughout the evening, I felt his lascivious eyes on me. I could swear he was undressing me with those covetous looks of his. *Such a pervert!* An inner resolve coming over me, I swore to myself, whatever dirty thoughts the pervert was entertaining in his hideous head, I was determined I wasn't going to be an easy lay and was certainly going to keep my thighs firmly clamped together. *No easy pickings, mister.* If he thought all this was pre-coital banter, he was in for a rude awakening. I wasn't going to be easy-peasy for him.

"You are truly beautiful, Marina. I would love to see more of you," Mark had remarked as he dropped me off at our students' digs following our maiden encounter in Piccadilly Circus, the heart of London. To my utter surprise, he had been gentleman enough at our parting to only give me a light goodnight peck on my cheek, a far cry from my paranoia.

But that Jewel Piccadilly restaurant date had only been the beginning of my tricky, tempestuous dalliances with irascible Mark Instone, GTN big wig. Much to my surprise, we were to meet several times again a few weeks following our first date. In no time, a clandestine relationship bloomed between us. I can't say he took advantage of me or that I wasn't attracted to him. That would be a blatant lie.

I gradually grew to like this man. Initially, I had tried to find fault with him, denigrate him as old and repulsive. Yes, defiant Marina Thompson was saying this, inwardly refusing to be manipulated by June, Elise, and the gang into having a relationship with this man. But inside my heart, another battle was raging, *you know you want him; you keep laughing at his jokes. You know you enjoy this man's presence and company. You keep looking forward to your next date, so why not go for it?* A clear counter voice kept reiterating this to me and in the end, I willingly succumbed.

Never underestimate the power of self-delusion. Yet I must admit, when I started looking at Mark with a different set of eyes, credit to him, I did see him in a different, positive light. Though much older than me, Mark had the looks, with his lithe, supple body, as I later found in our steamy marathon sex sessions. I guess all along I had been playing, plain denialism by blatantly refusing to acknowledge his enticing physical features. There was, however, to be a caveat to our relationship. Since I was the beneficiary of my second- and third-year scholarship from Mark's GTN company, it meant our relationship had to be under wraps, something Mark was keen to make clear as he wanted to avoid a scandal.

"Given I'm your scholarship benefactor, I'm sure you're aware it's completely unethical for us to fraternize, but who gives a flying fuck if we do this thing clandestinely. Get it?"

It was more an order, as with many of Mark's statements. Perhaps being too much of a manager had got into Mark's psyche and even how he related to people and conducted his relationships. In his mindset, he saw everyone as subordinates and underlings who had to be pushed and ordered around, stuck in a world where his word reigned supreme, and he didn't brook any rejoinders.

"Perhaps keep it low key and only share with your small friendship group, June, Elise, and the others if you have to," he'd remarked with a dismissive wave of his hand.

"Suit yourself, Mark," I'd flippantly acquiesced.

Besides, I was smitten by Mark's charm and persona. He had a way with me and made me feel so loved. Also, I found his wide knowledge of wines and alcoholic beverages somehow alluring. It set him apart as some kind of connoisseur, as happened one Valentine's Day when he took me to Kensington and Chelsea's svelte neighborhood's Launceston Place restaurant, famed for being Princess Diana's favorite, a fact Mark repeatedly flaunted.

"A bit of history for you, Marina, Launceston Place has some royalty in it. The late Princess Diana used to frequent it as one of her favorite spots," Mark remarked as he poured himself a glass of wine, took two long sips and savored the flavor, after which he proceeded to pour me my share.

"Really, Mark, is that your claim to fame then, dragging me here? Trying to impress me, are we?" I teased.

"Just saying. Here, try this dry martini, Marina, from the deep, South French Alps, you'll love it," he purred, a naughty twinkle in his eyes. "The French are renowned for their fine tasting wines."

I was inwardly impressed by his array and knowledge of French wines, given my own drinking prowess. The way he went on in his treatise about French wines, the man was certainly a connoisseur, but of course I kept my emotions in check. *Not wise to be overly eager, these are early days in the relationship.* I had learned the maxims of dating quite well, how it's constantly a game of wits, and so I kept my enthusiasm in check for good measure.

Chapter 24

Mother and Son Spat

"I think substance abuse is how you've put yourself on trial, son. It's judge, jury, executioner, and everything! All on you, like you're facing the firing squad. And you know what, Julian, I'm tired of all this shit."

"For fuck's sake, Mum, give me a break, will you! I am sick of all this bullshit also, just so you know, your self-righteous drivel and what have you. On trial for what? Don't you start on me with your silly, opaque analogies. I'm not up for this crap today."

"On trial for your personal losses. I hear you, son. I feel your pain and sense of loss but take it. As hard as it is, face up to it. You're not responsible for Evie's death or even your father's murder. What happened, happened, son. It is what it is. This doesn't make me callous, coming to terms with my own loss as a mother and a wife. I also lost my husband Jim as you know.

"It's been *eight years*, for heaven's sake, son. I'm sure Evie would have wanted you to move on, have a semblance of a decent life, not this self-pitying exercise and wreck of a loser you've become, taking solace, hiding in narcotics."

"Aaah, I see, Doris. You're now a mind reader? You know how I feel? Now let me tell you something, woman! You don't know how it feels losing a wife at eight months pregnancy when you'd been trying for a baby all these years, living through the motions of endometriosis, ectopic pregnancies, countless miscarriages, then one day, just one day, boom it happens, in cruel fashion. Boom! It all falls apart. It goes pear shaped.

"In one fell swoop that beautiful wife of yours, you've endured the pain together, which is taken away from you. Just like that! Now that is nigh painful, Doris! Not you sanctimoniously pontificating and moralizing at me. Now, get out of my sight, will you?"

"You're not guilty you know, son! No one is guilty at our losses. Perhaps only those who deprived us of our common bond, Evie, my daughter-in-law, your father, my husband, are the real culprits who ought to take the cane and not you and me. If anything, we're in this together, son."

"Now, I'll ask you again, like I've done all these instances when you refuse to engage with me. What's my place in this trial? It helps to talk, Julian. I am your mother for heaven's sake. Open up! Don't leave me out like you've been doing. I don't want to be left out. You're freezing me out. It's cold out there."

"You're a witness, Mum. You saw for yourself how Dad was murdered. How they raped Evie at gunpoint in Mazowe. See how your little, parsimonious speeches won't do me any good? And do you know what really gets to me? It's the thought of those vile miscreant criminals roaming the streets of Harare free, as they were acquitted in that sham trial they went through. And this is the spirit of ubuntu Zimbabwe, huh!"

"I cannot speak for those marauding pseudo-war veterans, but I am a lawyer for the defense, the wronged parties, Evie, and Jim my departed husband.

"And whilst we are at it, allow me to make my opening arguments, son. Ditch this junkie lifestyle persona you've been flirting with all these years. You're going nowhere, Julian, it's one cul de sac after the other you are heading to in this self-destruct merry go round gerrymandering you've become so accustomed to.

"You're equally culpable of this shit unravelling, festering on for so long. Take some responsibility; you're not saintly, you know!"

"Too late for that, Mum. This shit has caught up with me. And you know what? I'm in it up to the eyeballs. Swimming in deep shit with my junkie mates, but we love it. This is out of choice, Doris, we snort cocaine, out of our own fucking choice!"

"One thing for sure, it's only an idiot like you who refuses to change course, yet they're headed straight into a gigantic iceberg. You know what, son? Suit yourself! I'm so done with you, Julian," and with that Doris left me rambling in my cocaine infused treatise.

"I love you, Mum," I shouted sarcastically after her.

"Oh, I wish you did. There was a time when you did, but right now it's just the dope talking," Doris shouted back as she retreated into her bedroom, and I drifted outside for another joint.

Chapter 25

Marina Reflects

"In hindsight, I can see and interpret the events of my life in a new and different light. Now I can clearly see where I went wrong. And I'm not only saying this because my life is in limbo and I'm most likely to die here in prison."

"Excuse me, sorry to butt in, Marina, but please enlighten me here. It's getting a bit hazy," I said. "As you say from your harrowing tale, Mark put you through hell. Why on earth did you hang on to this toxic relationship for so long? I mean, you're not making sense to me here. A young, nubile university student like you at your prime? Surely, you could have managed to pull blokes much younger than the old geezer Mark, no offence meant of course."

"None taken, Rhys. To answer your question, though, allow me to revisit the precise circumstances of our meeting, how mighty Mark Instone of GTN Telecoms came into my life. Perhaps, only just, this may give you a perspective on how this man had such a massive hold on my life, if not a chokehold, which was nigh difficult to escape, let alone his vice-like clutches.

"Which woman would run away from such luxury? Being pampered, spoiled, and treated like royalty was one side; then there was the darker side, of course. There's always a darker side isn't there? But how can you ignore it when I had become the envy of most of my college friends, June, Elise, Myra, and the whole lot?

"Perhaps, I was in love. As the wisdom goes, love is a maze; once you get in it, you're pretty much trapped. Perhaps I was not in love. Perhaps I was in love…perhaps not.

"The Blanchett years did me some good, though. Taught me tenacity at a tender age, which came in handy in later years dealing with Mark and our difficult relationship, though part of my outward bravado was a façade to the outside world, and it is only now I can openly acknowledge this for what it was."

Chapter 26

Voices

Sometimes when I sit down in reflective mode like now, I hear no other voices except those of the past. That is when I see her again: Evie's beautiful face smiling back at me like an apparition, or like now, creased into an angry frown, reproaching me as she's been doing of late. Evie! Wait for me!"

It was as if I heard her say, *"You fucked it! The more you blame others, the more you prove it. Get a grip and leave Mum, me, Rhys, everyone else out of this! We can't be bankrolling your junkie lifestyle. Get used to it! This is your own shit! Swim or sink in it!*

"You wanna snort cocaine, then be your own guest and not bring us into it." Sanctimonious Rhys gleefully joins in, so as not to miss a chance to diss me. What else gives him the kicks other than his mindless sadism?

"Takes one fucker to know another one, miles away," I sniggered back at Rhys' sanctimonious put downs. The past week had been difficult, as both Doris and Rhys kept going on and on at me, banging on nonstop. How do you stop when others are not stopping?

"You're in a dark place, Julian, lump it or suck it. Better sign into rehab with Dr. Hinckley's Harare rehab clinic," Rhys admonished.

But I needed a fix. How else can I get my fix if I don't get to nick Doris' jewellery or any other household valuables which come my way? One must do what one must do. What people seem not to know? Downtown Harare, drugs didn't come cheap. And hearken, people, you don't really understand what it's like when one needs their fix do you? Now, don't you go tell me you do, because clearly you don't. Otherwise, we shouldn't be having this conversation.

What people don't seem to realize is, losing Evie and her pregnancy was the darkest period of my life, both her death and losing our unborn twins, coming on the back of our conception problems. So, don't you tell me you would have coped better, and I am not looking for your sympathy either? Evie's death left me smothered with an intense emptiness and loneliness. Clearly, you don't understand the enormity of this upon me. There is a void. How do I fill it? Do you even hear me?

Otherwise, you wouldn't all be wearing those snotty high and mighty faces looking down on me with your condescending stares. Take them somewhere else. Go! I don't need them. I'm done with sympathy. I would rather have practical assistance, someone who gives me money to buy more holy powder than all you sanctimonious lot.

Besides, I was running out of time now. They're closing in on me now. They were losing patience with me, the Chipangano lads. They wanted their fair share of their money for those drugs I'd been enjoying on credit or borrowed money, what have you. It hadn't been bad initially, as I used to pay in kind via my services as a local supplier for Munyaradzi's drug syndicate. As my traction increased, Munyaradzi started showing more trust in me. I became the linchpin between Harare north and the sprawling high density Southern suburbs divide, as I helped push the drugs among my white counterparts in Borrowdale and other surrounding affluent areas within the northern suburbs' vicinity.

"You're our invaluable link, Julian. You will also arrange for drug dealing and pushing with our Borrowdale clientele, but this will all be hush-hush, and we ensure we keep it under wraps." It had all been hunky dory as we'd sat down in one of Mark's safe houses in Harare Highlands where we executed and set in motion one of the most lucrative drug syndicates in modern day Harare. We had all the support we needed from the party's big wigs who, for greasing their palms with some fat wads of American greenbacks, turned their attention the other side. What a successful turnaround we had as our drugs and sleaze business grew in leaps and bounds.

To compound the facade of the business, Mark would fly from England, purportedly with charity aid and donations money meant for the underprivileged of Harare and other deprived communities in Zimbabwe.

Government ministers would preside there, amid glowing pomp and fanfare equally glamorized in the party's sole broadcaster, CCTV station. Of course, it was all part of the grand scheme in building and promoting a narrative of deception and hoodwinking people, especially as the local papers really went to town gushing about that media mogul: "UK based Zimbabwean telecoms entrepreneur continuously breaking new ground in charity and philanthropy work within and beyond Harare." But then our bubble popped sooner than we'd expected when our mule, Amanda Poulter, was busted at Harare International Airport. Then it all cocked up for us.

"I'm afraid we have to temporarily suspend operations for now," Mark had admonished us in that tense meeting at our Highlands safe house.

"What for, boss?" asked Munyaradzi, one of the over-eager underlings. "We have protection from the highest offices and corridors of power in the land. Why stop at this, a temporary setback? Surely, our connections, our immunity, will carry the day for us."

"I say we stop it, because it's not safe, and because I'm saying it as your boss," Mark angrily reacted. For a man who wasn't used to be questioned, he was increasingly rattled and considered it a slight from someone as low in the pecking order as Munyaradzi.

"Sorry, boss, whatever you say," a clearly wounded Munyaradzi whimpered in a climbdown of defeat.

Somewhat mollified by Munyaradzi's climbdown, Mark resumed speaking in a conciliatory voice.

"The terrain is rough at the moment, especially with the recent change in the country's administration. We have to exercise caution, as we may need to re-negotiate our contracts and fiefdom parameters with the new administration.

"Right. In the meantime, I have pressing business commitments to attend to fellas. I have a meeting with a high court judge assigned to our mule Amanda Poulter's case. So let me dash along to this meeting and see if he can kill off this looming prosecution. We can't afford the negative publicity and all the attendant mess which will come with it.

"Munyaradzi, you see to it that operations at Harare Airport cease until I give you and other divisional heads the go ahead to resume operations. You will need to co-ordinate with our point man, Brian Wharton, at the Avenues safe house."

Brian Wharton! At the time Mark mentioned that name, it had no impact on me. How would it when I knew no Brian Wharton? There was nothing new in Mark's modus operandi in ensuring how he strove to keep his business empire in clandestine mode so that most of the employees operated covertly and we hardly knew each other unless there was a need to.

"You're on a no-need-to-know basis," as Mark used to term it. "No loose ends, lads! The less you know of each other the better. It minimizes risks and undue pressure to the business."

Chapter 27

Doris

"And then he had a relapse and started self-harming. Have you seen his elbows, and the garish knife marks on them?" Mother asked me one morning.

"Who are you referring to, Mum?"

"Who else other than your brother, Julian? He's taken to slashing his elbows with a knife. His justification, as he says, is, 'It helps me cope when I need a fix and can't get it.'"

"Aaah, I see, and you seriously think mutilating your body, being a crazed masochist, is the way to go?"

"Whatever, Doris. Why can't you ever leave me alone for heaven's sake? It's my life, not yours. Let me be and do as I please," Julian had rudely countered. "In any case, it's the voices in my head telling me to do this! They keep telling me: *Do it, good old Julian! Do it! Do it! Go on, mate, slash those wrists. You know you want to. Just do it, you do love the sight of blood, don't you?*

"The voices?" I had retorted in total surprise. "Which voices, you fool? What are you on about? Is this you or the meth talking again?" I looked into his face inquiringly, my befuddled brain failing to process his balderdash.

"I just told you it's the voices didn't I, Doris? V-O-I-C-E-S! Can't you hear them yourself? They were making so much noise last night, I barely slept a wink. That's why I was pacing to and fro in my bedroom.

"And you know what gets to me? When they laugh at me, relentlessly taunting me, I'm a coward for not daring to spill more blood from my wrists and elbows. Damn voices. But I'm trying so hard! Why can't you be grateful at acknowledging my efforts? What do you think these scars are for?"

There was so much anguish and exasperation as he stretched his hands out to me, baring the garish criss-cross scars where the kitchen knife had done its permanent mutilation, leaving an ugly sight on his arms and elbows. Inwardly, my heart bled; this was not my son. *Where had good old Julian gone, my little boy of yesteryear I used to cuddle goodnight as I tucked him in bed at our Mazowe farm?*

I felt a cold shudder course through my entire body as a mother. Something didn't feel right with my Julian anymore. Call it whatever you want, a sense of déjà vu? You name it, but with his incessant voices companions I knew somehow we had entered new territory with Julian. This was a Rubicon moment, and I loudly shared my thoughts with Rhys.

"Rhys, I say, do you hear me, Rhys? I'm scared and worried about your little brother, Julian. Today has been the first time Julian alluded to the voices in his head."

The voices in his head were to become the centerpiece of his endless struggles, his demons. I couldn't help but reflect, there's a song to that, *Gloria,* by Laura Branigan, and by some strange coincidence I started humming the tune, "…the voices in my head!"

"What about reaching out to Dr. Hinckley again?" I threw this back at Mum. "Don't you think Dr. Hinckley's trazodone or olanzapine might do the trick if she ups the dosage, seeing Julian's behaviour has become increasingly erratic in recent days?" I said, seeking to reassure her and ease Mum's disquietude.

"Sounds like a plan. Will sound her out. I truly wish peace on his troubled soul. He's gone back to his old mates after all that progress he'd made in going cold turkey. But this is not our Julian anymore, Rhys. Julian is well and truly gone," I said, stifling the avalanche of tears welling in my eyes.

At times I tried to get to the bottom of these voices, hoping he would snap out of what I termed a daydream, but my interrogation always morphed into further misery and that awkward silence, as Julian was adamant that the voices were his friends.

"You see, Doris, unlike you and Rhys, the voices are loyal to me, as friends that is. They never judge me like you lot do."

There was that unmistakable sense of betrayal evident in his voice, eyes and demeanor as he continued babbling, lost in his hogwash.

"Perhaps, you need to consult a medium. There is this exceptional man, Chitakunye, in Domboshawa. I hear he's very good at exorcising these strange illnesses, like what's happening to baas Julian. They're evil spirits and this is child's play to Chitakunye," Sisi Maria, good old Sisi Maria, our long-standing maid, had implored and entreated me.

But I was having none of this bull crap medium talk. I stood firm, unyielding, even as it became increasingly evident Julian's screws were becoming looser by the day.

"Thanks, but no thanks, *Sisi* Maria," I said, after a long period of hesitancy and silence while I'd reflected on her seer recommendation.

"Why should we even entertain, let alone validate Julian's sickness by seeing a purported seer? All Julian needs is more dosage of his medication. The current dosage is now clearly weak and not doing its job," I had fiercely objected to Sisi Maria. "I know you mean well, love, but I'll let the Domboshawa medicine man pass. But thank you nonetheless, *Sisi* Maria. I really appreciate your kindness," I had said, squeezing her hand to show her my support.

Secretly, I felt conflicted with this whole idea of seeking spiritual divine help for what I clearly saw as escalating mental illness ignited by substance abuse and possibly unresolved grief at the loss of Evie, his wife, my beautiful and sassy daughter-in-law.

I do miss Evie. I say that from the bottom of my heart. She had a heart of gold for want of a cliché. I also miss my husband, Jim.

Part of my conflict stemming from *Sisi* Maria's suggestion was how I would explain seeking an African seer to my other friends like Dr. Jenkins, our family friend and his wife, Marian.

Where on earth, Doris, have you heard white people consulting dark mystical forces? How could you get involved, immersed in that voodoo black magic mess? It is not done! Are you descending into hell? I could imagine Marian Jenkins reproaching me in her uppity voice. In addition, how could I possibly believe in such things? *Perhaps it may work*, an inner voice whispered in my ear, further fuelling my inward turmoil and catastrophe. *Give it a rest will you, Doris?* Another counter voice retorted; I grudgingly went with this latter voice.

Chapter 28

Doris

Final Straw

"Really, sincerely, and from the bottom of my heart, fuck off, Julian. I've just about had enough of you, up to my eyeballs. Why can't you go away from where you're not needed and take a hint for heaven's sake?"

I wasn't taking any more shit from Julian's tomfoolery, and I was determined to stick it to him. This mother's molly-coddling strategy I'd adopted all along hadn't worked with him, now that he was so far gone in his downward spiral and descent into hell. Perhaps I had reached the end of my tether.

There was always a febrile atmosphere which fettered in the house whenever he was around. Today I felt there was something in the air, and I wasn't prepared to put up with Julian's antics anymore. Something's gotta give.

"How many times have I bailed you out of your self-inflicted junkie woes? Tell me! And when is this ever going to end, with your ceaseless manipulation, blackmail you name it? It's not servitude nor criminal to be one's mother. You should know that!"

"Try something better, Doris! Is that your leverage, bludgeoning me with relentless questions?"

"How dare you have the effrontery and temerity to answer back to me and utter such disparaging remarks? I am your mother, for heaven's sake!" My voice bristled with limitless anger and venom as I let rip into Julian.

"Why would I take umbrage at that?" I replied incredulously, shrugging my shoulders in disbelief. 'As I've always said to you, Doris, drugs chose me, I didn't choose them. What a complete ass clown you are!"

"Don't be ridiculous! And while we are at it, watch your mouth, young man, that's no way to talk to me when you live under my roof, enjoying my charitable benevolence.

"Now let me put you straight, young man, once and for good. After tonight I want you out of my residence. You've crossed the line with your whole substance abuse and chaotic lifestyle, and I'm sure I'm not the only one here who shares these sentiments and misgivings," I said as I glanced at Rhys. He had quietly walked into the room in the middle of our melee and was all the while nodding his head in acquiescence as I spoke.

"I am not going nowhere, you two. Let's get this straight. I have as much right in this house as both of you. Last time I checked, I'm still my old man Jim's son, and no way you're evicting me, throwing me to the wolves, just like that. It's not happening."

"Well, we'll see about that, Julian. You heard Mum's sentiments, and her sentiments, which I happen to share, will pretty much prevail. That's the end of it all. This matter is now closed and not up for further discussion. By noon tomorrow I'll see to it that your sorry ass will be out of here!"

"I ain't standing here taking any shit instructions from you, Rhys. You can forget about this, mate. Your ego has become so inflated you think you co-own this place. Stop lecturing me. You and I are siblings and no one is cleverer than the other or has the monopoly of wisdom to dictate to the other how to live their life."

I was fired up and continued, "You're one to talk, Rhys! You think I don't know your dirty stinking gentleman's club secret in Avenues? Next time, think twice before you open your gob, or I'll blow your cover.

"Okay, I need to be clear with you here, Rhys, and let me enlighten you, however you may seek to downplay whatever I say as junkie stuff. But the thing is, I am well-aware of your sordid secret, the whorehouse in Avenues and your rent boy business. And not only that, but I've also known this for a long time.

"Truth be told, Rhys, you're not as squeaky clean as you've hoodwinked Mum all these years. Goodness knows, you're just as fucked up as I am!

"And while we're at it, before you lecture me on what is right and wrong, do you want to come clean to Mum and me on why you think it's okay to sponsor a whorehouse in downtown Harare?"

I'd piqued Rhys' interest; I could see his eyes were dilated, his mouth agape at what I had just said, and I carried on with much renewed fervor in my voice.

"So, next time, before you dismiss me as a junkie, think twice! Not all that emits from my mouth is hogwash, unlike you and Doris."

"You know what, Julian? Sometimes I can't believe the shit that comes out of your mouth." I sarcastically laughed off his remarks. But inwardly my heart skipped; I was perturbed, in fact, that he knew about the Avenues sex ring. *How much else did he know of the full extent of my duplicitous lifestyle?* I pondered to myself. *Did he also know that we supplied the very drugs I lampooned him for taking, day in and day out?*

I felt sick with the bile rising in the pit of my stomach as my stinking hypocrisy came back to haunt me. But I braved it out and switched to my alter ego bluff and bluster personality, challenging, "Who would believe you, you pill popping rambling idiot! Now you are making up stuff about me again. Very well then. Mum, you know what he's like, a junkie through and through, and don't dignify the rantings of a lunatic.

"Who are you now, the Pope pontificating on morality? How dare you malign and insult my integrity with falsehoods?" I was rankling with rage, foaming and frothing at the mouth, as I glared menacingly at Julian, my fists clenching and unclenching in unmitigated rage.

"Cut the crap, Rhys! You really are a useless liar. You and I know what I am talking about, so better you shut your stinking gob."

"Or else what?" I retorted.

143

"Just try it," he spat back. "You keep pushing me, I won't be liable for whatever will come out of my mouth, moreso in fully exposing your longstanding duplicity. You really don't know who you are fucking with, do you?"

I ignored his dismissive condescending tone, which I knew for sure was a bluff, but Julian was on a roll; his tongue was loosened, and he couldn't help himself.

"Don't you get tired with this level of hypocrisy, Rhys?" he defiantly shot back. Just looking at you utterly exhausts me. But where do they get hypocrites the likes of my brother, Rhys? Where are they made? Poor Doris doesn't really know the true nature of her goody, goody two shoes son, does she?

"You clearly underestimate me don't you, Rhys? Just because I snort some powder and I smoke weed doesn't make me stupid. Give me some credit. I'm not that stupid. For years I've known your shady lifestyle and how you make money, but as you're an adult I saw it as none of my business to get involved. But seeing you can't lay your slimy, interfering hands off me, then it becomes my business! And I can tell you this, from now on, the gloves are off with you! No more pussyfooting with you, Rhys."

Somewhat caught in a trance-like silence, the mighty voluble Rhys appeared wide-eyed and momentarily stunned into silence, quite a far cry from his usual bluff and bluster swag.

"Perhaps, too many things in life cannot be reconciled, as mother has persistently rammed down my throat each time she reproached me for cavorting with my demons. What a stroke of irony, if only she knew the duplicitous nature of her beloved son, Rhys," Julian said.

Doris was too dumfounded by the unfolding spectacle that had rendered her speechless; she constantly switched gazes to Julian, to me, to Julian, to me, after which I angrily stormed out, hurling unprintable expletives, possibly in a clearly calculated damage limitation exercise.

Julian really didn't know what to say following my weird response to his unmasking of me before Doris. Much as I denigrated Julian as a pill popping junkie, it became clearer to him that his supercilious brother was

144

equally messed up in the head, especially in his own estimation of his self and inflated ego. I really didn't know what to do.

Chapter 29

Inferno

There was something in the air that night. Swedish pop group Abba had a song to that effect, *Fernando*. Ominous dark clouds covered the full moon, obliterating its glow as if to foreshadow whatever lay ahead. Call it a sense of déjà vu; perhaps it was because of my earlier spat with Julian that somehow, I had this feeling of unease as I lay in my expansive bed, turning and tossing between the sheets, struggling to close my eyes and have much-needed sleep. Then miraculously I must have drifted to sleep, or so I thought. Still, I don't think I ever managed to shake off that feeling of impending dread and doom.

Time and again, I tried to suppress the internal monologue that kept looping through my head that something just wasn't right. Call it premonition, I don't know. I had this persistent sense of uneasiness I couldn't shake off.

Sleep has eluded me since Julian started his antics. Every night I have had to contend with fruitless searches for sleep. Perhaps this explains why I am ratty and irritable with everyone else at this house.

"Madame Doris' crying has known no pause since Baas Julian descended into his hell hole downward spiral. There is a terrible spirit in this place, and these people need help. I wish they could listen to me for just a day. They can be fixed," I've heard Sisi Maria speaking to M'koma Eddy every now and then, but I pretended to be oblivious to it all. It's a coping mechanism I've developed, deliberately waxing my ears to insulate myself from all the shit associated with my family. Julian's melancholia has been nigh depressing and has sucked dry the joy of others. It's been stifling just being around him.

***

"Fire!"

"Fire in the master bedroom! Help!"

Wild, agonizing, terrified and shrill screams erupted from Doris. I scampered out of bed and barely put on my boxers, dashing to Mum's bedroom in the expansive west wing of the house. *What could have possibly caused the fire?* This and a thousand other questions crossed my mind as I dashed into Doris' bedroom, where a strange spectacle of a distraught Doris greeted me. She was frantically trying to put out the flames from the upper end of her bed by the pillows, where the raging flames were unchecked.

"Get a blanket!

Water, to smother this!"

"*Sisi* Maria!"

"M'koma Eddy, we need you here," I bellowed at the top of my lungs as I sought to contain the situation. Huge reams of blazing flames engulfed Doris' bedroom, cruelly devouring and ravaging everything on their way, not least her long curtains which the fire selfishly and hungrily swallowed.

It was at around the same time that I noticed the silhouette of my brother Julian slumped on the floor, but still conscious.

"Julian! I say Julian, are you alright?" I was shouting at him in frenzied deafening tones. "Julian, do you hear me? Answer me, will you?" I was speaking to him while my other attention was consumed by the fire I was valiantly trying to contain with the huge blanket I had managed to extricate from the wardrobe. Doris appeared to have slipped into a zombie-like trance. It took bellowing in her eardrums for her to snap out of her stupor. "Water, Mum, get buckets of water, we're succeeding with the fire, can't you see?"

Meanwhile, I had knelt by Julian's side after seeing the small flames of the fire subsiding.

148

"Julian! Julian, speak to me what happened?" I earnestly entreated him.

"I... I... I did it, Rhys," he was gurgling to speak amid thickish blood spluttering from his mouth, some gushing out through his nose and ears. It was a hideous spectacle. There were also rivulets of blood furiously oozing out of his chest. I somersaulted to a nearby drawer and managed to drag over a piece of cloth to plug the gaping wound on his chest.

And then, I noticed it, the first time, the huge, gleaming, butcher knife laying not far from Julian. It was the type of knife used to dissect proper cow carcasses in meat factory abattoirs. A thousand questions coursed through my brain as I tried to process this incriminating crime scene.

"I had to do it, Rhys! Julian goaded me into it, bragged he'd set my bed on fire to get back at me for threatening to chuck him out of the house."

I turned around to confront an ashen-faced Doris. She was like an apparition from a horror movie standing before me. Something didn't seem right with this surreal spectacle.

"Do it, do what, Mum? You're not making sense. What's going on here?" I asked, pressing the rag hard on my brother Julian's blood-soaked chest and looking at his now limp, lifeless body. Then and there, I knew we'd lost him. Even though I had no medical knowledge, I knew Julian had taken his last breath on earth. There was no life there anymore. It had ebbed from him. But even as I struggled to process this, Doris' sobbing jolted me into the present reality, and I knew I had to pull myself together, if only to enable me to navigate the Herculean crisis which now lay ahead of us as a family. This was full-bloodied murder staring my mother in the face and it wasn't a difficult decision for me to make, the plan formulating in my mind.

Marina, who had been quiet all along, interrupted me, "What did you have in mind?"

"What did I have in mind? You dare to ask me such a mundane question, Marina? What does every son do to protect his mother?" I threw the question at her as if it was her fault.

"It's a no-brainer to me," she said. "A son must do what must be done! Period."

"Exactly, Marina! Now we're on the same wavelength. And from that moment on, my assertive side took over as I spoke firmly to Doris, both my hands holding her head, ensuring I was staring into her terrified eyes.

"Now listen and listen very hard, Doris, will you? You will just have to listen and commit to memory what I'm telling you here. From now on, I'm in charge and my word goes. Do you follow?"

Poor Doris was so far consumed in terror and fright, she could only nod to show her acquiescence.

I told her, 'This is what we will do. Julian is gone! He's gone for good, and nothing is going to change that. But there's something we can change, and it is that I'm not suddenly going to let a seventy-three-year-old woman who happens to be my mother languish in gaol over the accidental death of her junkie son. The first thing, we have some work to do tonight, serious graft if ever there was. Here, take a couple swigs of this stiff scotch, you will need it!'

To Marina I said, "Up to now, I am not sure where we summoned the strength, Marina, but throughout the dead of the night, with picks and shovels, Doris and I managed to dig a shallow grave in our back garden where we were able to dispose of Julian's body."

"What of M'koma Eddy and *Sisi* Maria, were they privy to this? Were you not scared of them stumbling upon you both during this macabre incident?"

"That's the thing, Marina. Strangely enough, both M'koma Eddy and *Sisi* Maria slept throughout the whole thing. In fact, it later turned out *Sisi* Maria had been off duty that weekend, so I had only M'koma Eddy to worry about. But from the events of the following days, it appeared he didn't notice anything was amiss."

"What of your friendship groups? Were you not at all concerned they would notice your brother's disappearance?"

"Aaah, not unless you have a junkie for a brother who leads a Bohemian lifestyle and tended to come and go like the wind as Julian did, then you knew you were safe. I had no qualms in this respect, as this tended to be Julian's modus operandi most of the time. He could disappear for days on end, and even some of our friendship group, like the Jenkinses from neighboring Vainona, had come to accept as the norm not seeing him each time we had our get togethers. The same goes for *Sisi* Maria and M'koma Eddy; it was pretty much a given that Julian could have these long unexplained absences from home, then resurface whenever he wanted."

"No fear of girlfriend or partner raising the alarm?"

"You're joking! Julian had no time for a relationship. That requires time and commitment, two things he was quite mean with. The only real thing he had time for was his crystal meth, *mutoriro* and his sleazy nocturnal deals with his criminal underworld, downtown Harare underlings."

"Looks like you had it all planned, though I hate saying it like that. This is your brother we're talking about, for heaven's sake, a person you were once close with, before this fine madness set in."

"True, I'm with you there, but what options did I have, other than protect and look out after my mother? You forget I'd had previous brush-ins with the Zimbabwe criminal justice system following the brutal murder of my father at our Mazowe farm. Yet to this very day, the criminals who deprived my father of his life still walk scot-free.

"So, what justice can I get from such compromised courts, even if I had decided to come clean with this? None. No justice whatsoever. In any case, why should Mother suffer relentlessly with no respite?

"By Jove! Hasn't she suffered enough? Losing her husband, her daughter-in-law Evie, pregnant with twins at eight months, her son Julian to drugs. The list of Mum's ordeals is nigh infinite! For heaven's sake, the poor woman deserves some respite, which is where I made the right judgement call and promptly stepped in to save her from the vultures that Zimbabwean courts are."

"I hear you. I am not judging you, Rhys," Marina said to reassure me.

"The judiciary in any country should be the ultimate bastion of truth and scrupulously comply with both the letter and spirit of the law and constitution. If this doesn't happen, and the public loses faith; then the entire justice system is undermined.

"From my experience and yours, Marina, the judicial officers arguably rank as the greatest betrayal in the political history of this country, a separate arm of the state but reduced to some party caucus. So sad, very sad!

"Even as the entire world witnessed during the chaotic land invasions of white-owned farms, the judiciary was left with egg on its face, exposed for what it is, an appendage of the party, as they brazenly stood aside and did not dare raise their legal might to stem this nonsense. And you tell me I could get justice in such courts.

"The tyrannical system creates pseudo democratic structures to mask its evil character. The whole legal system is now designed to shield the obtaining dictatorship from external scrutiny. And don't forget, Doris and I being white Zimbabweans makes us enemies of the state by default, given the regime's modus operandi. So we would have been unlikely to get a fair trial, which is why I ended up doing what I had to do.

"You also seem to forget that highly publicized drug smuggling case of one certain Amanda Poulter, busted at Harare Airport with a 6 kilo consignment drugs stash. Despite the ensuing hullabaloo at the time, where did that end?

"Amanda was later released on bail and her case disappeared in Zimbabwe's deeply corrupt maze of the criminal justice court system. So, there you are. That's justice for you in Zimbabwe, Marina."

"I get that. You're very much on point in your appraisal of the rogue legal system obtaining, but perhaps the last question from me, Rhys is, after all your well-choreographed facade, how were you outed? How come you ended up getting nicked? That's the part I don't understand at all. Please do shed some light."

"Aaah, what can I say, Marina?" I shook my head at her to underscore my sense of exasperation.

"Call it the night of long knives. That's what got to me in the end."

"Night of long knives? Was there some inside betrayal on your part? But how could that be, as both M'koma Eddy and *Sisi* Maria were not privy to all of this. Enlighten me please. I am none the wiser here."

"Forget about 'night of the long knives.' Perhaps confession night is more like it, Marina. I am my own enemy here, love. I blurted it out to the old Bailey following a nasty road traffic accident in Ruwa. We were travelling back to Harare with my friend Julius when this *kombi* driver speeding away from the police ploughed straight into my Jeep Wrangler, ruthlessly clipping my passenger side where Julius was seated. That sent him flying out of the car and landing in the middle of Ruwa's main road, in the way of an oncoming timber-laden heavy haulage truck which tragically smashed him into smithereens.

"It is only now I am brave to even talk about it, Marina, but the shock of seeing Julius being mowed to death right before my sight tipped me over the edge. I was a complete utter nervous, wreck, mumbling gibberish as the police tried to take a witness statement from me. I kept rambling on incoherently, 'I'm sorry. I didn't kill him. Please let him live, officer. I can't have two deaths living on my conscience. Please help me, officer. I can't do this anymore. The first one, like this one, was an accident, believe me.'

"I'm told it initially took four police officers to calm me down by the Harare-Mutare highway, but even then, that proved inadequate. It was not until I regained consciousness from the heavy sedation at Wilkins Hospital that the inadvertent horror of my self-incriminating confession dawned on me with a jarring effect. I promptly requested my legal counsel to help me recant my earlier statement. Try as my legal counsel, Jonathan did to have my earlier statement rescinded, Harare Central Law and order cops were having none of it."

"They said, 'As far as we're concerned, your client made a warned and cautioned statement of a very serious nature, and until investigations are concluded to establish the whereabouts of his brother, Mr. Julian Williams, then I'm afraid your client and his mother, Mrs. Doris Williams, remain possible prime suspects linked to the disappearance of their kin.'"

"But it remains hazy to me, Rhys. I don't see how a purported roadside traffic accident confession connects you to the murder of your brother, both you and Doris," said Marina, giving me both a searching and sympathetic look.

"Aha, I haven't yet come to the crux of the matter, Marina, have I? I could have religiously stuck to my traumatic delirious confession story as indicative of my shock, but then homicide and forensic detectives from the CID discovered and exhumed Julian's body from our poorly dug shallow grave in the back garden of our Borrowdale Brooke home in what became one of the most high-profile media circus cases in recent years."

"You're joking, right? Not only did they make that all important discovery, but they also exhumed your brother's remains from your home garden?"

"Precisely, Marina, that is the case. That is what happened, and from then on, it was a roller coaster for both Doris and me as things pretty much went downhill.

"You can quibble with other things, but not when a physical body is there with pathological reports and forensic science-backed experts baying for your blood. To cut a long story short, the discovery of Julian's body was a defining game changer, if I may say. The last nail on the coffin. Our fate was pretty much sealed by this."

"I see. Any potential leaks who may have outed you?"

"You know, I've tried to think about it all these months I've been here in Chikurubhi. But I doubt the police had any external assistance to the garden secret."

"Really? What about M'koma Eddy and *Sisi* Maria?"

"I doubt it. Besides, M'koma Eddy was fast asleep on the night in question. *Sisi* Maria was away for the weekend, as I've said before. So, I doubt it's anything to do with them, and in any case, their loyalty to us has always been impeccable in my estimation.

"We go back a long way to Mazowe farm days. M'koma Eddy and *Sisi* Maria are decent beings, I would say. They're pretty much part of the family if I may add.

"On deep reflection, my stuporous confessions were certainly my undoing, however hard Jonathan my legal counsel tried to claim them as inadmissible. Still, they set in motion a cathartic series of events which have led to mine and Doris' incarceration here."

Chapter 30

Marina

Road We've Travelled

My relationship with Mark has been troubled for as long as I can remember, seeing how he relentlessly abused me physically, followed by his over-the-top remorse. He always apologized profusely, promised to change, but never changed. I guess I'm an idiot for staying that long in a pointlessly painful, challenging relationship.

Mark's shenanigans were always a recurrence of the same old script: "Sorry, sweetheart. You know I love you and can't help it, right? I am a global figure, and it will surely ruin me if you go public with this. Besides, who would believe you? I've got the financial and legal largesse to make things difficult for you, so just don't get carried away. Remember how the Amber Head-Jonny Depp abuse trial ended?"

There always seemed to be an ominous threat to the way he threw that last question at me and left it hanging in the air. Then bizarrely, the blatant bribery cycle would follow with him taking me on those expensive getaways abroad to European capitals, particularly Berlin, Amsterdam, and Copenhagen. The upshot was, I became the envy of my uni friendship group, June, Elise, Myra, and also within our residence hall.

In the early days of our relationship, when I was still at Durham uni, Mark's abuse was more subtle; it came across as more emotional/mental abuse. I tended to make excuses for him, putting this mistreatment down to the stresses of being a high-profile businessman. *What a hopeless loser!* I bet some of you are lampooning me for not picking up the red flags then, but hey ho, it's much easier to be judgemental when you're out of love than when you are in the thick of it.

Looking back, hand on heart, did I stay because of the money? Was it my mercenary motives? I don't know, but as June, good old June, used to say, many times, "You know you never struck me as a masochist, Marina, especially given the rough and tumble life we had at Blanchett. But the more I look at your dysfunctional relationship with Mark, the more I think you are only staying in this farce because it suits you."

"Suits me how so?" I shot back at her.

"Well, think of this, poppet. Besides the money and lifestyle Mark exposes you to, I think you're also staying because you love the chaos."

"Love the chaos?"

"Of course, you do, love, how else does such an intelligent erudite lassie like you deliberately disrespect yourself like that with Mark's silly antics? You two seem to thrive in the chaos together."

"Well, that makes me a smart whore then, accusing me of hanging on because of Mark's financial perks and fat bank balance. You're a complete bitch! I can't stand you!"

"Oh, spare me the moral platitudes, Marina; been there, heard these before. You and I know you like Mark to keep the champagne and cocktails rolling!"

"It's a difficult one, June, but much as my brains tell me a big no, my heart lies with Mark. Besides, he's talking of relocating with me to his home country, Zimbabwe."

"Relocating to Zimbabwe? Oh, oh my, Marina, Zimbabwe? When? That's big, that's certainly huge."

"Post completion of my degree, he wants me to be involved in the day-to-day running of GTN, his telecom company in Zimbabwe. He says all will be above board. 'I'll pay you a competitive salary just like any of my executive employees, Marina.' Those were his words to me, verbatim."

"And what did you say to this?"

"I said, 'I need more time to mull this over, Mark. You've just thrown a huge surprise at me without giving me any prior indications.'"

"He said, 'Of course, munchkin, you can take all the time you need in the world to reach your decision. But think of the perks involved, not only in the monetary sense, but a rich culture, warm climate, and a friendly people.' June was clearly impressed with this and certainly egged me on."

"Is that how you eventually moved to Zimbabwe then?" Rhys asked.

"In a way, yes. He did manage to convince me, the smooth talker and dandy charmer he is."

"'Look Marina,' he said. 'Don't take this the wrong way but I think you need to try out this Zimbabwe option. Trust me sweetheart. It's not like you have family ties here. So, why not take the plunge, love, and see for yourself what it's like. Two years is all I'll give you in the first instance.' He spoke persuasively, waggling his two fingers at me as if to drive home his point."

"'Two years for what Mark?' I challenged him."

"'Two years to check out for yourself what you make of your foray in Zimbabwe. If you don't like it after two years, then you exercise your option to return to England.' But I bet you'll love it,'" he'd said, a wicked glint in his eyes."

"That weekend, we flew to Barcelona as he tried to woo me, all in a bid to make me acquiesce to the Zimbabwe dream. He need not have worried himself needlessly, as I was already sold on the idea but was only playing hard-to-get. I didn't want to appear too eager to him, lest he change his mind. Tell me, what sort of fool would decline a godsent opportunity to relocate to a warm country like Zimbabwe?"

"Unbeknownst to him, the first few days he'd mentioned the Zimbabwe story, I had surreptitiously checked it out online and, oh my, I liked what I saw and read about Harare and its iconic landmarks, *Domboshava, Mutirikwi Lake, and Mukuvisi Woodlands,* among others. I was going to say yes to the Zimbabwe dream, but the bastard would have to sweat for it first, like he

157

did in Barcelona after we spend the entire weekend exploring Catalonia's famous landmarks and rounded the day off with a memorable visit to the famous *Nou Camp,* Barcelona Football Club playing ground.

"That evening, as a prelude sweetener to the night, I gave him a blow job like there was no tomorrow and left him panting for more till he begged me to stop. The next morning, we made hot passionate love again, followed by a surprise sapphire diamond encrusted ring. He gingerly placed it on my breakfast plate and in romantic fashion went down on bended knee. 'Marina, my love, would you be my fiancée? With this ring I'm asking your hand to be my one and only fiancée.'

"'Yes, yes, my love,' I gushed my acceptance of his unforeseen proposal which, I must say, despite my astuteness at reading situations, I hadn't seen coming.

"After breakfast we sealed it all with another amorous sexual liaison in the hotel's jacuzzi. It was undeniably seductive, Mark's tongue gently encircling me, which hardened me. For the first time, I experienced the utter pleasure of a man going down on me. My undercarriage was thoroughly wet, I was ready and literally begging for it from Mark. He didn't disappoint, as he went on to ram his stiff cock into the diamond between my thighs, much to my delight; I egged him on, cooing relentlessly with delirious pleasure. Following this holy treat, I reciprocated in kind and gave him his much-needed Zimbabwe acquiescent present.

"I licked him like there was no tomorrow, the tip of my tongue tantalizingly nice on his manhood, as I sucked on it like an ice-lolly on a sweltering summer morning, with my other fingers expertly playing with his balls, much to his delight, accentuated by his cooing like a dove in heat, 'Oh Marina...Marina, I love you honey...' He groaned with immeasurable pleasure as our bodies coursed with a cacophony of ecstasy which blinded us in toenail-tingling sensations.

"'That's it, naughty boy,' I said, adding, 'Offer to relocate to Zimbabwe accepted Mark.' And that was it, we celebrated in style with yet another ferocious lovemaking moment. My bottom was sore for several days afterwards. I did struggle to walk following the Barcelona marathon sex sessions. We both had an insatiable appetite for sex, each of us as bad as the other in this respect. I knew how to please men; that was my specialty, well-honed during my university days before Mark was on the scene.

"So, you see, contrary to how my friendship group perceived our relationship, things were not always bad and grim between Mark and me. By the time I completed my degree, Mark, and I flew to Zimbabwe to commence a new life, which I hoped would eventually culminate in something bigger. June, my longstanding loyal friend, came to Heathrow Airport Terminal 5 to see us off and she was in floods of tears at our parting, floods of tears, as if someone had passed on. June can be such a drama bitch! Why was she in such torrents of tears, embarrassing me like that? One would be forgiven for thinking there was a bereavement.

"Part of me understood her feelings of despondency and sadness. Inwardly, I was equally emotional, though I strove valiantly to hide it. It was understandable June was emotional, for she was my only family to talk of in England from our days back at Blanchett's Goodhope Convent. June was more like a sister and brother all wrapped up in one for me, the sister and brother I never had.

"'Look after Marina well, Mark,' she'd jokingly admonished him, though there was an air of seriousness and earnestness in the way she said it."

"'What do you mean look after Marina well? You know Marina is a diamond to me,' Mark had playfully sparred with June in Terminal 5 check in lounge, as June's body language betrayed her misgivings.

"We flew British Airways first class to Zimbabwe, via South Africa, especially as Mark had insisted, 'I wouldn't know how it is to fly any other way, Marina.' Not that I was complaining. Why would I, travelling in such exquisite opulence? I told myself, *there is my man, Mark, and if he wants to flash the cash, then let it be!* I wasn't the least fazed by his exhibitionist streak. It was an overnight flight, and after a brief stopover at OR Tambo Airport in Johannesburg, the next morning we resumed the short one-and-a-half-hour flight to Harare, which was soon to be our new home."

Chapter 31

Sisi Maria

For as long as I can remember, I have been a Zimbabwean national. My mother, Mbuya waTapera, used to tell me when they migrated from Mozambique into present day Zimbabwe, then Southern Rhodesia, that she was heavily pregnant with me. I was one of the babies born at Baas Jim's Mazowe citrus fruits farm clinic, the enterprising iron corrugated-roofed white house clinic, so named after its all too white color. The clinic itself was a brainchild of baas Jim's wife, Doris, a kind-hearted soul who was later to work tirelessly upgrading the clinic for the years I grew up. She also sourced anti-retroviral drugs for HIV-positive people in and around Mazowe community.

In view of my birth in a little Mazowe farm clinic, I am a Zimbabwean. I don't really get it why my foreign parentage or ancestry comes in and should be constantly thrown in my face, used against me to whip me, to remind me *I do not belong. Maybe I don't belong* after all, given the incessant vitriol against our lot, black immigrants. There are moments when I've had this fleeting doubt that maybe there's truth in what they've been saying all these years. *Maybe I don't belong?* But today, I am having none of these thoughts. I am very much a Zimbabwean like everyone else, and no amount of this politicking in the name of looking for votes will make me feel any less Zimbabwean. For what world or habitat have I known, other than my beloved Zimbabwe? So, why seek to divide us and displace me?

I had thought the xenophobia I went through would pass with the birth of my very own son, Tapera, but how wrong I was. I may as well have tempted fate by speaking too soon. It broke my heart, the litany of moments I have had to intervene and explain to Tapera not to take to heart the snide remarks from some of his peers, the xenophobic slurs thrown about to a young lad, *mabvakure,* a derogatory term for foreigners, loosely translated, "those who came from foreign lands." Thus, many times I found myself reflecting within myself at this abounding xenophobia, which seemed to have gone a notch further and escalated in post-2000 as Mugabe upped his incendiary rhetoric seeking re-election.

"What of our children? Why were they being denied Zimbabwean citizenship? The national identity cards registrar, a crude old, obnoxious relic, anachronistic dinosaur not fit to be in that office, repeatedly parroted the mantra; renounce your Mozambican citizenship first. How can we renounce something we've never had in the first place?"

How many times do I have to overstate it to be taken seriously? I am Zimbabwean now and will live the Zimbabwean way of life. I am not hankering over a past I never had or have lived long to remember, unlike what I'm being forced to accept as my nationality. Is it any wonder my son Tapera ended up crossing the border to *Egoli* Johannesburg after the only country he'd ever known spat him out?

"But mama, there's no future for me here," Tapera had remonstrated with me, not once, not twice, not thrice but for umpteen times. Deep down I knew he would eventually throw in the towel and leave, as happened that fateful Saturday morning when I could tell something was up with my boy. Earlier on, he had sounded agitated on the phone, "Mama, do you have time to spare? I have to see you, it's urgent."

"What is it?" I had shot back. "Can't you just say it and refrain from needlessly alarming me. I'm an old woman and don't do emergencies. I have high blood pressure. If you've just impregnated a girl, just say it, and see whether I'll reproach you."

"No, Mama, it's not that. Will you take me seriously for once? It has to be done in person. I will drop by in the morning." And that was it, the line went dead. And here he was, my boy, with his seemingly ground-breaking news to me.

"Can I make you breakfast?"

"No thank you, Mama, I have to go. Sorry I don't have much time. It's now or never, Mama." He spoke matter-of-factly, avoiding eye contact, and my heart skipped, even as I hazarded a guess at what was coming next.

"Don't you think you need to give it time and wait a bit, son? Things may well change." I was embarrassed at the insincerity in my own voice and inwardly felt ashamed at subjecting my only son to this hellhole that was Zimbabwe.

"But Mama, you know that this place will never accept me, *MuSena*, as they call me, a derogatory insulting term denoting my purported Mozambican heritage and ancestry.

"How many times have we been in this merry go round rollercoaster seeking for my national registration, citizenship documentation from the registrar general's office, and still the song remains the same: 'You are not Zimbabwean but Mozambican; go back to Moza to renounce your citizenship.' You know very well I've never set foot to Moza in my life, so how can I renounce something I've never had in the first place?" he countered, my silence only further escalating his sense of frustration and agitation. Each time this happened, Tapera's stutter became more pronounced as he struggled to string together words and sentences coherently.

I felt for him, as I did on this occasion, inwardly blaming myself at not having done enough to seek medical intervention to address his stuttering. It had started way back when he was nine, when his father abdicated on his paternal duties and blatantly refused to have anything to do with the lad.

"They are laughing at me at school, Mama. They, they, they…all…all…make fun of my stutter. I had to punch one of the boys, Damien, and yet Miss says it's my fault."

"Well, violence is not the answer, Tapera. How many times have I told you this? I will speak with Baas Jim, and perhaps when he takes the next batch of oranges to Harare, he can take you with him to be seen by a speech therapist."

Madam Doris had suggested this to me before, the kind-hearted woman she is. But the speech therapist visit hadn't happened, not because of the Williamses' fault. They were good people to me and my boy. *Baas* Jim's life was cut short by those marauding youths masquerading as war veterans, but that's for another day.

I can't believe how time flies. That had been many years ago, when Tapera was going through primary school being bullied on account of his identity and ancestry. Fast-forward to now, he's a grown lad, my boy.

"Mama, are you even listening to me? Are you not going to say something to me?" Tapera's shrill voice jolted me out of my mid-morning reverie.

I could only look at him in utter sympathy and that was all he needed to carry on his anti-Zim diatribe. "So, I'm saying, Mama, if the song is on auto-repeat for so long, then about time I change the dance routine instead. There's this man at work, Lovemore, he has a contact who will arrange fake papers for us to start work in Johannesburg as soon as we arrive. All I needed was transport fare which I have from my savings. This is it, Mama, I've come to say farewell to you."

And with that he hugged me for a good few minutes, holding me tightly to his bosom, as I silently sobbed, after which he retrieved his small bag holding all his 21 years of possessions. And with that he was gone like the wind exiting Zimbabwe, another statistic like his friends who had also left the country in droves earlier, as the Zim economy nosedived into a tailspin. That for me was the sad story of Zimbabwe and her people, the born frees like my son, Tapera, who had grown up and never knew what it meant to hold a job, let alone feel a payslip in their fingers. I must say, I am relieved though; my boy Tapera's good judgement had seen him not dabbling in the now rife crystal meth craze which had ruined many teenagers' lives. They all seemed to seek solace in this burgeoning drug and other attendant drugs, *mbanje* and *broncho* among others.

Meanwhile, in a cruel fashion, the sole broadcaster *CCTV* radio station kept playing those anachronistic, if not insulting tunes: *ivhu kuvanhu, rambai makashinga*, land is the economy, literally translated, keep on holding on, we got our land back and now in our land lies future industries and well-being for the nation. Of course, nothing could be further from the truth, as these twisted fuckers well knew, I silently cursed under my breath and spat to underscore my revulsion at the ruling establishment and their subterfuge.

Inwardly, I knew my son Tapera had a valid point, legitimate concerns for feeling aggrieved at a mother society which had spat him out of its mouth as if he was vermin. No one deserves this kind of treatment from their motherland. His father had disowned him and so had his country of birth, surely there has to be some let up of some sort in this world. Life had dealt me a cruel hand. With my son's coming of age, I'd thought I was on the brink of something great, but out of nowhere, I had this curve ball thrown my way. And Tapera had finally relented, throwing in the towel, with his decision to emigrate to South Africa.

I couldn't withhold my welling tears anymore. I was just knackered; my body felt like shit. I guess, I was feeling a tad sorry for myself. More tears made inroads down my cheeks.

I also felt like my son; I found myself resonating with his affinity for Zimbabwe. It is the only country we have ever known. We pretty much grew up here. This is home for us. This "go back home" talk by politicians is frankly not on. I know in my exchanges with M'koma Eddy, a Malawian immigrant working for Baas Jim, we tended to concur that Zimbabwe was now pretty much our habitat and there was no going back to a land we had never been to anyway.

"Agree with you absolutely, Tete Maria. How preposterous of the politicians to even suggest this xenophobic rhetoric," M'koma Eddy remarked.

"Well, Mugabe wants to win an election, doesn't he? He's pushed into a corner with his ruinous economic policies, and this election is a must win for him, by hook or crook, and what better way than to make fellow Africans of foreign descent convenient scapegoats. See, we are easy fodder for his scapegoating, and the fact that we are employed as laborers by white commercial farmers makes it even worse for us; we are enemies of state by extension, a charge axe wielding war veterans never ceased to remind us. 'Whose side are you on here? It's either you're with us or the white people, our enemy. That's what the President tells us; we listen to our President,' these war veterans, some young enough to be in Tapera's age group, would often charge menacingly at us, with hostile bloodshot eyes to underscore how high they were on weed."

"Yaa, I get that, Tete Maria. I'm not that educated like today's youth, but the few remaining history lessons I remember are, in history, dictators always pick on minorities as perceived enemies. Didn't Hitler do it with the Jews? And now *M'dhara* Mugabe is doing it with white commercial farmers and by extension to us black farm laborers?"

"Oh yes, last week's election rally was ugly. I'm told there was a lot of violence and Sisi Eriza from the neighbouring farm lost a few teeth when she got caught up in the violent post-rally melee. And to think she was only coming from the shops; she didn't even attend the rally. It was well nasty. I hear Mugabe gave it to us in his anti-whites/anti-farm laborers' diatribe: 'Let me tell them we have degrees in violence, and we must strike fear in the hearts and minds of our enemy, the white men and his kin, not forgetting their workers, totemless people: *vanhu vasina mutupo.*'"

"Really?"

"Of course, he did spout those incendiary inflammatory statements and I overheard *baas* Jim saying they are now living in fear around the neighboring farms, as sporadic reports of violence are erupting with some of these pseudo-war veterans besieging farms. Each morning, Baas Jim says, all commercial farmers do a roll call via walkie-talkies and mobile phones, checking on each other to ensure everyone has woken up safe from the night. It's increasingly scary out there with the 'war veterans' having set up squatter camps at most commercial farms."

"One thing for sure, I can tell you this, *Tete* Maria, that bastard Mugabe and his sycophants will never have my vote for as long as I live. How can I ever forget how we were sadistically rendered homeless and jobless, all the 200 workers on Baas Jim's farm, when our accommodation was razed to the ground by the war veterans, along with Baas' sprawling estate of the orange tree orchards? What kind of callousness was that all about?"

"You're telling me, *M'koma* Eddy, resorting to scorched earth policy towards your fellow brethren, your kith and kin, all in the name of land reform. Displacing the very people you purport to want to help gain a foothold on land? I'm sorry, if it were a joke, then it could be on them, these merchants of violence. Sadly, the irony of their actions is lost on them.

"After all these years that Tapera has been away, now I can reflect, and perhaps it's fair to say I now see things differently, the scales having fallen from my eyes, so to speak. More so, the xenophobic jingoism in our papers hasn't helped in fostering integration in our increasingly fractured society. Hasn't our ignorance and fear of immigration got us into such a mess? And what a shitshow of a government for exploiting that fear to shirk its own responsibilities. All ugly! All very difficult to repair now. Sadly, every so often, every single time we bear the brunt of it. Little things, digs, sneers, a superior stare, but they all add up. God! Have we not learned anything from the xenophobic attacks and violence in other parts of Africa?

"For some of us, like myself, *M'koma* Eddy, we may have become immune to the relentless migrant-bashing from the establishment. But what about our children like Tapera, who had in the end decided to jump ship and crossed the border into *Mzansi?* Was this not in itself self-defeating, given South Africa's very own xenophobic wars and violence of yesteryear?

"Sometimes I feel like saying to Tapera: 'Goodness if you like where you are stay. This place has less and less to offer.' Strange for me to harbor these thoughts, the very things Tapera used to say before he relocated to *Mzanzi.* But you know what, Tapera my son? Perhaps after all these years, the scales have fallen off my eyes. I do get it now. If you do manage to get your own family there in South Africa, then bear in mind, son, your children should support your decision, not try to pull you back. You can put your roots down now and make them strong wherever you are. Home is where the heart is.

Chapter 32

Muted Voices

A View from Joza

I wish I could say *Egoli*, the city of gold Johannesburg, has been a bed of roses, but I can't. That is not to say it's not been a worthwhile exercise, my exodus. Leaving Zimbabwe was the best decision I ever made for my long-term mental health and perspective. I was tired of the relentless xenophobia and deliberate exclusion. Why did it have to be nigh hard for me to get a national ID card like my fellow citizens?

I realized how disgustingly close-minded and judgmental I was before, and how there is so much more to life than following rules and scowling at people who choose to be different. I have made friendships in Johannesburg, and I am particularly close to one Chris from Malawi, my mate in dodging immigration woes, my all-time partner in adversity.

"You know, Chris, as much as things may be a tad hard here, leaving Zimbabwe remains a master stroke on my part," I often remark to him as we bounce ideas off each other. "Diaspora taught me tolerance. In terms of social toxicity Zimbabwe is the Chernobyl disaster equivalent of a toxic society."

"Good for you for admitting that, Tapera. And well done for seeing where you needed to grow and doing it! We need that kind of candor, however brutal; it will allow us to grow as individuals as we split from our broken amniotic fluid. Look at me, I'm far away from home like you. Why? Because Malawi failed me.

"So, I certainly resonate with your sentiments, Tapera, it rings true what you're saying. In fact, you just made me realize a possible solution to all my problems."

"And how's that?" I threw this brickbat back at a bemused Chris.

"Well, imagine how we are now. We've come a long way, living in these foreign lands, navigating, negotiating our way in the treacherous, murky waters of the diaspora. Steadying the ship. But whatever happens, there is no going back, mate. We are here to stick it out."

"Love this from you, mate, and to be honest, we all feel the same way. The bait dies before the fish, but they both die on the same hook! And so, we say, power to us for we're the future!"

"Absolutely, mate, the story of migration is never a single story as the party beyond the borders would like us to believe. The point is, people are leaving Zimbabwe and never looking back. That's the point that must be impressed upon, that when home no longer feels like home, you leave. Our story is relevant and must be heard. We refuse to be silenced by our existence in the greater diaspora."

Chapter 33

Sisi Maria

The Big Lie

The gruesome spectacle it is, of threadbare fellow farm workers trudging by the roadside, in the rain and cold, women, children, husbands, with their personal belongings on their heads, some huddled by the roadside with nowhere to go. Others walk alongside Harare-Mazowe main road with all the little possessions they've managed to salvage from their razed living quarters, razed by the fire of the war vets, still haunts me at the time *Baas* Jim was brutally murdered and hacked thereafter by the war vets. The picture of staggering despair was written all over the haggard, emaciated faces of the over 200 displaced farm workers, itself another damning indictment of this chaotic land redress. It hurt me to the core witnessing this unfolding humanitarian tragedy of epic proportions. Some of these now homeless people had been as close to me as family for all the years I stayed at *Baas'* farm. Not many had been lucky enough to be taken in and offered a new lease of life, as Madame Doris had done to M'koma Eddy and me by inviting us to move with them into their Borrowdale home after the mayhem.

According to the war vets, our crime was that we were enemies of state and accused of supporting both the whites and the new opposition party, the MDC. But then I caught myself thinking, *is it as easy as that, just being enemies of the state? Or, better still, are there no underlying factors that necessarily made white folk of Zimbabwe enemy of the state? Are they simply innocent?* Look, for how long would a tiny minority hold on to vast swathes of land amidst all this poverty. Would that be sustainable? So, next is South Africa! They must watch out…"

"Muri vatengesi, about time you know this; you're all traitors and there is only one place for traitors, six feet under!' The bloodshot, zonk-eyed leader of the war vets, a dwarf of a man called Mujubheki, had shouted at us, with his rag tag army in tow all high on weed, aggressively acquiescing, continuously pumping clenched fists in the air as they chanted party inspired slogans.

"Down with the whites!"

"Down with their appendages and minions, the blacks who collaborate and support them."

"We listen to our president, *Zimbabwe for Zimbabweans, Africa for the Africans. Africa is no white man's land,"* the war vets and their leader had carried on, bellowing their racist vitriol hate speech.

We were far too cowed and terrified to say anything, our voices muted by the omnipresent threat of sadistic violence underscored by their AK 47s, pangas and machetes. Besides, we were still stunned by the sudden murder of Baas Jim we'd just witnessed.

I was never in doubt the war veterans meant business that Friday morning they invaded Baas' farm. There was something in the air that morning, which just about underscored the grimness of events to come. The brooding Mazowe clouds were at variance with the chirping birds and sweltering sun. *Has the weather gone amok then?* I kept asking myself inwardly as I processed the strange weather unfolding that day. Call it a harbinger of things to come. How was I to know of the grisly shenanigans in the offing?

They came and they looked like they were prepared to shoot. But first they beat all male laborers, and they beat me and others as well, with clenched fists and cuffs amid swearing expletives on account of our skewed loyalties, taking the white man's side as had become their rallying cry.

Somehow, in the chaos of the melee, following Baas' brazen killing, we managed to get away.

We just ran. We just ran as fast as our terrified feet could take us. It was a very long way; we ran through the Mazowe forests, all the way oblivious of the lurking dangers of the usual rampant python snakes, prickly thorns and piercing stones on our bare feet. It had become a matter of life and death then; there had been no time to put on shoes or any decent clothes, as we were all in shock following Baas Jim's gruesome killing!

Under cover of the ensuing cacophony of confusion, with red tracer bullets being fired in the air by war vets leader Mujubheki and his fellow mercenaries, we hurriedly scurried and slipped away from it all.

Exhausted, frustrated and barely eating, we sought shelter among the Mazowe village communities who, I must say, treated us with kindness during our few days of displacement following the farm's takeover. Baba Munyanyi, a local secondary school teacher in the vicinity who used to frequent Baas's farm to buy chicken eggs, clearly commiserated with us at his sanctuary, which he gladly opened to us that red letter day.

"Aaah, nyika yaakuenda kumawere vanaTete. The country is going down a precipice with these uncoordinated land seizures. Mark my words, *hezvi ndiripano, kuri kuraramaka, tichazotaura."* Munyanyi had spoken, wringing his hands in utter dejection, as he resumed his philosophising sermon, his face a spectre of disappointment written all over it.

"Look, I was a *mujibha* myself, a war collaborator during the bush war of independence of this country and have no time for this bullshit baloney! Fast forward many years; I am a history teacher at Chipadze as you well know. I believe in land redistribution like my fellow black brethren. It's a well-meaning historical imbalance which ought to have been addressed long back; no one faults that, but you know what riles me most, *wanaTete?"* He paused, throwing the question at us as he surveyed our faces like he expected us to disagree with him.

As we could only nod in acquiescence, he resumed speaking, his voice now conspiratorially low like he was afraid the war veterans and their spies were eavesdropping outside. "What stinks with the whole thing is the haphazard manner in which it's being done! There's no logic behind this wanton plunder, scorched earth policy and madness obtaining on the ground.

"We're not idiots' contrary to what Mugabe and his sadistic hoodlums think.

"This is all about political survival under the guise of wresting land from the whites, and I say it again today, the country is going down an irreversible slippery slope." Munyanyi spoke with such a pained expression on his face, eyes wizened, underscoring his concern. Myself and my friend, Renika, we felt for him.

Many years later, as the country's fortunes careered from one catastrophe after another, the economy in a perennial tailspin, Munyanyi's now prophetic words: "the country is going down a precipice," kept haunting me, and in those words, I found resonance as I came to terms with the tragic failure of leadership in our country.

As surreal as it is, just like that, at the whims and caprices of a failing, geriatric tin pot dictator, we had been made homeless as Mugabe was driving his populist land reform agenda. Except it really was all done for political self-preservation expediency as Mugabe sought to shore up his waning political stock. There is no disputation; land should have been distributed equitably in Zimbabwe. No one faults this important premise, but what we have issues with is the haphazard, violent, vindictive and chaotic manner it was carried out, which ended up reducing the nation from a once vibrant jewel of Africa to a mere basket case. And I know my views here were shared by the generality of other farm workers, as we'd talked about this many atimes.

Surprisingly, in all this palaver and unfolding chaos, no one dared question Mugabe why this much-needed land reform hadn't been done in the first twenty years of his reign, such that it now constituted an emergency in the twilight of his political career. Could there be ulterior motives behind this sudden volte-face change of heart? I often heard it said that the matter was more complex, and that Mugabe was tugging on an otherwise genuine matter, land imbalance in Zimbabwe. Mugabe may not have been the matter itself. The matter lay under layers and layers of skewed historical events and Mugabe may have been scratching the surface to save his political life. He was the proverbial child who accepted to go on an errand because the trip would take him closer to individual dreams...

Besides, it didn't take long for the con to unravel to some of us that this fast-track land reform crusade was a power retention facade for a failing administration which had to cling onto power at all costs. From the picture unfolding in the country, it was not the largely poor, landless blacks who were being allocated seized land from the whites, but it was now being parcelled out to those closely aligned to the party's bigwigs and their cronies. More like a "you scratch my back, I'll scratch yours" scenario.

For the greater part of my kith and kin, who hailed from Mozambique, Malawi, and other southern African countries, and were now homeless courtesy of this land expropriation drive, life couldn't have somersaulted in a worse turn. One minute we were well housed, the next minute we were at the mercy of the unwelcome streets. Harare, it's stray dogs and ever-present street kids soon became our new habitat and allies. As my friend Renika later recounted to me, they ended up sleeping in plastic and wooden constructed shacks, packed like sardines, as some of the displaced farm laborers and their families set up a shanty squatter camp: Hartcliffe, near the outskirts of Harare. These squatter camps were an unfolding time bomb waiting to explode, as they were not fit for human habitation and did not have water and ablution facilities. I still remember vividly that chilling phone call from Renika, amid gut wrenching sobs as she broke the heartrending news to me, "I have nothing else to live for, Maria, there is a vicious outbreak of cholera and dysentery here. It's wreaking untold havoc. This morning we lost my daughter Tawana. She couldn't make it, the fourth child to pass on at the camp this week..."

"I am so sorry at your loss, my sister Renika, anything I could do to help?" my voice choked with emotion as I commiserated with my friend and felt her loss and pain.

"Thank you, I know you want to help, but what about my other family here with me, my other three children? Where would we go, who would house us where we can get access to clean water and money to access medical attention?"

In my heart of hearts, I knew Renika was spot on. I too had limited financial independence, as I was surviving on the benevolence of Madame Doris in her employ as a housemaid and had my modest servant's quarters at her Borrowdale residence. Once in a while, my son Tapera would send me some sustenance money from South Africa. It wasn't much to write home about, but at least I could get by. Still, I commiserated with my friend Renika at her loss. My heart went out to my friend and to all the other mothers and inhabitants of the now disease-infested squatter camp.

Meanwhile, the big lie was increasingly becoming clearer to me and others. With the unfolding land reform, a new norm had arisen; the party big wigs were increasingly profiteering out of the land grab as they proceeded to charge genuine landless people huge sums of money to go and peg out plots of land under their new lordship. The wheel appeared to be coming full circle so soon, as the land was just being transferred from white farmers to blacks connected to the party. The whole thing was akin to a country being run by a Mafia cartel which ruled by fear and brute force, and we, the common populace, dared not speak out for fear of brutal reprisals; we'd seen the war vets meting it out in exaggerated fashion, sometimes with the assistance of the party-aligned police force.

The police had increasingly become an appendage of the party, used to do its dirty bidding particularly during pre- and post-election periods, ballot stuffing with ghost votes, and torturing opposition supporters, while at the same time turning a blind eye to the party supporters' blatant transgressions of the law. You couldn't make this stuff up; it was unfolding in a purportedly independent African nation.

It was heart-breaking stuff for all of us, the generality of the farm laborers witnessing the deliberate ruin and destruction of a cohesive way of life and livelihood Baas Jim and his lot had struggled to build over many years being razed to the ground by these so-called war veterans. More poignant and hurtful was witnessing the carnage at Mazowe, which typified similar ruinous developments unfolding at other neighboring farms taken over, as large-scale commercial farms were reduced to mere slash and burn subsistence plots.

"It hurt us all, this gruesome spectacle," M'koma Eddy used to jokingly remark. "Tete Maria, if these youngsters' young enough to be your son Tapera are war veterans, then I also qualify to be a war vet."

We both shook our heads in disgust at how surreal things were unfolding in our country. We were aware of the duplicity surrounding the land invasions and how in reality these purported war veterans were unemployed youths manipulated and drilled in the party's warped ideology and schooled to intimidate the citizens. Some would boisterously blurt it out as the weed took over and loosened the tongue.

Years later, our scepticism has been vindicated. All this land grab did not improve our lot's mundane lives. Our people continue to live a life of abject poverty and penury. They are still living a life of subsistence. A once-feted jewel of Africa nation is now a basket case. One can't help but wonder, *Aaah land reform, what was that all about? What was the point really?*

My mind flickers to *Baas* Jim when he was alive. Each time he used to take us to Harare in his Jeep Cherokee, the road to Harare used to pass through prime farmland. Prime farmland typified most of then-Zimbabwe's countryside landscape, but driving along similar roads now, it's evident the country has become a land of wreckage mirrored by the ghost towns, disused farmhouses which were taken over by those with limited or no skills to effect productivity, notwithstanding the avalanche of propaganda to the contrary.

All we have with other old timers' farm laborers like M'koma Eddy are memories galore now, of *Baas* Jim and those bygone years at Mazowe farm, where my son Tapera cut his teeth into adulthood.

"Tete Maria, how can we ever forget Baas Jim and his contradictory character traits, the strict disciplinarian he was on *nyaya dzebasa,* matters to do with work?" remarks Mkoma Eddy amid hearty chuckles.

"I bet that makes us unique as people, doesn't it?" I shot back at him, sarcasm clearly in my voice. "Much as Baas Jim was a strict disciplinarian when bellowing those instructions to us in the sweltering Mazowe sun in the orange tree orchards, I feel it was all out of good intentions on his part to increase productivity on the farm. Still, for all his attention to detail, it was counterbalanced by his kindness, I would say, M'koma Eddy."

"True, on point, Tete Maria, I absolutely agree with you on this one. I'm sure all of us, his former farm laborers, can't fault Baas Jim's kindness; that's not in doubt, but it's always funny to me when I look at his other side. Remember I used to playfully say of him behind his back, 'a man of many jackets, he was.' All in good humour of course. Nothing malicious."

177

"Oh yes, I vividly recall your banter in relation to this. Have you forgotten how he used to go on and on about his eldest son Baas Rhys, and how it was high time he should get himself a wife and stop tagging along like a puppy in his mother's dresses, the grown man he was?"

"That's hilarious, Tete Maria. Look at it now. So many years have passed since Baas Jim's death, yet Baas Rhys is still a senior bachelor. I don't see him as the marrying type, though he appears to be a sharpshooter with women…"

"No way, M'koma Eddy, Baas Rhys is far too serious to get into a relationship, let alone settle with a woman. I swear the man is married to his work."

"You could be onto something there, Tete. The two brothers, Rhys and Julian, couldn't be any different. They're like chalk and cheese, for want of a cliché.

Chapter 34

Elusive Zimbabwe Dream

Black on Black

Ironically, the land reform drive has been exposed for the sham it was with the passage of time, as Renika, M'koma Eddy, and I are wont to share in our reminiscing. Whereas in the heydays of the chaotic invasions in the late 1990s-early 2000s, whites like *Baas* Jim and neighboring farmers had been targeted, several years later, it now appears a new trajectory had been reached. The shift has now changed to some black landowners being equally targeted and displaced from their farmlands, some in similar fashion to *Baas* Jim's case, where an owner had legal freehold title deeds and proof of purchase, as happened to the family of one war vet, Chitapi.

But there was a *raison d' etre* why the establishment were unleashing the might of the state on Chitapi's widow, MaKhumalo. Chitapi's son was a constant, rabid critic of the establishment, calling truth to power. Now anyone will tell you this for nothing, anyone who knows the party very well. They're a vindictive and petty lot who do not brook any dissent, let alone criticism. And we all knew Chitapi's family were being persecuted on account of their son Dumi's freedom of expression.

"Aaah, this is politics of vindictiveness by this so-called second republic, can't you see?" said M'koma Eddy to Renika and me one afternoon. "I see it clearly for what it is, a desire to punish Dumi and use him as an example and deterrent to other would-be government critics. Ha-ha…wisdom will kill me one day, *wanaTete*.'" Then M'koma Eddy went into gales of laughter, looking at us wistfully following his purported insights. As if to say, "See? I'm well smart."

Every so often, once he'd had one too many to drink, I would also overhear *Baas* Julian vent his disillusionment on how the revolution had gone wrong; it was now eating its own children, as he'd said one fine evening when he sat talking in the garden with both Madame Doris and Rhys. That was a rare spectacle, though it gave me joy to witness them as a normal family again, seeing them like yesteryear, getting along well together, even though these truces tended to be transient. We were having a late afternoon braai which had transitioned to evening, and so everyone seemed a bit cheery and garrulous. Add on to that some alcohol, with *Baas* Julian chain-smoking weed, then a perfect recipe unfolded as the tongue became loose.

"I know I rarely agree with you, Rhys, brother, but on this one I fully concur with you; you see these guys targeting a late war veteran's property, then you know we're not all safe here. There is no security of land tenure in Zimbabwe. It is open seas. The Zimbabwe dream continues to be elusive."

"True," Rhys said. "Without the respect of property rights, no real investors will come our way."

"Yesterday it was the white man, today it's the black man. When will this all end? I was under the impression land reform was all about correcting historical imbalances and injustices. Yet those connected to the party continue to enjoy multiple ownership of farms with unfettered hindrance," said Madame Doris, not to be outdone as she joined the fray.

"This is all very sad. Who would have thought black Zimbabweans would become victims of their own government being dispossessed of their privately owned land in the name of land reform?" said Rhys. "What kind of black empowerment works by disempowering blacks? This seems to be someone who is just greedy and wants to take where there will be no capital investment required! Absolutely corrupt tendencies here!"

"Better we be quiet and shan't say a lot, Rhys, lest we be accused of sour grapes, having lost our own Mazowe farm," said Julian, whose tongue seemed to have become loose with each gulp of alcohol.

But the Williamses weren't wide off the mark. Renika, M'koma Eddy, and I had tended to have similar conversations, especially as the case of Dumi, being the son of a renowned nationalist war veteran, had ignited widespread sympathy and condemnation from various people within and beyond the country.

"Land to the party plays the same role as the army, the police, and the captured judiciary. That is, land is deployed as a tool for control and co-option, and as an oppressive punitive mechanism to punish and settle political differences with those the regime considers the enemy," said M'koma Eddy, amid stares of admiration and shouts of 'Bravo!' from everyone else."

"This is not land reform, it is political harassment, M'koma Eddy," Madame Doris said, as she carried on speaking.

"Forget about their pettiness for once, but for me the irony is that Dumi's father was a political giant in the establishment. A politician of note, an outspoken icon who, incidentally, lies at the National Heroes Acre, an honor conferred upon him by the very people who are now persecuting him in the name of land reform."

"You can't make this stuff up, with this lot."

"Isn't land reform about addressing the racial imbalance on land ownership? And now we have a black government depriving its black citizens of land? I don't get this. Someone please explain this to me like I'm a six-year-old," a seemingly drunk Julian said, pupils now dilated.

"We never had land reform in Zimbabwe. Forget it, mate! Believe this, you'll believe anything. We had political weaponization of land hunger around the year 2000. That's why land reform remains chaotic because it is being used as a political tool.

The clause that the land belongs to the state is being abused to force people to patronise the system," quipped Rhys.

"You're telling me, brother! That clause has become a staple in political transaction by this Mafia.

I see it for what it is. We are drawing toward the next election period and they are taking land from other people in exchange for votes. What a sham strategy. But it's nothing new here. Been there, seen this before," said Rhys, before resuming his tirade.

"This violation of property rights is so depressing. I pray Dumi wins against this madness."

"It can never get worse than this. How on earth can a government just wake up and take privately-owned farms just like that? At the drop of a hat! Second dispensation my foot."

"It was never about land reform in the grand scheme of things. It was about *chefs* and their greed. Once they started ignoring property rights, it was just a matter of time before it affected everyone, and not just the whites, most of whom bought their farms legally anyway," acquiesced Julian as he refilled his glass with more alcohol, his unsteady hands spilling the beverage on the ground.

"As depressing as it is though, it reminds me of a poem we studied at school back in my GCSEs, something along the lines of *Not my Business,* an apt poem which decries citizens' indifference to the suffering of fellow citizens, a 'so long as it doesn't affect me' mentality. But now that it's affecting our brethren, it's come closer to home. Chickens coming home to roost kind of scenario. Look, and hear me out. I am not rejoicing at this unfolding tragedy that's happening to Dumi and other blacks on the receiving end of this kleptocracy. Far from it, but all I'm saying is, maybe now you will see that it was never about land reform from the start. It was about the party's greed," M'koma Eddy chipped in matter-of-factly.

"But you guys were all so blinded by your hatred for whites that you all thought it was great at the time we were at the receiving end of this.

"But now the wheel has come full circle.

"It's painful, isn't it?" Julian asked rhetorically.

"Shoko inonaka ichaitira vamwe, kana yoitiwavo, yoti kwangu kudiki," the monkey enjoys it, shafting others, but when it's its turn to get shagged, it cries foul, my hole is small, don't do it," said M'koma Eddy, breaking into uncontrollable laughter at his crude naughty sexual monkey analogy in relation to land being taken from whites. We all loosened up at M'koma Eddy as excitable chatter and chuckles floated around the vicinity.

"These vampires will never get tired. How can they allocate privately-bought property to someone else? Expropriating such a productive farm, what political hocus pocus," Rhys said.

"Well, your amnesia surprises me, Rhys, unless you're being flippant of course. For did we not lose our farm in similar circumstances as Dumi here?" said Julian. "This is madness on steroids if you ask me, brother.

"Now they are grabbing land from the natives. The establishment cares for no one except themselves. It's foolish for us to think these reptiles will change, mark my words."

Rhys replied, "I was only being flippant, to borrow your word, Julian. I do share and feel your pain, my brother. This evil regime will stop at nothing to persecute its imaginary 'political enemies.'

"Look at the regime's unashamed pettiness as they try to stifle democratic discourse and dissent through systematic intimidation and harassment of chief critics like prominent journalist Hopewell. A whole cabinet presided over by vindictive clowns seeking to seize goats from a journalist going about their legitimate, professional duties highlighting the shortcomings of a government which has largely failed its citizenry."

"True, it beggars belief, their obsession with trivia, *goats,* and striving to dispossess a fellow Zimbabwean of a piece of land he inherited from his ancestors. Besides, as we speak there are no working cancer apparatuses in our hospitals, and only a few dialysis machines on their last legs, yet for highlighting this, journalists like Hopewell and others gets needlessly pilloried and persecuted with frivolous charges with illegal detentions slapped on them.

"It's no wonder the regime will never transform both the commercial and common lands into the Freehold titled land because land has been instrumentalized both as patronage tool and as coercive and control mechanisms.

"Hopewell's issue is the microcosm of what happens to all of us for daring to have alternative political views."

"True. If you look at it, this war vet's son Dumi's case is in many ways similar to Hopewell's case. Same script, different actors.

"More so, the daily racist vitriol in our papers only helps in further fomenting and fostering divisions along racial and ethnic lines in our increasingly fractured society. Every time, we bear the brunt of it.

"The hollowness of their land reform echoes loudly when they take productive land from a black family whose patriarch was a national hero. I know that there could be other views and visions, but I am convinced the land reform is merely a political gimmick they deploy vindictively. Meanwhile, the elusive dream carries on unabated," Julian quipped as he dredged the last swallow of his ale, a philosophical air written on his face.

Chapter 35

Eastlea

Settling down in Harare was much easier than I inwardly anticipated, even though I had been looking forward to the move. Still, one always has niggling feelings of unease and doubt. Within no time, Mark and I had acclimatised to our new Highlands life in a posh suburb on the eastern side of Harare. I instantly fell in love with Eastlea, moreso our plush expansive apartment. But there were huge surprises looming for me in my relationship with Mark, nigh Herculean developments.

Frailty, thy name is trusting too much. Or is it naïveté?

In no time, I cottoned on to the strange goings and comings at our Highlands abode. Every other day at our flat, there were always strange men coming and going. It was like the flat was a haven and revolving door for these dodgy looking, God- forsaken scoundrels and ruffians. Mark ensured his meetings with these unsavory characters were always held in a secure disused part of the apartment to which I had been given robust "no-go" instructions.

"Business is business and should never be mixed with one's personal life," Mark remonstrated firmly, his hands raised for emphasis. And each time I enquired of these weird visitors' purpose and relevance in Mark's life he wouldn't hear of it and would flippantly dismiss me.

"Look the other way, darling, and allow me to do my business dealings. You just worry about my bank balance and more spending money, more holidays and the perks which come with it. That should be your prerogative. The minute you see those dwindling or stopping, then, Aha, we can have a chat. Get it love?" he had said to me with an annoying condescending air.

It wasn't a question: it was more like, "Keep quiet, I don't want you poking your nose into my business." Part of me was scared to probe further, especially given the resurgence of Mark's hitherto dormant temper and his brutal physical bashing of me that escalated in our Eastlea flat. The man could just lose it over a minor misdemeanour or misunderstanding; he would blow his top and thumb me to pulp. They were horrifying, harrowing moments for me, especially as I felt more vulnerable and isolated being so many kilometres away from home, England.

During those dark days of our relationship, I took refuge in my work at GTN Telecoms head office in Msasa Park, where I doubled up as a chief operating telecommunications executive and also offered human resources training opportunities to the wide array of our staff dotted around the country who would often throng Harare for our periodic training seminars. I threw myself into my work as a diversion from Mark's crassness and abrasiveness.

In my immediate department I had a talented pool of colleagues. Emmy, the human resources director, a talented pretty, mid-thirties lassie from Mutare, reported directly to me. Emmy quickly became a friend I could trust and turn to during my tumultuous home life with Mark. I also bonded with Emmy because we were both avid readers and members of the Harare Book Club, which in a way also offered me the much-needed escapism from my marital woes with Mark.

We did book club sessions twice a month, which suited me well, as it offered me a chance to unwind from my difficult existence with Mark. The book club sessions also opened other possible friendship opportunities for me besides Emmy. Many times, both Emmy and Harare book club sessions saved the day for me. Even though I trusted Emmy, I struggled to open up to her about my troubled private life, although she sussed me out correctly, I think.

Often, she would remark raising her disquiet with me, like on this downcast Thursday morning I had been late to work, which was unusual for a stickler for punctuality like me. But then I'd had a rough night with Mark, and it couldn't be helped; my whole body ached from the hiding and pummelling

I had taken, courtesy of Mark's vicious blows and kicks. Putting on concealing make-up was a right effort and took an exceedingly long time, which subsequently led to my being late at work. The dark sunglasses also had done a lot in concealing my bruises, or so I thought.

"I know it's not my place to say this, Marina, and you're well within your rights to shoot me for saying it, but don't you think you need to put a stop to these relentless physical assaults?"

"Physical assaults?" I tried to feign surprise, but Emmy wasn't falling for this hogwash from me.

"My sister Marina, hear me out, I'm speaking to you as a friend and a colleague. How long do you have to carry on like this, putting on a happy couple facade just so you protect Mark?

"I know he's my boss and I'm overstepping my brief here. Even saying this may well get me fired, but how many times have you come in here sporting a black eye hidden under your dark glasses?

"I know it's none of my business really, but this may well end in tears if it goes on unchecked especially now, given the frequency of your coming in with a bruised face, broken limbs, what have you.

"You can't keep on covering for him. Already the boardroom corridors are abuzz with your dysfunctional relationship with Mark. And you know what, Marina? It hurts me terribly to hear the litany of snide remarks being bandied around behind your back."

"Oh, fiddlesticks! There's nothing like what you're saying here, Emmy. That's just workplace gossip. All is well on the home front with Mark. In fact, we couldn't be happier together as a couple." I had fobbed off Emmy just the same way I used to brush off June, Elise, and my other friendship group at Durham in England.

People didn't really understand and get it. Though a rough diamond here and there, there was the other Mark they didn't know, privy only to me in the privacy of our bedroom and in between our sheets. The sex beast he was, who always left me satiated with his wide repertoire of sexual prowess and expertise. A satyr of note if ever there was one. Mark was something akin to what legendary godfather of soul James Brown called, *Sex Machine,* for want of a better phrase.

My fertile mind flickered to a graphic flashback image of a recent shag with Mark, always prefaced by his usual role play scenario. "I promise you champagne and lots of celebratory sex, my love, if you let me passage through those pearly gates of heaven," he'd said, the mischievous smirk on his face, which somehow managed to turn me on and had my juices down below in overflow.

"Of course, mister handsome, heaven is yours by the close of business today," I had coyly remarked as I unbuttoned his shirt, with my tongue exploring his in a passionate snog.

Our lust and libido were insatiable. We were constantly at it like teenagers.

In no time, Mark was thrusting in-out-in-out rhythmically into my lady bottom with wild abandon and frenzied excitement, ramming his manhood into the inner depths of my crevices, and the friction from his bulging cock made me come spectacularly. Our bodies exploded into a surreal orgasm that gave us toe-tingling sensations. I involuntarily squirted some extra juices as I gushed, "Holy fuck, Mark, that was epic." I applauded him as he heaved off me, a huge, contented smile creasing his face.

"Did you come?" he mischievously asked, his fingernails circling my still hard and erect nipples.

"One hundred and one percent!"

Despite his age, Mark had that boyish handsome face and charm, both of which I found to be immersive. I revelled in his lovemaking that always left me fully satiated. *Which kind of idiot would walk away from this?*

Besides the mind-blowing sex, being with Mark gave me a flamboyant and colourful social life I wasn't prepared to lose just like that, at the drop of a hat. This was too heavy a price for me to pay. Tell me, which sane woman would have wanted to willingly give up the trappings of dating a gregarious global telecoms mogul like Mark? The stakes couldn't have been higher. For starters, there was the social capital which came with the constant flow of rich expensive champagne. Expensive jet skiing holidays in Europe's capitals were too ghastly to contemplate losing. Then there was all the incessant, obsequious sycophancy, the adulation at public gatherings during his ceaseless charity work. Being introduced as Mark's other half was not something to toss down the drain. My relationship to Mark gave me immense respect from the gentry of Harare. I loved how the global media kowtowed to me as Mr. Instone's partner of greatness, and I literally had them drooling, eating out of my hand with the innumerable interviews and quotable quotes I would often come across, staring at me from leading magazines and newspapers.

Once British *Vogue* magazine ran a front cover story of me as an eminent, upcoming woman of color on account of my mixed-race heritage...a woman of color doing very well in Zimbabwe's telecoms industry. The interviewer had been fascinated and probed deeper into my reasons for relocating from England to settle in Zimbabwe. Of course, I had played to the gallery, giving well-rehearsed soundbites on how working for Instone's GTN was the thing to be lauded, how I was enjoying being a role model to disadvantaged young black kids, blah...blah...blah...all the palaver to raise my profile. Call me vain, I know...

"As a corporate entity we stood at the cusp of helping other marginalised groups in sub-Saharan Africa, particularly the girl child. We see it as our overriding social duty to attend to these groups."

That interview had gone well and earned me plaudits at GTN's boardroom. Even grumpy old git Mark had been visibly impressed and couldn't stop gushing, "Well done you, Marina, for flying our corporate flag high and reinforcing our corporate responsibility ethos. Way to go, love."

Granted, Mark's indiscretions, his deceit and treachery, were legendary, but where did this all fit for me in the grand scheme of things? The long and short of it is, this was a life of opulence and privilege I wasn't prepared to give up, and if it took a few physical rumpuses, then so be it. After all, Mark always assured me, "I love you dearly, hon. I can't help it if I give you a minor thrashing or tickle. I will go for therapy, trust me love. I can't help myself; I have sex addiction issues. It's these woeful inner demons troubling me which need exorcising from me."

Hear me out, those who are quick to pass judgement on my being ditzy. It's not that I'm dumb when I chose to ignore my husband's indiscretions and heavy handedness. By Jove, I'm a clever woman, a BSc electrical engineering graduate from Durham University, a top-notch elitist UK University for that matter. But why did I hang around for so long, turning a blind eye, something which troubled my inner circle of friendship group not least June, Elise, and Emmy? Perhaps, for the most part, it was easier to turn a blind eye than confront the truth. Not to mention the lucrative perks which came with being Mrs. Instone. I am not stupid. I knew very well that without Mark's influence and social capital, I would be a non-entity, thus it made prudent sense to hang around. Besides, which idiot would be silly enough to want to shoot the goose that laid the golden egg?

In any case, there was always a stash of alcohol in our expansive home distillery to see me through my abiding blues with Mark. As the abuse and downward spiral in our relationship escalated, I took solace in the holy waters, alcohol, creating an even greater chasm between Mark and me. I had turned to booze to nurse the outrage with my dysfunctional marriage. I have always loved my drink, and whenever the chips were down, the holy waters of gin and tonic, Valium and Baileys certainly did the trick for me. But as the physical bashing escalated, even these meant increasing my alcohol dosage. That was how I graduated into spirits and strong brands like whisky and Glenfiddich. My mind flickers to my undergraduate years; at Durham, it had been an open secret I was the campus' top guzzler. One lecturer often chided me in tutorials, "Oh, you're the infamous Marina, who drinks like a fish and parties daily," amid raucous laughter from my class.

"You know you are a proper guzzler, Marina, don't you?" June and Elise would often remonstrate at my drinking prowess, as if they were any better, which made \ their tone-down-a bit protestations all the funnier.

"Talk of the pot calling the kettle black," I constantly laughed at the irony of their protestations.

Perhaps June had sussed me out correctly, way back during those uni years; I was in it for ulterior benefits, but I didn't want to admit it.

But Mark was a man of contradictions. He also had the other side, the suave charm and amiability which enamored him to Harare's top echelons in business, politics and social circles. It's not like he was a monster through and through. Hear me out before condemning me; I'm not making excuses for him. Far from it, Mark had many sides. The man could be generous with his cash. I certainly quenched my insatiable desire for anything designer labels designated, ranging from my Louis Vuitton luggage, Pierre Cardin bras, Gucci handbags, Christian Dior, and Balenciaga paraphernalia, and an array of Salvatore Ferragamo shoes, not to mention access to GTN's company credit card with an unlimited credit limit at my disposal. Then there was also the small matter of unlimited mobile phone entertainment allowance. I enjoyed being the boss's other half.

A year after settling in Harare, Mark had arranged a small discreet wedding for us, held in the picturesque Nyanga fauna, Eastern highlands, a sprawling landscape area exceedingly beautiful to savour to the human eye. The area is nigh beautiful and captivating as I later recounted to both June and Elise in England over a WhatsApp video call.

"If ever you get the chance, girls, then a road trip to Nyanga is certainly worthwhile and you will absolutely love it. Trust me. Put it on your bucket list, girls, you'll thank me later."

"Your uploaded pictures on Facebook gave us the lowdown, super slut." June teased.

"Oh really?" I said excitedly.

"What do you mean, 'oh really,' with your feigned surprise, knowing very well, you've always been an exhibitionist of note, Marina," they'd both teased, laughing. Unfortunately, we abruptly lost our internet connection which unceremoniously terminated our call.

Troutbeck Inn was an exhilarating sight, even more impressive at close quarters as I relished it in person. No wonder I was so gushing in my praise of the Eastern highlands area of Zimbabwe. We got married at this opulent Troutbeck Inn in Nyanga, among a few guests, close business associates, and Mark's corporate and political circle of friends. Credit to his being a connoisseur, Mark had ensured the wedding was done in style, with the exquisite beige chandeliers providing a befitting evening backdrop in unison with our wedding apparel. It was an extremely beautiful ceremony in which we exchanged our commitments to each other.

Mark surprised me with a 19-carat diamond-encrusted gold ring he had bought from a famous Hong Kong designer, Ja-Hwe. In addition, my wedding dress had also been purchased from a designer in Manhattan. It was all top-notch stuff, very much a sublime wedding. I was overwhelmed with emotions. That night I cried, overjoyed with joy and happiness as I buried my face in Mark's broad, comforting shoulders.

Our exceptional lovemaking following our wedding went a notch higher, as Mark and I explored each other's bodies with a ferocity and hunger hitherto unseen by either of us. I felt wet and receptive as Mark's fingers playfully stroked my lady bottom. My body pulsated with pleasure as I reached multiple orgasms. Having fully come, buoyed by Mark's drumroll semen galore dripping down my thighs, now it was my turn to pleasure my man. I fully straddled him across his hairy chest as I expertly worked my nimble fingers on his "little Jonny," as we called his male organ, till he became hard again. All this time Mark was cooing in frenzied pleasure, I gingerly placed little Jonny inside me in the warmness of my thighs, after which I started rocking Mark, and mighty Mark went delirious with wild screams as his body responded. All the while, he was shouting my name, "Marina! Marina, sweetheart!"

"Yes, yes, take me my love, I'm all yours," I gave him the validation and affirmation he needed. I had multiple orgasms galore that night as Mark torpedoed me into the throes and vortex of limitless ecstasy and passion. A red-letter night it was in our post-coital history. Afterwards, we sprawled naked on the bed, spent as we savoured our marathon love making, entwined for a long time in each other's arms, longingly gazing at each other.

Whatever our gripe, one thing for certain, I can never fault our lovemaking sessions. They were always special, a treat between us, something to look forward to. And Mark did know just how to endow a woman. The man was an expert in that respect. Perhaps I had met my match. Could it be our intimate sex bonded us in a Stockholm syndrome kind of way for me? For someone who had been nearly sexually abused by sister Tendai's pedo-husband lascivious Walter, then a blooming teenager at Blanchett's Goodhope, I had taken to sex the way a duckling takes to water. I found sex liberating and intoxicating.

"You know that near rape incident should have permanently scarred and turned you off sex for good," June was wont to remark each time she chided me for my rampant sexual guns misfiring as she termed it.

"Well, I am not cut from the ordinary cloth, am I? I can't help it, if I love sex," I would say, rolling my eyes at her. "Not my problem if men drool over me and think they can get a shot at shagging me. Besides, I find it desirous and a huge turn-on to be craved by such multitudes of suitors."

"But have you ever wondered, Marina, your oddball obsession with nooky only became more pronounced after your near rape encounter with sister Tendai's weirdo hubby, randy Walter?"

"You're such a bitch, you know that! Why are you trying to sabotage my happiness?"

"Takes one bitch to know one," sniggered June, with a deprecating roll of her eyes.

"Aaah, I see, June, so somehow you've turned out to be this super clever child psychologist who's trying to make out I developed sex addiction behavioral problems because of that pervert dude. Good on you, sex therapist counsellor. When did you graduate from medical school?" This tended to be my default dismissive position to my friend June each time she broached the subject.

"Whatever, horny vixen!" June would sarcastically give it back in equal measure. And perhaps years later, on my honeymoon with Mark, I found myself reflecting, *Could there be some "truth" in June's sentiments i.e., the correlation between my high sexual libido and that weirdo who nearly took my virginity away?* Otherwise, why is it that men were always relentlessly following me. Once, after being caught in a compromising position with the laundry man at Blanchett's Goodhope, Madame Blanchett had mercilessly ripped into me, "Can't you get it, Marina, that what all these men want is to get in your knickers, nothing more, nothing less? Once they get that thing between your legs, then that's it, they're on the move, on the hunt for the next target." It was a bit of a shock for me to hear pious Blanchett utter such profane language as she used to diss it as unseemly. The poor laundry man, Toby, a young Scottish lad, lost his job following our improper association, and once more, I found myself a talking point amid the corridors and the girls at Blanchett's convent.

"That was then and what happened in the past should remain in the past. I'm now a married woman, so what can go wrong?" I firmly muttered

193

under my breath, pushing away these thoughts. I was bent on enjoying my honeymoon with Mark. In no time though, the honeymoon truce was over. The strange goings-on at number 19 Langley Road, Eastlea resumed at breakneck speed this time. I knew my husband was a very powerful and important man, given the global nature of his GTN Telecoms business, but what I couldn't get round my head was why he needed strange looking, down and out ruffians like Munyaradzi, Onai, and others coming to confer with him in the dead of night.

Not only that, but our driveway was always a hive of bustle and activity, jam-packed with the latest land cruisers, Lamborghinis, Aston Martins, Rolls Royces, Bentleys, Ferrari F8 and state-of-the-art Mercedes Benzes of Harare's rich and famous. More like a "Who's who?" list, I could recognize some of these faces from the media as big wigs of the ruling party. Once too often, I overheard snippets of conversations of a disturbing nature, which left me cold in my tracks, sweating profusely. I couldn't reconcile what I was hearing with who I knew as the man I had married. And for crying out loud, I could never reconcile why such a high profile, successful businessman as Mark was embroiled in the dark arts of Harare's criminal underworld. Yet hadn't I been viciously warned on numerous occasions to steer clear of Mark's private business dealings by the man himself? Reflecting on how chilling that threat had been given to me, I held my tongue and my nagging disquietude.

A subtle threat I picked up in one of his hush-hush meetings with his weirdos had been, "I'm speaking on behalf of the party, believe me when I say this comrade. Let's say the party will turn a blind eye to your drug empire if you up your monthly donations to us. Don't forget, there is also the small matter of your Telecoms license due for renewal later this year."

Being the consummate master at guile, Mark appeared to have risen to it, with, "The party and I remain long-lasting friends. Our friendship goes back in a long time. Consider it done, comrade. I will be instructing my financial director to oversee upping our acknowledgment/subscription to the party."

And that had been it; this tacit bribery gave Mark a free pass to do as he pleased in his other shady deals and dalliances with Harare's criminal element, Munyaradzi, Onai, and the lot. I knew my husband had an important ally, one shadowy fellow criminal mastermind, Brian Wharton, whom I had never met. His name and secretive persona and influence permeated and reverberated around Mark as the supreme mastermind with whom he worked closely.

Occasionally, when Mark had one too many, his tongue loosened and he would brag with no end about the immense power of his connections with the big wigs of the party and the establishment, in exchanges with Billy Piper, another white Zimbabwean, and close business associate who was heavily involved in mining concessions and safari game hunting.

"You see, Billy, this is where you get it wrong, your obsession with a squeaky-clean image. Take it from me, that won't get you anywhere. Been there, done it. It doesn't work here, at least not in Zimbabwe."

"That's you, Mark, I prefer doing clean deals. That way, I sleep tight at night, no loose ends, and no comebacks whatsoever."

"'I prefer doing cleans deals,' Mark couldn't help laughing at Billy's naïveté, mimicking him condescendingly. "I tell you I wouldn't have got this far without the party's protection. If you can't beat them, may as well join them. Look how my fellow white Zimbabweans who have not supped with the devil have been clearly fucked by the system, fucked back-to-back, that is. Why do you think, some white Zimbabweans fraternize with the party as MPs? Do you think they really like a party which has brutalized their kith and kin over the years? Dispossessed them from their land? It's a no brainer to me, Billy.

"The party is mightier than any being here, and their will goes. Why would I ever want to antagonize, let alone be in bad books with them?"

"Suit yourself, Mark," Billy said. "I'm afraid we operate by different standards. Perhaps our difference in personality makes our friendship unique."

Chapter 36

In the Gutter

His deadpan expression always unsettled me. I could never tell what was coming next. At times, it was the harbinger of the fisticuffs to rain down relentlessly on my body, fast and loose, with the constant shoving, pulling of my hair, and kicking of my groin...punctuated by unprintable expletives directed at my female genitalia.

As I settled down into the mundane drudgery of married life with Mark, it increasingly became clear there were just too many facets to this man's character and life which kept cropping up each time I thought I had seen the worst of the monster's dark side. This man was a living, walking enigma. Perhaps a flawed genius? Not to mention how difficult he was to live with. My constant misgivings were especially accentuated with the gradual realization of my husband's other sphere of life to which I hadn't been privy hitherto. No sooner than I thought, *Aha, now I know the bastard and his wily ways,* there would be another slip up or revelation which threw more questions at me.

One evening, for example, came the jaw-dropping revelations at the discovery that Mark also ran an illegal sex ring in downtown Harare comprising a brothel in the Avenues area, complemented by a discreet gentlemen's arrangement plan for those of an alternative sexuality. The latter required extreme secrecy and discretion, given that homosexuality is outlawed in Zimbabwe. The brothel business was discreet and upmarket, run by Mark's trusted white buddy, that recurring name again, Brian Wharton, who resided in posh Borrowdale Brooke, one of Harare's affluent northern suburbs.

I'm told the brothel's rich clientele included some of Harare's big wigs, and some dirty old pot-bellied men from the party were amongst the regular punters. With money floating around, discretion was a commodity which could easily be snapped up for a price in Harare, a maxim Mark had come to realize early on; he capitalized on in his litany of business interests sprawling all over the country.

Again, snippets of conversations increasingly became a useful device for plugging holes in my husband's duplicitous life, like how I stumbled on this Harare whorehouse-sleaze club news. Hear me out though, before the morality brigade takes their knives out on me. It's not like I set out to deliberately spy on my husband, possibly he got complacent and reckless. At times, these meetings were held in our spare bedroom next to my home office, since the previously isolated west wing of the apartment was being refurbished. The wall between my home office and spare bedroom was wafer thin, which explains why conversations meant to be confidential easily filtered into my ears, and I had to exercise a great deal of discipline in not making the slightest noise; had Mark got wind of my "snooping," the consequences would have been ghastly for me.

"Given our success with the Avenues fun house, I propose to rename it: Avenues Recreational Club." That was Mark's unmistakable gruff voice.

"Or rename it Montagu Club," added another voice.

"Let's face it, the majority of our clients are Harare's well-to-do residents, coming here to de-stress after a hard days, tough week, you name it. So, what we do here is provide a secure, fun recreational service, contrary to what our detractors may say.

"And I dare say, I would be one to champion discreet adult fun. About time this country opens up and becomes forward-looking in its approaches to these matters. I lived in England for umpteen years, and most men go to whorehouses and strip clubs. It's no big deal if I throw in a payment from our patrons for facilitating this service, is it? Look at our neighbor South Africa, they're quickly catching up on the gentlemen's club fun, so why not us? About time we here stand up and be counted."

"Why can't we have our own upmarket brothel? Sounds cool by me. People want sex, we discreetly provide a service. Why should anyone quibble with that? We are there to indulge our clients' sexual fantasies that is our remit and core business. Forget about GTN Telecoms, that's our cover to shield prying eyes from our other nocturnal activities…" I could hear the voices droning on amid my gob smacked face trying to process all these unsavoury disclosures."

"Just one question, Marina?"

"Fire on, Rhys."

"You talk of this mercurial character Brian Wharton being your late husband's extra hand in his other dark business. Did you ever get to meet him?"

"Why no, not at all. Mark was a sly old fox and he made sure I didn't get to mingle with his coterie of unsavoury characters. I knew of the small fish acolytes/underlings like Munyaradzi and Onai, but I guess it's because they were low down in the pecking order and perhaps Mark couldn't care any less that I knew these ruffians."

To my entreaties or inquiries, or when I wanted to do some digging, he often threw me the cheeky retort, "Just ensure you enjoy the moment and keep an eye on the bank balance like Skyler in *Breaking Bad.*"

"Clever bastard!" Rhys said as he stood up to signal our session for the day was done.

Chapter 37

Five Avenue Café

"I just had to talk to you, Marina," said Harriet, one of my book club friends. We'd finished our session and had escaped to Harare's Archipelago Five Avenues café. Harriet continued, "I gather you've been having a terrible time at home. Have you ever considered divorce? Could that be a viable option for you out of this morass?" Ruvheneko, our other book club mate, was also with us for this Saturday afternoon catch up. I waited for the waiter to take our orders before responding to Harriet.

"Not really, Harriet. Look, Mark brought me from England, and I'm fairly settled in this country. I like it here. I wouldn't like to rock the boat. Eventually, maybe he will change for the good as he always promises me. Let me give him time."

Harriet's sense of despondency was written all over her face as she exhaled her frustration and said, "Fine. Suit yourself, Marina, but always know I'm your kind of doppelgänger, always out to look out after you, mate."

"You don't understand, Harriet, the stakes are heavily stacked against me in any potential divorce with Mark. Besides he's so well-connected and powerful, he would bribe the high court judges and leave me to hang out to dry in any divorce settlement. I know Mark; he has a vindictive and nasty streak in him. I've seen it rearing its head every so often when he loses his marbles."

"But the point is, Marina, is this what you want, shackled in a loveless marriage if only for the material trappings which come with it? Ask yourself this question, and in your heart of hearts you'll know what you want."

I couldn't answer her, and I prevaricated, looking for a logical, credible explanation without finding any. The lump in my throat was growing huge. How could I find it within myself to openly admit it to her face without being rude to her as my friend? Mark's dodgy business dealings afforded me a certain lifestyle I was now accustomed to and wasn't keen on losing. Not at all. How could I willingly give up the high social status, wealth and lifestyle that came courtesy of being married to Mark? I simply couldn't. I wasn't dumb!

Sensing my discomfort, Harriet veered off the subject to safer waters as I aimlessly picked my salad with my fork. *Goodness knows, man up, Marina,* I silently mused to myself.

"I get it," Harriet said. "Marriage needs compromise and commitment. But equally this shouldn't ever be a one-way street whereby the other party is treated as a doormat. At what point does one draw the line, Marina and declares enough is enough?"

"But Mark has always told me he loves me, especially each time he beats me. Surely he means it and can't help losing his marbles with me," I countered defensively.

"Look, I appreciate you're all trying to help me out here, extricate me from this charade of a marriage as you may perceive it. But truth is, Mark is not a bad husband per se, he just has lots of business-related stress and sometimes wants to let off steam this way. I'm sure that explains those momentary lapses of madness which hog him. Trust me, beneath that rough, brusque exterior, lies a lovely man. It's just a few rough edges which need straightening. He'll come around eventually, my man will. I know he will."

Harriet and Ruvheneko could only exchange weird glances at this. But how else could I tell them there were other compelling reasons why I hung on? I really loved him. Why could they not get that? Is it hard to love someone even if they lose their temper with you once in a while? Now, don't give me that Stockholm syndrome bullshit, for that won't wash with me. Don't you try to do your psychotherapy shit with me; it won't work. Never will.

The consummate master in exquisite lovemaking with prowess in bed, Mark had perfected the art of sex with his protracted teasing and the sustained length of foreplay which always exploded into a crescendo of climax and a vortex of endless delight. I am yet to find a man who could leave me this satiated. Why would I want to let go of this? I didn't want to join the litany of the women at our book club who were constantly whining about how sexually deprived and unfulfilled they were.

And their brazen hypocrisy for daring me to ditch Mark, given their daily sad stories of lack of fulfilment in their very own marriages with their so-called role model husbands was staggering:

Hapless Harriet said, "My husband Jeff does it like a rabbit; in no time he's done, and he rolls over to the other side of the bed snoring annoyingly. It's not fair on me, is it? I'm not sure I can do this any longer."

Ruvheneko replied, "So, what do you reckon you should do then?"

"Look for a toy boy I guess," Harriet told her. "I'm so done with vibrators and all that talking therapy shit. It doesn't work with Jeff. 'Oh, I promise to change, honey. I'll get this new blue wonder pill. Should make you last the whole evening,' but it's all mere talk and no delivery. Jeff's bark is worse than his bite. I'm a young woman, very feminine and horny. Jeff is doing me a disservice, truth be told, girls. I love sex and I'm tired of pleasuring myself in the bathroom each time Jeff does his one-minute sex sessions. And all the while, he thinks he's taken me to high heavens. High heavens my foot!" She raised her nose in a disparaging gesture.

"Get someone at least fuckable," Emmy would often interject at these sex-starved vixens' woes amid chuckles from the whole lot.

Ruu told us, "Do you know that my husband won't go down on me? And it hurts because I know he does it with his mistress."

"How so?" asked Harriet.

"Because the haughty bitch told me herself in a nasty, vile confrontation I had with her when I saw her WhatsApp messages in hubby's phone and braved phoning this Jezebel whore! By Jove, I gave her a dressing down."

There was an awkward silence following Ruu's baring of dirty linen to the girls. Talk later resumed focusing on other issues, as if Ruu's revelations were nothing to write home about.

Inwardly, I felt for Harriet; I equally felt for Ruu and the whole other lot who bitched about their husbands' ineffectual sex drives. Out of respect to Mark, and as a rule, I never discussed our private sexual encounters. I rationalized within myself, that was for the two of us within the confines and privacy of our bedroom. But I knew in my heart of hearts that I certainly didn't want to be like them, moping and moaning about how sexually inadequate and frustrated they were. And for that I hung on to Mark, notwithstanding our other difficulties. Perhaps fulfilment in bed was an additional variable, a price worth paying for all Mark's palaver at being a shit husband.

What short memories both Harriet and Ruvheneko had. Their bedroom frustrations typified their usual moaning and bitchiness, yet they want me to leave my well-endowed man Mark. No way am I settling for this. In the end, I tactically veered our conversation to safer harbors away from their manipulative talk to ditch my husband. *Who do they think they are, telling me how to live my life?*

Chapter 38

Book Club Moments

"I changed the locks on an abusive partner and took his stuff to his mother's house. She opened the door, looked at the bin bags and said, 'Well, I don't know what took you so long.' I can't tell you how that one sentence bolstered my courage."

"So, Marina, you have to find within your heart the courage and conviction to walk out of this toxic relationship with Mark," said a visibly dejected Ruvheneko as we all huddled in our usual after-session catch up and gossip. In tow were the other girls, Harriet, Emmy, and Liz.

"Funny you say that; my own mother had to pull up my brother over the appalling way he treated his girlfriend. She called him to order and remarked to the girlfriend, 'You deserve better, and I do not accept the way he treats and talks to you. I never raised him to be like this, and that's what's knocking my head sideways. I know I'm not responsible for his actions as a man but for fuck's sake I feel it,'" remarked Emmy, before continuing to speak.

"Ever since Louise ended her toxic relationship with my brother, she has become good friends with my mother, whom she always thanks for saving her from her son. Bizarre it may appear, but that is the way things are. They even meet for Starbucks coffee."

"And how did your brother take it?" Liz butted in.

"How did he take it? Pissed off to high heavens, but who cares?" replied Emmy before she continued.

"You want a productive happy relationship with your woman, then accord her the respect and dignity, simple as," Mum would firmly say to Rob in her no-nonsense voice.

"So, Marina, when you hear us relentlessly banging on about your issues with Mark, it's because we care for you, sister. You're a woman of letters; we're not trying to run your life. Far from it! Affirmed Emmy.

Liz added, "It crushes us seeing your spirit wilt under the gargantuan millstone of this stifling marriage, depriving you of happiness."

"Been there, done it, girls. Why do you think I remain unmarried at 37! It's out of choice; besides my last relationship made me wiser in retrospect," remarked Emmy in a brief pause.

"When I used to ring my mother-in-law for help, her answer always was, 'I don't want to get involved Emmy. Sort out your mess together.'

"After a few more visits by the police in the small hours, and trips to accident and emergency, I found the courage to leave. So, one day, you'll realize you did the right thing, girl."

"When I sought help from my father-in-law, care to know what the bastard said? My father-in-law said to me, 'This could put my son in prison,' and turned it round on me. We never spoke again."

"That's despicable, Emmy!"

"You're damn right it is. We never spoke again."

"We're right to challenge this awful behavior. I'm the mother of sons, and I will always call out their bad behavior. I raised them to consider others, be polite and kind, their age is immaterial. Do unto others, regardless of their gender, ethnicity, what have you, is how I've brought up my lads."

"Just know you're amazing for calling out this behavior, even when it's an indictment of someone you adore. That's brave, honest, and very difficult, and makes you one of a kind.

"There sadly aren't enough of us willing to recognise the men we love can be abusers too," Harriet quipped, joining in the fray.

"Truth be told, Marina, I really don't know why you're with him. He'll not improve, he'll just grind you down until you're broken," remarked Liz, before continuing speaking.

"How many months have we been at it, toying on relentlessly about Mark's playboy lifestyle, his bed-hopping and brazen brutality on you? No need to answer; that's a rhetorical question, love, but it's all loud and clear to us. The leopard will never shed its spots. Today, you're sporting a black eye. Who knows what it'll be tomorrow? Get out before it escalates to something ugly, I would say."

"Totally agree with Liz, Marina," said Emmy. "I think this thing has run its course. You've given it your best shot. No one will judge you for heaven's sake. In fact, we will applaud your bravery and forthrightness."

"Don't think we're idiots, Marina, we do get it. Staying with the abuser is another form of trauma response. Staying is a coping mechanism where the brain denies the incident; that's why we've been fighting in your corner," remarked Emmy in her dishing of newfound wisdom as she carried on.

"I'm glad Rob's girlfriend spoke out. 'I thought about how things were, and how they were likely to be, and got out intact,' she's ever saying to both Mum and me, and we're saying, so can you, Marina. Embody and take on the change you want.

"You do not get plaudits for foolhardy heroism. Just be pragmatic and save your sorry ass."

"If I were Mark's father, without wishing to sound creepy, I'd be having a serious man-to-man talk with him. If you can't treat women right, you are on the slippery slope to treating everybody like dirt. It's not clever or manly. Is it any wonder there are increasing murmurs of grumbling from the Msasa Head Office work force? Reports are that the man has no ounce of respect towards us. He treats us like dirt under his feet," remarked Harriet, turning to the others for support, and finding Liz acquiesced with her.

"I must say we're not surprised, given the short shrift treatment he metes out on you. The mettle of a man is easily measured by how he treats his woman. Mark is a knob. I'm sorry, Marina."

"His dad plans on having a word with him," I said. "His dad is disgusted with certain aspects of his treatment of me. His dad has never treated me badly I'm his queen and I know it. His dad doesn't understand how his son can treat a partner like this. Many times, he's credited me for taming Mark, but as you all know, I'm not sure about taming this rogue beast. All sounds like a big lie to me."

"Someone is clearly fucking with you here, Marina. Forget it and move on for heaven's sake. Why give him the satisfaction by jumping at the bait? Walk away, for heaven's sake. Have some self-respect, woman," remarked a visibly agitated Harriet.

"With hindsight, I must admit Mark was a master at fucking with my brains. Goodness me, no wonder I stayed with him all those years, notwithstanding how he treated me like shit and his doormat. Though to be fair to him, had the abuse been so brazen while we were still in England, I wouldn't have been taken in by Mark's incessant 'come with me, lets settle in Zimbabwe' dream. Did you know, the sly old dog he was, all along I wasn't aware he engineered some subtle bribery to my uni friends in England, June, and Elise, buying them presents behind my back. All makes sense to me now, their last-minute switch in allegiance, as they gushingly encouraged me not to let up the decision to move together to Zimbabwe.

"'Go on, Marina, you'll love it in Zim,' they had said, much to my surprise; Elise and June had previously been lukewarm when I broached the subject to them. Then, boom! Before I knew it, they were onboard, just like that. Frailty, thy name is thirty pieces of silver."

"Funny you say that Marina," Emmy said, clearing her throat. "I always wondered why you were so daft as to want to ditch your cushy life in England and come in tow to a third world country in the hands of the abusive prick, your husband." She spoke eying me up inquiringly, searching my face for a cogent explanation.

"Well, what can I say, Emmy, perhaps, today I better come clean with you all, my book club friends and sisters. There is something I've never openly shared with anyone, which explains why I moved in with Mark and agreed to relocate to Zimbabwe."

"And what could that be?" they asked in unison, their interest piqued.

"A few months after Mark floated the Zim idea to me, I discovered I was three months pregnant. That discovery was a game changer, even though I had been inwardly harboring thoughts to settle in Zimbabwe with him. But with the prospect of a baby on the way, the decision to move to Zimbabwe was no longer a question of personal choice. It just had to be done! Having grown up in a chaotic family life myself, in a crappy foster care home, I couldn't fathom my unborn child experiencing a similar checkered childhood as mine."

"We get that, Marina, but that shouldn't blind your logical thinking," Ruvheneko said. "Sorry to sound crass, but what became of the pregnancy?"

"What happened to my maiden pregnancy? I lost it, girls, curse of the third trimester." There was an awkward silence following my revelation, then commiserations from the girls.

Emmy resumed the conversation, "Mark is an abusive prick, Marina, and there's no way of sugar coating this. It's high time you call him out for his wayward and bully boy tactics."

I knew I was too happy to play the contented housewife charade because I knew which side my bread was buttered on. But the events of the past few months had been horrendous for me. I'd been admitted to hospital with a broken rib cage sustained at the expert hands of the boxer, my husband. "I fell off the stairs, I was too drunk," I had glibly lied to the nursing sisters at the hospital who, judging by the way they raised their eyebrows in disbelief, hadn't fallen for that yarn.

Looking at my reflection in the opposite wall mirror, it echoed my inner turmoil and shone a light on my troubled soul. The mirror reflected dark rings under my eyes. I was clearly stressed and in need of proper sleep. Many times, my anxiety kept me awake at night.

Tears choking me, I couldn't help but remember there had been a time we'd been happy together as a couple, long before the abuse kicked in... those skiing holidays in Swiss resorts and Italian escapades. My husband had become a stranger whom I couldn't bear to be around any longer than I needed to.

I went quiet for a few minutes, reflecting at this. *Crikey! What got over my good sense?*

They were correct. In fact, they had been correct for a long time, my book club friends, and June, Elise, and the whole lot at Durham.

Mark will not change. I do not see him changing from his wayward actions. I can't say, hand on heart, I didn't know this. I knew it in my heart of hearts, my man was not for turning, even though I had valiantly tried tucking these inconvenient truths far away. Then Emmy's voice roused me from my momentary trance.

"Look. Marina, for how many months have we been banging on about this? No one is trying to interfere or run your life here. We all want you to be happy, though it seems unlikely with randy Mark. Truth be said, we just want you to be in an honest and happy space, mate."

"Ever wondered why I prefer to be alone and not indulging in relationships? Fact of the matter is, I don't tolerate a toxic relationship. I always make sure that I walk out of a relationship before I get trapped," remarked Harriet. "I've had to be thick-skinned though with the litany of abuse hurled at me, 'sad ugly bitch, weirdo, super-spinster,' you name it."

"Come to think of it, have you tried having another baby, Marina?"

"Why? What for, Ruu? Surely you don't believe I am one of those fuckers who've bought into the anachronistic notion that a baby can save our marriage. Far from it, a baby is no solution to my woes with Mark. Besides, I'm past childbearing now with my early menopause kicking in. Not a chance in high heaven for motherhood."

After a long inward battle with myself, pondering the insights of what my friends had said, not only today, but during the entirety of my relationship, my troubled marriage to Mark, somehow, I had the moment of epiphany. I raised my head with a genuine smile and remarked, "Fine ladies, the die is cast. Tonight, I am speaking with Mark about our future."

"Bravo, sister!" It was a jubilant shout from all of them, as they stood to cheer me up, back slapping me, happy to see the unfolding bravery of universal sisterhood finally energized as I sought to take, articulate, and make a principled stand against "toxic masculinity."

There was a real mood of bravado within me. I really felt there was a groundswell of it, a sense of "it's now or never." I inwardly smiled, enjoying this new direction of my thoughts. Living with Mark was a sick, twisted game, and I was tired of this existence. I wanted out of this whole charade, and today had to be the day I set myself free. My book club girls had offered me the opportunity to reset my life. Maybe my friends were right after all. It was time to leave, to get out of this dump. This was no way to conduct a marriage the way Mark did. There had to be a better life or alternative out there. Besides, there had to be some sense in our universal sisterhood. Increasingly, my book club girls became my confidantes and anchors and I'm sure they had my interests at heart.

As I inserted my key into the front door keyhole, I couldn't help but reflect, *why had I put up with him all these years? The man was full of shit! I think he was just plain shnoop.*

Chapter 39

Exorcising Ghosts from Yester-Year

Only from the legions of horrid hell, I told Rhys, can come a devil more damned than Mark! "I said to him, 'There's a very vile type of nasty in you, Mark. For so many years I've put up with your boorishness. You were happy to treat me like a doormat as you went about transgressing every cardinal value point of this marriage. Well, not anymore I'm afraid. Especially now, with your vile revelations, things will never be the same again between us.

"'For so long I was prepared to play along to your bullshit in this dysfunctional marriage, but not anymore! You have betrayed, abused, and reviled me for so many years, and for this you deserve your comeuppance. Take that, and that bullet again!' I had bellowed at him, emptying the bullets into his now limp, lifeless body.'"

"I hear you. I get you, Marina. In retrospect, now that you've had time to reflect, how did you feel after gunning down your husband in cold blood like that?"

It felt like an accusation coming from Rhys, but I ignored that sanctimonious tone from him.

"Yes, I am being facetious. Forgive me, but I felt a form of release at Mark's death at my hands."

"Relief?" Rhys shot back at me incredulously.

"You heard me correctly, Rhys, no need for the sanctimonious vibe with me. Relief tinged with freedom. By the time the police came to remove me from the crime scene, I was still trying to process the enormity of the

tragedy, though I gave off confident vibes to them. My husband or father --
however bizarre you took it, had died in cold-blooded murder at my hands.
And in a way his death would be my deliverance from our twisted oddball
relationship and everything which had been wrong with it.

"Of course, I hate the cruel fashion in which I had discovered he was my
dad and how I blamed him for goading me into killing him. I'm not a
narcissist, sociopath bitch, as the media spin has been putting it out there.
I'm just a woman who went through hell and snapped when she reached
her tipping point. So, don't judge me; no one has a right to, for they haven't
walked the road I walked with Mark Instone. Mark was a difficult man to
live with and to love all those years.

"For crying out loud, the paternity revelation was shattering and nerve-
wracking, it staggered me into unparalleled silence. I felt my senses go
numb. I became dazed and confused as I failed to process what was
happening to me. *Could I be in a terrible nightmare?* I reflected within myself,
pondering the fluctuating fortunes life had thrown at me. *How was it possible,
I had been caught up in an unnatural, incestuous relationship with my own father? How
could this be happening to me, Marina Thompson? I'm Marina for heaven's sake, smart,
sassy, intelligent and clever. This can't be. This kind of thing only happens to dumbass
girls and not people of my ilk!*"

I flicked my eyes to the man who was supposedly my father, a man with
whom, for over six years of my life I'd been physically intimate, shared
some secrets of the very deepest personal nature. And now, by a strange
coincidence unbeknownst to him as well, he had just outed my parentage.
Not only that, but he also alluded to the very circumstances of my
conception in a derisive, belittling way, casting aspersions on my late
mother.

I wish I could say he'd looked remorseful at the avalanche of jaw-dropping
news he'd just told me. But he wasn't. If anything at all, a leering, mocking
smile curled on his evil lips. And then he said something which threw me
into a seismic vortex of emotions.

"You can't sit there blaming me with your accusatory eyes, Marina. No one
is to blame here, but your mother, who hid you from me, persistently
obstructed contact and could only fob me off with her pathetic, fake stories

of your demise, like telling me, 'I'm sorry Mark, but I lost that pregnancy in my second trimester. There's no baby to talk of.'

"Really, she would go on and on, stringing me along with her incessant lies, changing her story multiple times about your existence or non-existence at will. But what can you expect from hookers? Once a hooker, always a hooker. They have no shame at all, their lot. Hookers and liars, inseparable bed fellows. And now look who's having the last laugh?" he asked mockingly, laughing at my horror that he could find amusement in such an earth-shattering discovery to me.

As if that wasn't enough, he went a notch up further in his twisted, weird, macabre humor, saying, "Blame it on Sophie the bitch, not me. Had your mother played ball, then all this wouldn't have happened."

Looking at him, hearing him incredulously, I couldn't believe my ears at this horseshit drivel. His cold harsh words slowly dropped on me like bricks from a skyscraper. There was something maniacal and fiendish in those gleaming, evil eyes, moreso the unsettling laughter, as he dispensed cruelty to me, now his newfound daughter.

Call it deja vu, but I had unspeakable feelings about this man, that somehow things wouldn't end well between us following this horrendous disclosure which had numbed me; I was in a state of shock, utter disbelief, humiliation. I was experiencing a vortex of conflicting emotions at all this. Nor did it make things easier that Mark was casually stoking the embers and the fires of an already incendiary situation. My mind spun, b*ut surely, what had I seen in this man all these years? What had made me hang on to such a fiend?* I was none the wiser.

"Stare into my eyes and tell me it's not true. I dare you, Mark!" I bellowed at him in sky-high anger and outrage.

"Of course, it's true. How else could I have said..."

"Stop!" I vehemently shouted at him. "Just stop will you, Mark. This is my mother you're insulting, a dead woman for that matter. Where is your sense of propriety, decency, and respect? We are human beings, for god's sake, and that sets us apart from animals!

"I won't have you trample on my mother's name and good memory; however bad things may have been between you and Sophie."

And then Mark did the unthinkable. He stood up, advanced toward me menacingly, and slapped my cheek harshly with his open palm. It was a stinging, hard slap, followed by three additional slaps in quick succession, which left a burning, stinging sensation on my cheeks.

Quite dazed and disoriented I could just about manage to hurl a blood curdling scream from the inner bowels of my being, "Get out of my sight, Mark! I never want to see you again. You filthy pig! Oh my god, this can't be happening to me!"

But he wasn't done with me yet. He grabbed at me, aiming for my head, but missed me by a whisker as he lost his balance. His head went bang, right on the sharp corner of the glass table in the apartment. I could hear him bellowing in pain amid obscenities, cursing and swearing both at me and mother's genitalia, which further incensed me. By now my thoughts were on one thing: the cabinet drawer in the master bedroom where he kept it.

I sprinted to the master bedroom, yanked open the door, and almost flew to open the top cabinet drawer. And there it was, a gleaming revolver, just as it was when he had tutored me how to fire it all those years ago. I could feel it heavy in my hands, a good sign to me it was loaded, much to my delight. A maniacal frenzy of euphoric joy engulfed me as I darted out of the bedroom back into the living room where a helpless spectacle of Mark, big man Mark, greeted me. He was sprawling in an uncomfortable heap on the floor. All I could hear was his pitiful self-whimpering, quite a far cry from his usual bluff and bluster big man bravado. It must have taken him a few moments to recognize the gun in my hands trained on him. That loosened his hitherto tied tongue.

"Now, don't be silly, Marina. Will you put that thing down please"

I must admit, I was quite taken aback hearing the mighty Mark utter the magic word: please.

"Too late, Mark! Now is not the time anymore. By the time this evening is over, you'll be joining my mother Sophie, the woman whose memory you lambasted and insulted earlier on. But here's what'll happen first. I'll make it slow and painful, and to show you I'm not bluffing, here's an introductory sweetener." With that I fired the bullets into his kneecap, immobilizing him.

As I thought of all those years of physical and emotional abuse at the hands of Mark, it filled me with a renewed vigor and enthusiasm and an added maniacal frenzy. I stabbed him relentlessly, having thrown the revolver on the floor beside him, and grabbed the knife from the kitchen. His cries for clemency only further egged me on, giving me a strange orgasmic feeling. All the while I was hurling insults at him, "This one is for you Mark, stick it to the man for all the times you were a dickhead to me. Fuck you, Mark!" I spat as I plunged the blade further into his now lifeless carcass, a malevolent smile curling my lips. Somehow, savoring such a spectacle, I experienced an unexplained greater sexual frenzy coursing through me, which made me picture myself as some sort of reincarnated *Killing Eve* master assassin, Villanelle, and I wasn't even ashamed of this.

With Mark, I had only ever experienced a dangerous, hurtful brand of relationship, and I felt this was my crowning moment. By now, I was totally oblivious of his wild terrified, horror screams. Our flat neighbors opposite us found me in a pool of Mark's blood as I straddled his chest. I have never felt so satisfied with myself.

"Perhaps it was all the pent-up energy of your toxic relationship over the years let loose," said Rhys.

"Possibly. Seeing Mark at my mercy was my comeuppance moment. It gave me a fiendish delight to see Mark crumbling before me, and I found myself consumed by creepy maniacal laughter."

"But would you not say, was it not also the cruel revelation he was your father which tipped you over the edge?"

"Most likely the shock of it, given our prior amorous liaisons. At least that's what the prison shrink is trying to drive me into writing, an admission statement in this respect, so we plead insanity, but I'm not having that. I won't take the easy way out, Rhys. As callous as it sounds, this man might have been my father, but he wronged me in many ways, wormed his way into me as his scholarship benefactor, subtly manipulated me along the way. How was I supposed to say no to his advances? And each time I tried to walk out on him, he would be all nice again and promised to change his ways, which never happened of course. I guess I was a sucker to continually fall for his lies. And then there were those abortions!"

"Abortions?" Rhys gasped.

"Yes, abortions; you heard me correctly, Rhys. Three times he talked me out of seeing through my pregnancies with him. This coming on top of my maiden miscarriage. What kind of a man is he, who shirks away from responsibility?

"Bizarrely knowing he is my father now makes me sick to my stomach. I don't want to talk about it, the abortions; above everything else, this upsets me further."

"Fair enough. What about your encounter with the neighbors when they found you firmly planted on Mark's blood-riddled chest? What transpired after that?"

"'I feel like vomiting,' I blurted to them as I felt bile and nausea rising in me. I started retching and vomited continuously for what seemed an eternity. The last memories I have here are blurred and hazy, Rhys, but I remember waking up in A and E and repeating my nausea plea. 'I need to vomit,' I said to the clearly bewildered faces peering at me. 'I feel sick, I need to vomit!' I repeated.

"The words had barely left my mouth when I vomited some yellowish stuff onto the A and E floor. I remember I continued to vomit and retch uncontrollably onto the floor. Everyone was running around for me. I passed out again, the second time that evening.

"Talking about all this, reliving the horrors of Mark, saps my energy and wears me out. I think that's it's for today, Rhys." I stood up, my eyes moistening, and left him mouth agape at the bizarre revelations of my life.

Chapter 40

The Expose

"Now let me get this straight, Marina, how did you actually discover Mark was your biological dad? That bit remains hazy to me."

"From a fucking diary, can you imagine? Snippets from my mother's diary were among some of the important papers and documents he never wanted to touch, nicely tucked away in Mark's study.

"Can you imagine the gut-wrenching shock to me, Rhys, as excerpts and snippets of recrimination jumped out of Sophie's diary to me? A diary I'm sure she never thought I would be privy to. And in a cruel fashion, just like that, I was jarringly made to realize my true parentage and conception. And bizarrely, I had been sleeping with the man who was my father all those years. I mean, nothing ever prepares you for this kind of gargantuan catastrophe."

But more cruel revelations which further incensed me, and possibly sealed Mark's fate, were laid bare in an excruciating fashion. From the same diary, I discovered that Mark had been my mother's pimp during her difficult days of settling down in 1970s London as an illegal immigrant, playing cat and mouse dalliances with the home office immigration system. Turns out, Mark was renowned as the fixer for undocumented immigrants who were swallowed up by his nocturnal seedy brothels. Mark was known to run an underground pimp house in London's notorious Soho district, akin to Amsterdam's red light district zone, and like a lamb to the slaughterhouse, that's where poor Mum Sophie had met her tormentor and architect of her ordeal and subsequent problems.

And so, an inner resolve wedged within my heart at these cruel discoveries. That evening, I imbibed with glasses of whisky as I girded myself for the eventual showdown with him. I was determined to get to the bottom of what had really transpired between him and my mother and the sheer cruel coincidence of their meeting in England.

"I know this sounds pathetic, Rhys, but I wouldn't have done it, had he not been crass about the whole thing and in a way goaded me into it: 'Oh Sophie, that stinking whore. How can you possibly know of her? We met in England, and she told me she aborted my pregnancy; then later, it was, 'I lost the pregnancy at three months.' Last I remember, some idiot fucked her and took responsibility for what I assumed was my daughter. Through Sophie's stories, your existence kept changing by the day, akin to the way she changed her knickers with different men. One minute you were alive, one minute you were not there anymore, another minute she wanted child support money. So, what do you believe as the gospel truth in the end? Can you blame me for my blasé attitude?

"But that bitch wouldn't let me have anything to do with my ward, even when I later picked it up that my daughter had been placed in social care by Her Majesty's government. And now you'd like to claim somehow, as surreal as it sounds, you and Sophie are somehow connected? Oh, my word, what bullshit you spew Marina. What will it be next? The pope is pregnant?'

"Looking at him in disbelief, trying to process his bullcrap, I felt an utter sense of betrayal at having shared my life with such a prick. Mark had been part of my life, privy to all my private stuff. Yet here he was unashamedly disparaging my birth mother. I was apoplectic, seething with unmitigated rage.

"Well, that woman you so disparage as a whore is my mother, Mark, and I won't let you disparage her memory," I countered defensively, the anger mounting in me as I prepared for a duel with him.

"Forgive me, Marina, I love a bit of a tease." The odious smirk on him was unmistakable.

"Am I supposed to feel honoured?" I had a cacophony of emotions; my outrage was escalating by the minute. I felt the tears well in my eyes. But I swore under my breath, I wasn't going to give him the satisfaction.

"Your mother my foot," he sniggered back at me contemptuously, oblivious of my rising ire. "If she's that, mummy of the year, why did she dump you into a social services home then?"

"She was a victim of drugs, and you are one to talk, Mark, given your thriving drug empire in Harare. Have you ever paused to reflect at the litany of lives and dreams decimated, ruined by your drugs, all those youngsters who've become victims just like my own mother Sophie, a young Zimbabwean immigrant alone, pregnant in England, far away from home, and with a dick of a partner like you? No wonder she didn't want to have anything to do with you?

"Unlike me, she was brave enough to stand up for what she believed in. Bravo to Sophie, after all these years! I give her my respect and a thumbs up to her intelligence at leaving you, a brute of a man!"

"Oh, shut up Marina, will you, and spare me the needless dramatics."

Rhys butted in, "Looking back, do you have any regrets though, at the whole thing?"

"As callous as it sounds, I felt no sympathy at Mark's death, revelling instead in his ignominious end for one who so put himself on a pedestal as an untouchable. God, how it gave me a rush in my blood! The monster was gone and gone for good for that matter. Inwardly I had mentally prepared myself to encounter my fair share of justice for my misdeed. I must hasten to say though, following my freedom and exit from my tumultuous marriage, my healing has been long drawn out, both physically and emotionally. My inner emotional scars and psyche will take ages to completely heal, this testimony to an abusive relationship. The end normally defines the whole. More and more, I look at the way things have panned out as a befitting trade off, having Mark's life in exchange for my freedom even though bizarrely, the hangman's noose is now an immediate spectre dangling for me."

Chapter 41

Fallen Scales

"Hang on a minute, Rhys, am I getting this right? There is one thing which remains hazy to me in this grandiose tale of your brother's colorful life and infamy, something I've meant to raise with you ever since you narrated your fateful night of falling out with your brother Julian.

"Let me jog your memory by taking you back to something you said earlier, and you perhaps may shed some light on this grey area I have here. Something is not adding up for me, here."

"Go for it, I'm listening, Marina."

"Who exactly is Brian Wharton? The shadowy but ever-present figure, whose name and seemingly mystical omnipresence rings a bell in me as my husband's number two man or deputy. What did Julian meant when he accused you of harboring a sordid, dirty secret, because come to think of it, Rhys, the name Brian Wharton does ring a familiar bell to me, like I keep saying."

"What sort of familiar bell?"

There was a heightened tension in Rhys' voice as he posed this question. Anxiety and alarm registered on his usually choreographed face. It made the penny drop for me and I only just managed to refrain from jumping out of my seat, animatedly saying as much. Moment of epiphany, so to speak!

"Oh, my fucking word, Rhys. Are you fucking shitting me? Now the penny has dropped! The scales have fallen from my eyes! Brian Wharton, the shadowy figure, the one who could never be physically seen yet had a towering influence in Marks's business empire. You and he? So...so... you are Brian Wharton? You've been Brian Wharton, incognito, under the radar all along? Masquerading as the role model, squeaky clean son to your long-suffering mother? Are you not? Deny it! Otherwise, how would you have known so much about Mark, and now juxtaposing your craftiness vis-à-vis your brother Julian's outburst on the dreadful night he lost his life?"

So many questions, a flurry of them, an avalanche, were raining non-stop from me as I aggressively badgered Rhys. My eleventh-hour deduction now seemed to make logical sense, as it fell in line with his own deceased brother's remarks: *"Truth be told Rhys, you're not as squeaky clean as you've hoodwinked Mum, all these years. Goodness knows, you're just as fucked up as I. The thing is, I'm well aware of your sordid secret, the whorehouse in Avenues, and your rent boy business. And not only that, I've known this for a long time. Give me some slack. I may snort some powder, but that doesn't make me stupid..."*

Julian's words were themselves a damning indictment of this fraud sitting before me, the grand master of deception himself whom I had unashamedly befriended in Chikurubhi all these months, treated as a friend, a confidante, pouring my life's story to him.

Julian's words repeatedly replayed into my mind, only they had greater poignancy now in enhancing clarity as the scales fell from my hitherto blinkered sight.

"Are you going to answer me, Rhys?"

He could only stare at me like a snake, mouth agape. *Was it shame, embarrassment that his grand subterfuge had been found out?* I wondered to myself.

"Rhys, are you not going to say something? I demand some clarity and conversation from you? You can't deny me conversation."

Still no response, which further heightened the veracity of my clever deduction as to the identity of Mark's right hand man, the elusive Brian Wharton, who'd seemingly remained in the shadows all these years, yet his name and presence had a pervasive influence.

Oh, my word, how could I have been so blind at the obvious? No wonder the devious questions from master criminal Rhys: "Have you ever seen this Brian Wharton yourself? Do you know what he looks like?" All along, the poor bastard was in defensive mode trying to conceal his tracks, while at the same time hoodwinking me as a friend. He kept staring at me as if zonked out on narcotics.

I looked furtively at her, all the guilt and acquiescence palpable on my face. How could I deny it? My double dipping, duplicitous, well-choreographed life of lies and deception had spectacularly come crashing down like a house of cards. And perhaps I deserved it for being such a brazen hypocrite all these years, hoodwinking poor old Doris, Mother, who hitherto still reckons I am the paragon of virtue, the role model son.

Perhaps, Marina and even Julian were right. I deserved everything which was coming my way now. Talk of poetic justice!

"Are you not even going to answer me, Rhys? Brian? Whatever name you're going with today? Look me in the eye and tell me what went on between you and Mark. You're not gonna bullshit me on this one, it won't stick," she upbraided me, the sharp tone of her voice jolting me out of my trance.

I had no choice now but to come clean. My lies, subterfuge, had crumbled to nought; there was no way out. Kudos to Marina for sussing it out just like my kid brother Julian, who had long sensed my revolting hypocrisy at the time. He had characterized it as such and called me out on it, although I had strenuously denied it and sought to pour cold water on it, capitalizing and consistently rubbishing him as a junkie whose words shouldn't be taken seriously.

"Fuck my family, we've always been twisted, cursed if you like. But I'm afraid your reading of my identity is correct, Marina. I did assume the nom de plume Brian Wharton as a convenient façade for my nefarious activities with the down-and-out louts of downtown Harare, as you've sussed out. And not only that, but I am also sorry for what I'm about to say next. Forgive me, Marina, but I'm sure you already know the next bombshell before I even say it..."

"You twisted pervert, Rhys. Now it all makes sense to me. Every word you've ever said is a fucking lie! You're a fraud and you've been a fraud all this time. Oh, my fucking word! Get away from me. Come to think of it, I shouldn't put it past you; you may have killed your own brother and put the blame on poor Doris!

"So, you're also the supposed right-hand man of my late husband Mark, the much-touted Brian Wharton, whom I never met, yet his influence reverberated like an earthquake in my husband's professional life. What a twisted fuck you are, Rhys?"

I could see I had rattled her, or better still, the mask falling from me, my true identity revealed. That and the emerging extent of my criminal shenanigans being revealed just about tipped her over the edge and she was in no conciliatory demeanour with me.

"But, why, Rhys, why the deception...? Why did you have to demonize your very own brother, daily debasing him to your mother, yet you had bigger and viler demons to contend with? I am so disappointed and done with you, loser!"

"What...what...can I say, Marina," I struggled to string together a coherent response, mortified at my outing. "I...I... can't really say anything, but perhaps, I will need to find peace with Mother and own up to my misdemeanours," I pleaded with her.

He bored his piercing eyes into me as if I were his saviour, the errant schoolboy vulnerability evident on him again, but this time, I wasn't falling for it. I said, "Leave it, Rhys. What for? What difference is it going to make to Doris? She's in failing health, bless her. This protracted incarceration, with no end in sight, is already wearing her down, and I tell you, your cruelty will only finish her off. I'm sorry to be so crude but I had to say it to you in no uncertain terms, Rhys.

"You've not been a very nice human being I'm afraid, and if ever you're to make any atonement to Doris, then let her not know anything which will further distress her. She's been a great mother, from our exchanges, but you've failed her big time, Rhys!

"Not to mention those youngsters in downtown Harare you did wrong. I know my husband Mark strove to conceal the shady aspects of his business, but there was no way I would have ever thought part of the seedy business was in facilitating a whorehouse and drugs empire. I did have a whiff of suspicion about the latter, and some superficial knowledge about it, but I never had concrete proof to vindicate my suspicions.

"Oh my God, you crafty, slimy, conniving weasel, Rhys. All this long you've been stringing me along, hoodwinking me, pretending to be this soft, nice gentleman, yet you had your fingers deep in it, in cahoots with my vile husband. What a sly fox you are. Now it all makes sense, your asking me whether I had met Brian Wharton, just to ensure your tracks were covered. All those carefully designed questions you kept throwing at me in that forensic style of yours.

"And those youngsters in downtown Harare. What a vile, disgusting human being you are, Rhys/Brian, whatever your real name is. You dirty, old man!"

It was then that I lost it, stood up, and lunged at Rhys full steam ahead, kicking and hurling invectives as I began walking away, seething with enormous rage. This revelation had certainly further unhinged me.

I could only hang my head in shame as images of my misdemeanours and infamy with Mark and the syndicate flashed through my mind. "Sorry, Marina," I sheepishly mumbled to her as she ignored me, the look of disdain and revulsion on her face quite a powerful spectacle.

"I know I deserve it, your contempt and derision. Look, I'm not proud of some of the things I've done, Marina..."

Giving me further evil looks, she left me still protesting my piety. So, there it was. I had been caught out after all. My guilt and shame were all too consuming.

Acknowledgments

In putting together a book of this magnitude, I am conscious of all who have contributed to helping me throughout the years, and of the debt of gratitude I owe them.

My wife Priveledge, my first reader, has consistently supported and encouraged me without any hesitation. You're a true diamond, I love you dearly.

I am grateful to the NAMA adjudication panel for according my debut novella *Diaspora Dreams (2022)* such a lofty accolade, a nomination in the *Outstanding First Creative Publishing Work Category*, as this has spurred me on to scale greater heights in my literary pursuits and to further affirm my literary passion.

Equally, I wish to extend my utmost gratitude to fellow writers and the writing community for their unwavering support to me. Notable are colleagues and friends, the inimitable Memory Chirere, the erudite Tariro Ndoro, and Stan Onai Mushava "our national treasure." You all rock! I can't thank you enough. Chirere, your enthusiasm is palpable all the way across the pond, as is that of Tariro and Onai and everyone at Kharis Publishing. It is such a pleasure working with you all, and I feel incredibly blessed to have you on my team.

Additionally, I'd be remiss not to give a well-deserved shout out to my esteemed publisher Kharis Publishing who have helped push this book to new heights. To Kharis Publishing, thank you for believing in me when I was ensconced in the depths of obscurity and recognizing my potential. Additional gratitude goes to the indefatigable Acquisitions Manager James Clement for relentlessly attending to my avalanche of emails without a single complaint.

Andrew Chatora

Last but not least, thank you to my children, Brooklyn Manatha and Alexis Pernilla who constantly bear the brunt of my petulance during my writing spells. I love you both so much. You are the future!

About Kharis Publishing

Kharis Publishing, an imprint of Kharis Media LLC, is a leading Christian and inspirational book publisher based in Aurora, Chicago metropolitan area, Illinois. Kharis' dual mission is to give a voice to under-represented writers (including women and first-time authors) and equip orphans in developing countries with literacy tools. That is why, for each book sold, the publisher channels some of the proceeds into providing books and computers for orphanages in developing countries so that these kids may learn to read, dream, and grow. For a limited time, Kharis Publishing is accepting unsolicited queries for nonfiction (Christian, self-help, memoirs, business, health and wellness) from qualified leaders, professionals, pastors, and ministers. Learn more at: <u>About Us - Kharis Publishing - Accepting Manuscript</u>

Author Biography

Andrew Chatora is a Zimbabwean novelist, essayist and short-story writer based in Bicester, England. He grew up in Mutare, Zimbabwe, and moved to England in 2002. His debut novella, *Diaspora Dreams* (2021), was approvingly received and nominated for the National Arts Merit Awards (2022). His second book, *Where the Heart Is*, was published in the same year to considerable acclaim. Chatora's forthcoming book, *Born Here But Not in My Name*, is a brave, humorous and psychologically penetrating portrait of post-Brexit Britain. Chatora is noted for his acerbic and honest depiction of the migrant experience. Heavily influenced by his own experience as a black English teacher in the United Kingdom, Chatora probes multi-cultural relationships, identity politics, blackness, migration, citizenship and nationhood.

New Book by Author Coming Soon...

Born Here, But Not in My Name is the author's forthcoming book.

Read ahead the first chapter of the author's imminent book:

Born Here, But Not In My Name

Synopsis

Against the backdrop of 1960s-1970s England, two unlikely immigrants, Mustafa, a South London Somali cabbie, meets and falls in love with the enigmatic Polish lassie, Mariela, the dancer.

Born Here, But Not in My Name is deftly set against a backdrop of a burgeoning cultural movement of a London Windrush, from whence emerges a poignant story of repressed love, friendship, secrets, betrayal, and hope, as told through multiple characters in a tale spanning over two generations.

Chatora's characters are given much nuance in articulating their voices and realities in their lived experiences, from the idealistic, inquisitive Moira to the rabid white supremacist Briercliffe, whose warped worldview is becoming increasingly anachronistic in a fast-changing post-Brexit Britain.

This is a pertinent tale which shines a light on the minutiae ramifications of mass migration, what it does on migrant communities, and it offers marginalised and authentic voices their rightful place and platform to be heard – **Sue Quainton**

I

All Fur Coat, No Knickers

I married their daughter, no? My warthog totem walks their streets with British blood for the sons she bore me. Damn, her father even gave my three nappy-hair bastards their navy-whistle noses. Thanks to him, they can't help sniffing out every variant of the hate passed around on this island. My sons are Britishers too, you know. Yet their mundane playground experience has been a determined stream of "Fucking, nigger" every other day. "Fucking nigger, I'm gonna shag your mother on a hard cold floor till you fuck out of here to your fucking country." Full-blooded landlords, you see. They want us to be the first shipload of vermin to Rwanda even before Comrade Kagame signs his side of Brexit 2.0. I thank my father-in-law for sticking to the buccaneer whistle. Had my sons inherited his madness too, we would have never known the end of it. England has been around long enough for her towns to be layered on graves. So many of her medieval scoundrels too, and so many of their bones rattling beneath the foundations of polite society. No wonder so many people are mad these days, especially the old ones. So much madness you don't need special instruments to detect the contagion of it. Now, I don't eat the island's soft rice in a stay-at-home apron, but before I look over my shoulder, redneck scriptures will be flying into the empty space where my face was. So much Splendid Alienation being parceled out here. Enough to meet the swinging clipboard of my face at every 90 degrees. So many bloody Tories clawing at my balls with their Union Jack, I am much too stewed down there and up to here to know the end of it. If they can't stand my Tonga glow, why come at my little warthogs? Grandsons, I gave them to hound out with hate like diseased vermin. The more primitive the hate, the more mature the poison. I want to go. I want out.

In a few months, my family and I are leaving the UK. After 16 years, three children born here, a poisoned work environment, and many great friends and comrades, recent events mean we no longer feel welcome by many. We are moving back to Zambia, my country of birth. Tanya, my white British-born wife, shares my sentiments. Today, I feel sad that it has come this far.

"I am very sad too," remarks a dejected Tanya, her brow stitched up with weary furrows. "I don't feel too welcome here either and I was born here. I am going with you, Ray. This will be a journey of becoming for our sons."

Tanya barely recognizes the country she has known and loved. She is ashamed of how we have made EU and other world citizens feel unwelcome, but who is "we" anyway? The blatant racism this country has slipped into, the xenophobia, violence and alien threat now written into our – no, their – collective wisdom. I do not know. In fact, I do. This has always been there bubbling away under precarious politeness.

"I couldn't put up with Briercliffe and Pritti's bad vibes anymore. It's a clear case of constructive dismissal, but I don't have the energy to keep up with those two anymore," I speak my heart to Tanya and the three-dear staffroom comrades who have taken me to the Archipelago pub by Westminster Embankment for a quiet farewell do.

"Besides, Tanya has been very supportive about our move back to Zambia."

"I have always wanted our boys to have a connection with your country of birth, love. As much as it hurts uprooting ourselves from England, we just have to plough ahead," quips Tanya. "Who knows, but my feeling is, things will still work right."

"Post-Brexit, I think we have not made people coming to this country feel welcome anymore, wherever they come from. I can only wish you well, Ray," Chris butts in, one of the nice chappies from the PE Department who'd managed to make it to my farewell do.

"Look, I'm Scottish as you well know, but so many times I have been made to feel my views for seeking independence are like an act of sedition," remarks Chris.

"Which they're not," quips Moira as she carries on.

"Do you know after Brexit, out of six million encouraged to apply for settlement, only two million did apply. The majority have returned to their home countries."

Once more, for the people at the back, settled status is a non-choice for EU citizens. Either apply or become illegal. And everyone knows the English's unhinged hatred of illegals.

"Thank you for expressing so well the way I feel," says Nadine. "And we wonder why we have all these shortages, empty shelves, through-the-roof gas and electricity prices, high interest rates! This country is fucked."

"That's a brave lie, but then it's typically 'woke.' Nobody has been made to feel unwelcome." Vintage Briercliffe-Pritti nexus! Showing someone just how welcome they are by calling them a liar.

"Of course, you would say that, wouldn't you, Pritti?" retorts Chris with undisguised irritation. We have all been taken aback by Pritti, who had quietly ambled into the Archipelago within the last few minutes, our faces giving it away that she is unwelcome. *But there you are, like a bad penny she's popped into my farewell, as if she has not relentlessly tormented me in the department.* Perhaps Pritti has done it to give one little finger up my way.

"You can't deny a person's experience by calling them a liar," Moira chips in. She is pissed off with Pritti's show at this farewell do.

Who does she think she is, turning up like that where she's not welcome? Moira's menacing glare seemed to say, as Pritti walked in.

"Following Brexit, people you think you knew, talked to every day, have become different towards you, even in the school's playground when picking up the kids. So, if you never experienced that don't say it never happens," says Moira.

"You don't get to tell other people how they feel, Pritti. It's not your place," remarks a fired-up Nadine.

"It's true. My Spanish friend, whose daughter was classmates with my son, found that they could no longer vote. Lived in UK for 20 years. Voted in every election before.

"But somehow, post-Brexit, their names had been scored through on the voting list at the polling station. They left. No longer welcome. So, we hear you, and all resonate with Ray's experience here," Chris rages on.

"I am very sad, too. We all are, Ray," the whole lot at the table assented, bar a bemused Pritti who kept sipping through her drinking straw in her glass of alcohol. In a way, our Archipelago encounter led me to draw analogies with Ken Loach's social-realistic classic; *I, Daniel Black,* in which the majority of Britons on the right side of history unanimously ended up assuming protagonist Daniel Blake's persona and dubbed themselves, "We are all Daniel Blake." Hounded from the English department, hounded from Brentside, and now jettisoned out of England, the only country I had known, that had been the map of my dreams for so many years. The hypocrisy of the little England brigade was staggering. Chris's next words rouse me from my reverie.

"Pritti, how are you able to tell me or anyone else how we feel? I have met many people who were welcomed here once, and who now do not feel welcome. I have lived here for decades, and the poisoned attitudes lately make me feel like an alien. Are you even aware that during your famous referendum, hate and race crimes escalated? Religious crimes too towards the end of 2016?"

"It's no good is it, blaming everything on Brexit?" quips Pritti, finding her voice.

"Brexit is the greatest fraud of our time, thanks to devious British elites claiming to give control back to the people when, in fact, they were looking to duck the social responsibilities of a communal EU. Now we pay with our rights and spaces while the Tories and their tribe profiteer, left, right and centre," remarks Ray.

"You do tend to put too much spin on these things; I'm sure other immigrants have had a favorable Brexit experience," Pritti shoots back.

"That's not been our experience. My wife, who has been a British citizen for a decade, has been told to go home several times now. We would move if some ignorant asses hadn't voted to remove our freedom of movement."

"Pritti, it's not just the nationalist English ignited by Brexit who are doing this all the fucking time, fomenting division and xenophobia. It's the Home

Office with their opaque form-filling requests, treating foreigners like they're criminals."

"Patriotism means supporting people who live here. Grow up," Pritti said.

"Says a petty nationalist with a union flag on her classroom table and a white supremacist head of department, who thinks we are making this country great, and nobody is being made unwelcome. If xenophobia and racism are not the logic of Brexit, I don't know what other delusions we have to deal with here. I've seen the way you, Briercliffe, and the Brentside suits treat minorities at the school. Are you not even ashamed you are the reason this poor man is leaving?" Chris was going at Pritti, but had much to divert to regarding the situation.

"A welcoming country, where the home secretary wants to send asylum seekers escaping war and violence to desert islands and dictators' countries like Rwanda, what have you. A welcoming country, which deported British-born Caribbean citizens to countries they have never been to, wantonly denied them their medical and legal rights under the greatest scandal of all, the Windrush fiasco. I say hello! Give me a break!" remarks a fired-up Chris as he carries on.

"The irony of it is, the perpetrator of all this madness, your home secretary, is the daughter of an immigrant herself and admits her own folks wouldn't have been allowed in this country under the exclusionary immigration laws she's been crafting. I mean, you can't make this shit up!

"I was born here and walk around like an alien because I'm not a flag-shagging, pro-Brexit Tory. Pritti, fuck out of here and stop making excuses for you and your ilk," an irate Chris rants, heated up with the atmosphere at our table.

Pritti squares up to him before putting her own final word, "Whatever, Chris. What a sad little man you are, made uncomfortable by the hard truths of our country." She leaves amid counter-expletives from Chris.

Looking back at how we got here, I am not any wiser. What I don't get is, if ever there was an eligibility test on meeting the integration threshold in Little England, then I would pass it with flying colours. Why wouldn't I?

Lightning Source UK Ltd.
Milton Keynes UK
UKHW021556161122
412294UK00016B/134

9 781637 461969